"TURN AROUND," ADAM SAID SOFTLY. "I WILL UNFASTEN YOUR GOWN."

Victoria's heart hit her throat. "What?"

"Does your hearing fail?"

"N-No, of course not." Her cheeks flamed. "I just d-didn't expect . . ."

"That I would assist?"

A slight tremor racked her body at the thought of his hands on her flesh, then she quickly admonished herself. *The man isn't the least interested in—in—* "No. I, um, I just thought we might dine first."

He stepped behind her and reached for the row of pearl buttons down her back. "You thought wrong." He moved closer, his warm breath caressing her ear. "But then, you are wrong about a lot of things. . . ."

Books by Sue Rich

The Scarlet Temptress
Shadowed Vows

Published by POCKET BOOKS

Shadowed Vows

Sue Rich

POCKET BOOKS

New York   London   Toronto   Sydney   Tokyo   Singapore

This book is a work of fiction. Names, characters, places and incidents are either products of the author's imagination or are used fictitiously. Any resemblance to actual events or locales or persons, living or dead, is entirely coincidental.

An *Original* Publication of POCKET BOOKS

POCKET BOOKS, a division of Simon & Schuster Inc.
1230 Avenue of the Americas, New York, NY 10020

ISBN: 0-671-73626-4

First Pocket Books printing August 1992

10 9 8 7 6 5 4 3 2 1

Cover art by Donald Case

Printed in the U.S.A.

Chapter 1

London, England
1775

Hawk stripped off the last of his clothes and tossed them onto the polished hardwood floor. Flickering light from two candles danced over the pile of shimmering blue and the elegance of the stately bedchamber he had occupied for the last eleven months—in *her* house.

His mouth drew down at the corners, yet he could not even summon the energy to scowl as he wanted. He was too tired. Between his ongoing search for his friend's sister and the need to avoid *her*, he had pushed himself beyond exhaustion. Again.

Glancing at a bed, which sported gold drapings and a heavily carved headboard, he started toward it just as a clock downstairs chimed once. Realizing he had been up for forty hours, he felt a heaviness claim him, and he stretched out naked on top of the covers. He fell back into the pillows, enjoying the heat from a low-burning fire that soothed his weary limbs.

Soon he would go home. Back to America, back to the quiet serenity of his cabin deep in the Virginia forest.

He felt a moment's uneasiness at the thought of returning to the colonies. But surely after nearly a year abroad he had come to terms with his feelings for the wife of his friend, Jason. Hadn't he? Too, his search for Jason's long-lost half sister, which had kept him occupied day and night, was nearly at an end.

1

The infant, sired by Jason's father, Beau Kincaid, had been born without the elder Kincaid's knowledge. When her mother died during birthing, the child's uncle, in a fit of rage, gave the babe to the midwife and ordered her to dispose of the girl. Then he killed Beau Kincaid.

The midwife sold the babe to a childless couple from England who were visiting the colonies. Jason had learned of this shortly after Hawk's departure for London, and he had sought Hawk's help.

Sixteen couples had returned to England from the colonies with a daughter in the year 1760, and Hawk had spoken to, then dismissed, all but two of them. Those two he hoped to meet tomorrow.

But first he needed sleep—without having to endure another nightmare about *her*. He heaved a sigh and closed his eyes, then forced all thoughts from his mind. But strangely, in a far distance, he could hear a soft breeze blow through the Virginia pines, its low whistle calling to him. . . .

He was ten years old again, and he knew something was wrong. Shaking off the skitter of unrest, he grabbed a handful of mane, then swung astride his horse's bare back.

The pinto sidestepped and reared its head.

Shadow Hawk reached forward and patted the stallion's sleek neck. "Easy, Atar. You will frighten Jason's maid. She does not understand the way of a man and his horse." He grinned and glanced back toward Beau Kincaid's plantation house, then at the woman watching nervously from the porch.

Whirling Atar toward the bordering woods, glad that his lessons were over for the day, the boy made a face when he was certain the maid could not see. "Agh, why does *Notha* force me to learn the ways of the white man when he knows I only want to be a warrior like him?" From *Nikyah* he could understand this. After all, his mother was white. But his father, Flaming Wing, was a great Shawnee chief. He knew of men's ways, of warriors. Still, he sent Hawk to the tiny house Beau Kincaid had built for learning, certain that the white man would someday rule these lands. He wanted his son to be prepared.

Hawk did not agree with his *notha*, but he would never oppose him. He would meet with the white teacher each day—and hate it, especially now that Beau's sons, Jason and Nick, no longer stayed at Halcyon.

Shifting uncomfortably, Hawk shook off a wave of loneliness. He missed his blood brothers, longed to see them, ride with them. If only their father had not sent them away. If only their mother had not died.

Hawk felt something tighten in his chest. He knew how he would feel if it were his *nikyah* who walked with the Great Spirit. Wishing to rid himself of the frightening thought, he tightened his knees on the pinto and focused on the trail ahead of him.

Off to one side, he spied a dogwood tree bursting with pink blossoms. He jerked Atar to a halt and jumped down. Smiling now, he raced to a low-hanging branch and picked several flowers, remembering how his mother looked with them in her sand-colored hair. She liked flowers, especially pink ones.

Another rush of uneasiness poured into his belly. Frowning and unable to dismiss the feeling, he mounted, suddenly anxious to return home. He kicked Atar into a gallop . . . and prayed, though he did not understand the need to do so.

By the time he reached the village of his people, sweat trickled down his temples, and his fingers were cramped from clutching the flowers and Atar's mane. The smell of woodsmoke, roasting meat, and newly tanned leather filled his senses. Yet even these familiar, comforting aromas did not ease his spirit. He could feel the strain surrounding the Shawnee as he rode past the staggered rows of bark-covered *wegiwa*. Even the other children were quiet. They stared at him.

Upon reaching his dwelling, Hawk leapt from the horse and cast another confused glance at his solemn people, then tossed open the buffalo flap covering the entrance. He waited for his eyes to adjust to the dim light seeping in from the smoke hole at the top of the *wegiwa,* expecting to see his mother working at some womanly task. But when his vision cleared, he saw only his father sitting before a low fire, his back hunched. *"Notha?* Are you ill?" Hawk asked. His father should have been out hunting with the others. "Where is *Nikyah?* Does she go for the shaman?"

His father's gaze lifted slowly.

The pain etched in Flaming Wing's eyes nearly stopped the boy's heart. They looked dull. Lifeless. *"Notha?* What has happened?"

Flaming Wing stared at him sadly, then lowered his gaze. "We are alone, Shadow Hawk." His father's voice sounded broken. "For us, your mother lives no more. She has returned to the white man's world."

Hawk's grip tightened around the pink blossoms. His mother was gone? "Why?" He hated the way his voice cracked. "Did you quarrel? Is she angry?" He fought rising terror. She could not leave him. He *loved* her. His lower lip quivered.

"No." Flaming Wing's hands drew into fists. "I rode out with the others when you left for your lessons. She sent the trapper, Jed, to tell me of her decision—that our way of life was no longer acceptable to her. By the time he found me and I returned to the village, she was . . ." His voice trailed off. The cords bunched in his neck.

No. Oh, please, no. A thousand burning arrows pierced Hawk's chest. She could not leave him. He blinked quickly and glanced around the only home he had ever known. His mother's cooking pot, usually filled with steaming vegetables and meat, sat empty by one of the deerskin sleeping mats. Her board for shaping bread hung idle from a peg near his *notha's* warrior shield.

She was gone.

He looked down at the pink flowers still clutched in his fist. Opening his hand, he let the blossoms fall. As each flower hit the ground, pain burrowed deeper into Hawk's heart, turning, twisting, branding him with its cold, cruel mark. But he forced his chin upward. He would not let his *notha* see him cry. *He would not cry.*

Hawk lurched upright in the bed. He gripped the sheets and took a deep breath to still the thundering rhythm of his heartbeat. Even sheer exhaustion could not stop the nightmare from coming.

Rising, he knew that tonight, like so many other nights, there would be no more rest. He shoved his fingers into his hair and again cursed himself for coming to England. After all these years, the pain of his mother's desertion had nearly grown bearable. But since his arrival here, each day, each night, grew worse.

Lowering his hands, he glanced around the room and felt the stifling confines close in around him. He needed to get out of *her* house.

He opened the armoire and scowled at the rows of brocade and satin garments. For the hundredth time, he wondered what she had done with his buckskins.

Hawk tugged on a pair of tight breeches and a frilly white shirt that had been tailored just for him—Adam Remington, the fifteenth duke of Silvercove. Anger ignited inside him. How he detested the white man's title.

He shoved his arms into a brown redingote, knowing the night would be cold. It always was in this godforsaken country.

After stomping into black riding boots, he slid his ever-present knife inside the right one, then quit the chamber.

When he was halfway down the stairs, he heard his mother's door open and swore softly. The woman had the instincts of a she-wolf.

"Adam? Where are you going?"

Hawk halted his step and tightened his hand on the banister. "Out."

"Don't do this."

He ignored her and continued his descent until he reached the entry.

Alaina followed him down. "I know you're doing this to

punish me, son, but you're hurting yourself. If you'd only talk to me."

Alaina Remington watched the muscles tense in her son's back, his bitterness and stubbornness visible in every powerful line of his tall frame. A soft sigh escaped her lips, and she looked away. He had shut her out again. He would never listen to her reasons for leaving him all those years ago.

Her gaze drifted back to the lean, chiseled features so like his father's. She felt hollow inside. How close she'd come to losing him back then. How close she'd come to losing Flaming Wing. . . .

She forced herself to concentrate on her son. Over the years, she must have sent him two dozen letters, explaining what happened that day, but obviously he hadn't read them. He wouldn't still hate her if he knew the truth. Flaming Wing might, but not Adam. "Son, please—"

"Do not call me son." He swung around. "Or Adam. If you must call me anything, I prefer Shadow Hawk, or merely Hawk. But do not call me son, for you have long since forfeited the title of mother. And you are wrong. I do understand." His clear gray eyes darkened. "You left us. Life in our village offered no excitement for you. Flaming Wing could not give you the wealth you coveted." His voice grew hard, distant. "And I had nothing to offer but a child's naive love."

Pain gripped Alaina's chest. It was an old ache, a killing one she'd lived with for the past fourteen years. "Adam, don't . . ." Her words trailed off when she saw his mouth tighten at her use of his Christian name.

"Do not what, Mother? Do not remind you of the man you nearly destroyed? Do not remind you of the ten-year-old child you left behind?" A muscle throbbed in his jaw, and his voice deepened. "Do not remind you that you sent for me now only because I am the one person who can claim the duke's fortune for you?"

He truly believed that. He thought she only wanted him here to claim her father's money. Dear God. How she must have hurt him. He didn't even know her anymore. Forcing down the knot in her throat, she lifted her chin. "If you believe that of me, then why did you come when I summoned you? *Before* Jason learned his baby sister had been brought to England?"

He took so long to answer that she thought for a moment he wasn't going to.

"To distance myself from an uncomfortable situation," he replied at last, then laughed without humor. "Only to find I have merely exchanged one set of distasteful circumstances for another."

His gaze drifted over the elegant sitting room in the west wing of the London apartments, his scorn obvious. "But I now realize the other situation is more to my preference."

He lifted a black cape off the hook near the table and flung it around his wide shoulders, then turned toward the door. "As soon as it can be arranged, I will sail to America."

"But what of Jason Kincaid? What of your search for his sister?" She knew she was grasping at threads, but she couldn't let him go, not now, not until he understood.

He shrugged. "I have spent nearly a year in search of the girl—without success. If I learn nothing from the last two names on the list, I will leave the task to Jason or his brother, Nick." He reached for the doorknob.

"Don't go back, son. Not yet. Not until things are righted between us."

His stance stiffened. "There *is* nothing between us to right, madam. But if your concern rises from fear of a penniless fate when I leave, I will ease your distress. The treasured Remington fortune is yours to do with as you wish." Jerking violently on the gilded latch, he stormed out of the house.

As the door slammed behind him, Hawk closed his eyes. Damn her. He would not feel the pain of loving this woman who cared little for him. He would not hear her lies. No matter what her reasons, her excuses, she *had* left him, had without words shown her true feelings.

He felt a slow drumming in his temples as he looked down the steps toward Park Lane, the fog-shrouded street running in front of his mother's apartments. The old familiar feeling, the need to hit something, to hurt someone the way he hurt, nearly overwhelmed him, and he flexed his hands to relax the straining muscles. If only he could escape to the quietude of the Virginia forests.

Releasing a disgusted breath, he looked toward the dim, distant lights of the London docks over three miles away. He recalled the many times he had ignored aristocratic propriety by not only walking to but patronizing the disreputable Waterfront Tavern on the north bank—and his reason for doing so. Smiling wryly, he stepped away from the door and headed for the street. A brisk stroll and a visit to the tavern would allow him to vent his frustrations.

Victoria Townsend froze as a step creaked beneath her kidskin boot. She held her breath. Waited. Hearing no sound, she clutched the bundle tighter to her chest and took another step.

She brushed a lock of dark reddish brown hair over her shoulder and glanced nervously behind her. No movement came from the darkened stairway. With a shaky hand, she grabbed the oak banister to lighten her weight, then edged down the remaining steps.

When her boots finally touched the tiled floor of the entry, she started to turn, but the scent of lemon oil and wax wafted from the parlor. She stopped and peered across the wide, shadowed expanse to the opening. Memories overrode her fear for a moment. How often she had seen her mother in that room, directing the maids while they cleaned, even polishing the heavy rosewood furnishings herself.

Visions of the beautiful Alexandra floated before her, and Victoria could almost imagine her mother's slender frame standing beneath the arch. She could see again the gentle wave of silky dark hair, hear her mother's soft voice, which never seemed to rise above a husky whisper.

Victoria's grief returned. She would never hear that voice again, never look upon the exquisite face that now lay forever beneath the lid of a satin-lined coffin.

A board creaked overhead. The image of her mother vanished as Victoria spun toward the noise. Fearing discovery, she hurried to the back of the house as silently as her boots would allow.

As she raced through the formal dining room, the pocket of her skirt caught on the arm of a Windsor chair. Its leg scraped across the wood floor, bringing Victoria to a skidding halt. She tugged at the material while frantically watching the entrance. Finally she tore the pocket free, scurried to the rear exit, and fled out to the stables.

Inside the barn, she dropped the bundle she carried, then lit a candle before moving swiftly to hitch her mare to a carriage.

With the horse and conveyance readied, Victoria retrieved the muslin-covered parcel and tossed it onto the seat beneath the half canopy, then shoved open the barn door. Scrambling atop the single driver's seat, she lifted the reins, giving silent thanks to Paddy for teaching her to handle a chaise.

Dampness from the thick fog seeped through the layers of her green woolen gown and matching cape. She pulled the material closer, attempting to stay her body's incessant shivering.

An icy breeze numbing her cheeks, she guided the horse down the vacant streets of London. The animal's hoofbeats sounded hollow on the cobbled road. On and on, clip-clop, clip-clop, the eerie clatter rang off the mortared stones. Something moved in the recess of a foggy side street, and Victoria's gaze flitted about nervously. Murderers and thieves haunted the docks, preyed on innocent— "Stop it," she warned herself, her own voice somehow reassuring. "You're acting like a simpering ninnyhammer."

Suppressing a shudder, she pulled the reins to the left and turned the carriage down a narrow lane. Heavens, how she hated this part of London—the back alleys, the wharfs.

Boisterous laughter rose from a nearby public house on the north bank of the Thames. The Waterfront Tavern. Another shiver that had nothing to do with the cold raced along her spine. She snapped the leather to quicken the mare's pace.

She searched uneasily beyond the pools of light made by

the lamps on her chaise. Eerie silhouettes wavered over the rows of crudely built huts behind the warehouses that lined the alley she'd just entered. Human stench, the smell of stale salt air, and the reek of decaying fish assailed her senses. She quickly withdrew a handkerchief from her pocket and pressed it to her nose, her gaze never leaving the many doors looming like shadowy demons. Fervently she prayed none of the occupants would appear.

Only for Paddington McDaniels would she put herself at such risk. Only for dear, sweet Paddy. Her friend. The man who had always been like a second father to her—and of late much more a father than her own.

She inhaled against the pain of her father's undisguised bitterness, against the disapproval she couldn't begin to understand. If it hadn't been for Paddy, she couldn't have borne the last six months. Not after her mother . . .

Clamping down on the unwanted memory, she thought instead of Paddy. He had been there for her when Mama died. But then, Paddy was always there for her when she needed him. It was he who had tended her skinned knees, cuddled her after some childhood trauma, and dried her tears after a fight with her father over her unladylike behavior. And now for the first time *he* needed *her*. She wouldn't—*couldn't*—let him down, no matter what the sacrifice.

She focused again on the dreary street. Seeing a low flicker of light through the window of Paddy's small hutch, she felt the tension leave her. She had to stop worrying that something would happen to him. Though he couldn't get around well after his accident, he was recovering. And he *did* eat—she saw to that. How silly, this persistent concern.

Tugging back on the reins, she drew the mare to a halt, then quickly retrieved the package from the rear seat and climbed out of the chaise.

She knocked quietly on the door to Paddy's dwelling. It seemed to take an eternity before it swung open to reveal his tall, lean frame, dressed in what looked like cast-off rags.

"Ria? Ah, love, what are ye doin' out in the cold? Come

10

in, lass. Hurry, now, before ye catch yer death." He placed a thin but well-muscled arm around her shoulders and guided her inside the low-ceilinged room.

The feel of his sure grip never ceased to surprise her. There was a strength about him, a concealed power, and a keen awareness in those clear blue eyes that belied his often crude manner of speech.

"I told ye, I dunna like ye sneakin' out in the middle o' the night like this." He gave her a hard stare. "It's too dangerous for a young lass like yerself. I appreciate the food and supplies, darlin', but ye mean more to Paddy than all the fancy fares in Providence. Me heart would break if somethin' happened to ye, love."

Victoria smiled and set the bundle on a three-legged table braced against one wall, then lifted her arms and hugged the older man. "I've missed you."

"Yes, well . . ." He cleared his throat. "I've missed ye, too, Ria. When ye didna come on the Sabbath like ye always do, I figured this time ye'd listened to me and wouldna come again. I'd hoped ye'd heeded me warnings about the dangers here."

"Father arranged a hunt at Denwick on the week's end. It was impossible for me to get away with all the guests milling about."

At the mention of the hunt, she saw a flicker of sadness enter his eyes before he quickly turned away. She had forgotten how much he loved the chase.

"I wish ye'd forget about me, lass." He limped to a tiny fire circled by rocks in the center of a dirt floor and added another piece of precious firewood. Then after moving back to the wobbly table, he pulled out a rough-hewn chair and motioned for her to sit down.

It tore at Victoria's heart to see him like this—so unhappy and living like a street beggar, for heaven's sake! For her entire life, until six months ago, he'd lived above the stables at her father's estate, Denwick, in a large airy room. He hadn't been crippled then, or looking older than his two score years.

No. Then he'd walked tall and straight, his body hard, solid, much heavier. There had been a serenity about him. A contentment. And though his loss of weight hadn't detracted from his handsomeness, there was now a gaunt look to his features, that of someone whose very soul was haunted.

"Why did Father make you leave, Paddy?" Victoria asked suddenly. "No one will tell me—least of all him." Taking the seat Paddy had offered her, she watched the former groom. "Why won't you come back and talk to him? If you tried, he might allow you to return."

Paddy's eyes took on a faraway look, and he shook his head, causing firelight to dance over chestnut hair touched by silver at the temples. "No, love." He sat cross-legged on his pallet of straw and scraps of cloth. "The tiff between me and yer papa canna be settled with words."

"Yes, it can. I could persuade him to ask you back."

Paddy at first looked stricken, then quickly glanced away. "No, Ria. I dunna want ye to be stickin' yer nose into me affairs. Just let it be, lass. I'm content here."

He was lying; she could tell by the way he wouldn't meet her eyes. Besides, he loved Denwick. He had been the groom there long before Victoria was born. She knew the dispute between him and her father was related to the accident on the day her mother died. The earl had run Paddy down with a carriage. But it wasn't her father's fault. He had been hysterical. Her mother had just fallen into the lake, and he hadn't been able to save her. He had, in fact, been racing frantically to Denwick to summon help.

Standing, she crossed to her friend. She suspected that seeing Paddy every day brought back painful memories for her father, so he had let the groom go. But surely now, after six months, the earl would listen to reason.

Unmindful of the damage to her clothing, she dropped down on the floor in front of her friend and clasped his hand. "Let me talk to him."

Paddy's throat worked as if he wanted to say something, but he remained silent. Then, after easing out of her hold, he raised his fingers to her cheek and ran a thumb over its smoothness. "It's in the past, love. Leave it there." He lowered his hand, then nodded toward the bundle. "What'd ye bring this time?"

She sighed in defeat. Knowing that the discussion was terminated, Victoria rose, retrieved the package, and placed it in his lap. "Open it and see." She grinned. "And afterward I'll see if my gaming skills have improved."

Paddy shook his head. "Lass, I'll take no more o' yer coin. Do ye think I dunna kin that ye lose to me on purpose?"

Victoria blinked innocently. "Don't be absurd. Why would I do a thing like that? Surely you misunderstand. I merely have yet to master the game of cribbage." She chuckled quietly. "But I will—and soon. Then we'll see who cries foul."

Collier Parks cast a forlorn glance at the last of his money lying in the center of the table. Throwing his cards down, he rose and swaggered to the end of a long polished bar across the room, trying not to think about what tonight's loss meant. It pained him too much, and it wouldn't do to let the blighters in the Waterfront Tavern know of his hellish situation.

Stepping up to the counter, he slammed his palm down atop the chipped surface. "Pour me a hearty mug, my good man. The blasted smoke in here has fairly stripped the flesh from my throat."

Thomas Markworth, owner of the Waterfront, cocked a bushy eyebrow in Collier's direction. "Let me see the color o' your coin first, mate."

Collier glanced quickly toward the occupants of the room, then lowered his voice. "You'll get your damned money. Just put it on my tab."

The hefty, aproned barkeep continued to dry the tankard he held. "Seems ta me like yer tab's a might overdue. I'll no' be extendin' more credit, Parks, till ye set it ta rights."

"You'll get your money!" Collier's voice squeaked high with his anger. Then, remembering his position, he softened his tone. "Damn it, man. I'll have it within a fortnight." He knew he'd better have it if he planned on living out the month. "Listen, Markworth, I've an allotment from my father's estate coming soon," he lied convincingly, knowing full well he had gambled those funds away long ago. "I'll settle up then."

"Seems ta me I've heard *that* one afore."

"I know, I know. But this is different. The solicitors made an error last month. They've straightened it out now. I'll have your money before the month's end."

Thomas Markworth expelled an exasperated breath and tossed the towel aside. He filled the tankard in his hand with ale and set it before Collier. "Hear me well, mate," the older man said harshly. "If I don't get me coin by the end o' the month, I'll be takin' the fare outta yer miserable hide."

Too concerned with the drink before him to respond, Collier merely nodded. He needed this drink. Needed it badly. It helped stave off this last of the many threats he'd received. Bloody hell. Thomas Markworth would have to stand in line with several others if he wanted to defile Collier's person. Half of London sought that end.

Nursing the ale, wanting to make it last, Collier looked around the dimly lit room. Ten days. He had ten days to come up with payment for his vouchers. He was desperate, knowing what the consequences would be if he failed to do so.

He swallowed another sip and tried to think. He had to see Ria again. She was his only hope. He just prayed she'd saved enough from her allowance to see him through.

At the thought of his beautiful and quite malleable cousin, he smiled. He loved her beyond reason and planned to marry her when she turned eighteen—even though she didn't know it yet.

Just the thought of someday possessing her warmed his blood. Too bad she didn't have more funds available to her. If his blasted uncle wasn't so stingy, she would have. How did the man expect his daughter to exist on the paltry sum he doled out each month? Ria would be much better off if that bastard father of hers met with a sudden accident.

The tankard stopped halfway to Collier's lips. Ah, yes, now, there was a thought. The earl didn't have a king's fortune, but what he did have would keep Collier's skin intact for a good while. And Ria would give it to him. Collier had no doubt of that. The girl positively doted on him.

As always, thoughts of Victoria stirred his loins. In just two more years she'd belong to him. He'd lay claim to her dowry . . . and her bewitching body.

Too bad Uncle Richard was in such good health, Collier thought. If he were to die any time soon, Collier, being the only male heir, would gain control of Ria and her estate in its entirety.

Sighing, Collier took another swallow. He wished he had the courage to slit the old cock's throat. But he didn't try to fool himself on that score. He just didn't have the nerve. That was why he frequented establishments like this one. Whenever he needed a distasteful task performed, there were plenty of men here who, for a price, would do what Collier himself couldn't—at least not with his own hands. Too bad he didn't have more money, or more nerve. That would have solved all of Collier's problems—and Victoria's.

Thinking of the woman he planned to marry, Collier felt the tiniest pinch of guilt as he set his tankard down. If he hadn't told the earl what he knew, Ria wouldn't be suffering the man's hatred now.

Collier lifted his chin and squared his shoulders. He'd had to do it, he told himself. He'd needed money so desperately at the time. And Uncle Richard, for all his faults, had paid well for the information.

Collier's shoulders slumped. If only he could have foreseen what his uncle would do. But how could he have known how the earl's mind worked? That the man would go out of his head? And how could he possibly have imagined that his uncle would turn his wrath on Ria?

It wasn't often that Collier felt regret, but this one time he did wish he'd kept his mouth shut. He should never have told Uncle Richard what he'd witnessed.

He shook his head and forced aside the unfamiliar feeling of guilt. Ria could take care of herself. It would be far better to concentrate on something more productive—like how to save his own skin. What happened before was in the past. His future, if he was to have one, needed immediate attention. He had to get his hands on a goodly sum of money. And soon.

Chapter 2

The cold, damp air acted as a balm, soothing Hawk's raw nerves, so that by the time he entered the dimly lit, smoke-filled common room of the Waterfront Tavern, he had almost given up thoughts of battle. Almost.

Hawk eyed the noisy crowd. Most were seamen in port for the night, having arrived after long voyages. Hawk's gaze flicked briefly over a yellow-haired man standing at the end of the bar, staring in his direction. It wasn't often that men dressed in finery visited the docks. Although Hawk did recall seeing this particular one here before. And judging by the way he stared, the man recognized Hawk, too. Or, more likely he recognized the duke of Silvercove.

As he had so many times in the last year, Hawk moved to a table in the far corner of the room and sat down, his back protectively to the wall. Leaning against the rungs of the chairback, he waited with casual disinterest, watching, knowing it wouldn't be long before the merriment now humming through the large, cluttered room would turn into violence.

He mentally scoffed. The white man enjoyed strange rituals. But then, that was why Hawk came here. Maybe it was the white half of his blood that sought this odd ceremony—the laughter, the cross words . . . and the inevitable brawl.

A dark-haired barmaid stepped before him, her large quivering breasts barely concealed by the low-cut white blouse she wore. "What'll it be, love?" She leaned closer, allowing her neckline to gape, affording Hawk a clear view of dark, protruding nipples. She smiled and ran her tongue teasingly over her bottom lip. "We've lots ta offer a gent."

Thinking of Cassandra, the beauty who had shared his bed for the better part of a year, Hawk met the woman's inviting gaze without interest. "Ale."

Her lips thinned and she straightened abruptly, her dark eyes flashing. "Anythin' ye say, milord."

He watched with amusement as she spun around, stomped toward the long wooden bar, and snatched a mug from an aproned man. She returned to slam the frothy tankard down before Hawk, uncaring that the amber liquid sloshed over the sides onto the worn, scarred tabletop. Still smiling, he leaned back, then lifted the mug to his lips. It was going to be an interesting night.

The woman made several trips to his corner during the next few hours, but not once did she speak or smile. She merely collected his empty mug and replaced it with a full one before lifting her chin and sauntering off. Obviously she had taken offense at his lack of interest.

Hawk studied the woman as he watched her walk away again with his empty mug, her well-rounded hips swaying.

As she passed a table occupied by four men, a hand reached out and jerked her off her feet. She landed in the lap of a brawny red-haired seaman. Screeching loudly, she drew her free hand back and slapped his bearded face.

The sound echoed through the suddenly quiet room.

The man's massive shoulders grew taut, and the muscles in his arms bunched. His hamlike fist shot forward.

Hawk bolted to his feet. But not quickly enough. He winced as the force of the man's blow sent the tavern maid sprawling across the floor. She landed hard against the leg of a table, blood spurting from her cut lip. Mugs toppled at the impact, and the occupants jumped back to avoid being splattered.

Feeling responsible for the woman's ill temper and annoyed by the seaman's harsh act, Hawk stepped up behind him. "One who strikes a woman reveals his cowardice."

Gasps echoed through the crowd.

The red-haired man jumped to his feet. He spun toward Hawk, his bearded face bloated and red, a scar bulging over what should have been his left eye. "Och. What did ye say?"

Hawk arched a brow. "I do not repeat myself."

The red-haired man's piglike features stretched taut, and his single eye blazed. "Why, ye uppity, snobbish son of a wh—"

"Begone with ye, O'Ryan." The burly barkeeper stepped forward holding a musket across his chest. "There'll be no brawlin' this night. I'm still payin' for yer last romp. Now get outta here." He gestured with a dip of his head toward the other three men at the table. "And take yer lackeys with ye."

No one moved as O'Ryan stared at Markworth. Then his gaze flicked to Hawk, and a sneer curled his lips before he nodded to the barkeep. "Aye, matey. Anythin' ye say." He gestured to his companions. "Come along, lads, the air be gettin' foul in here."

Hawk watched O'Ryan and his men strut noisily from the taproom, knowing they would wait somewhere outside for him. Anticipation hammered through his veins, and a slow smile surfaced at the thought of the coming battle. Deliberately taking his time, Hawk resumed his seat and waited for the battered woman to deliver his ale.

When she approached him with a fresh mug, she smiled warmly, revealing a trace of blood at the corner of her lip. "Me thanks, guvner, fer steppin' in like that. But I hope ye know what yer about. That man ye set down is Dooley O'Ryan." She paused, obviously waiting for the name to register with Hawk. When his expression remained unchanged, she continued in a lower tone. "He's bad clear ta his dirty fingernails. Got rid o' more'n one high-born lord's mistress who got wi' child. Ever' time he comes here, he causes trouble. Without his eye patch, I didn't recognize him at first, or I'd never have raised me palm." She placed a plump hand on Hawk's arm. "Ye might watch yer back when ye leave, guvner. They's bound ta be waitin' for ye."

Hawk nodded and turned back to his drink. As the woman walked away, he thought of the way O'Ryan had struck her. Though Hawk was Shawnee and his people believed in controlling their women with force, he did not. There were much more pleasurable ways for a man to entice a woman to do his bidding. As always, thoughts of his village, of the women, brought on a feeling of warmth. But it faded as quickly as it had come when his mother's lovely face intruded.

Blood pumped anger into his veins, and he glanced at the tavern door, knowing Dooley O'Ryan waited just beyond it. That was why Hawk had come here tonight. Tossing back the last of the ale, he slammed the tankard down and rose.

The room swayed, and he blinked. He stared down at his empty mug, trying to remember how many drinks he had consumed. Unable to recall, he shook his head, then squinted before lumbering across the tavern's dirty, spit-stained floor to the front entrance.

As he reached the door, Hawk noticed the yellow-haired man had also set his tankard down and stepped away from the bar, looking as if he might follow.

Surprised, yet unconcerned, Hawk ignored him and pressed the latch. His stomach knotted. They were out there. He could feel their presence, sense the danger. His warrior blood began to drum softly. His nostrils flared with the scent of challenge. But when he opened the oak panel and glanced out, the street was deserted.

Not deceived by O'Ryan's obvious ploy, Hawk remained alert as he left the taproom and strode unsteadily toward St. James's Park. With each step, thoughts of his mother's betrayal churned in him, and he clenched his fists. Damp, salt-tinged air stung his eyes as he walked between rows of buildings, their windows closed and shuttered.

The stench of dead fish and rotting wood assaulted him. He curled his lip and turned his head. A shadow moved. His blood raced.

Then he saw them.

Expectantly he watched the four men step from a side alley and approach him. He gave thought to retrieving the knife from his boot, but quickly cast the notion aside. He did not want to kill anyone, merely to vent his anger. He just hoped they felt the same way.

He eyed the men again and just for an instant hesitated. He had battled many times in his life, especially during the past year, and had gained a dark reputation because of it. But he had never been up against men like this. What had possessed him to confront four of the biggest bastards on the London waterfront? They would probably kill him. Warily he watched the men trying to circle around him.

Water lapped against aged pilings as the men advanced.

He moved to one side.

One of the men attempted to slip behind him.

Hawk turned.

Laughter erupted from within the tavern, but Hawk would not allow it to distract him. Fighting—and winning —was what he did best.

A clublike fist came out of nowhere. It slammed against Hawk's jaw. The impact snapped his head back. Pain exploded in his face. Dazed, he shook his head and blinked. Then a slow smile tilted his mouth. He curled his fists . . . and swung.

By the time Hawk limped away from the fight, every muscle in his body was screaming from abuse. His head thundered like a newly skinned drum, and blood from a dagger wound soaked his fine linen shirt. So much for fair play.

The knowledge that the four sailors lay on the dock battered and bruised pleased him. And he did not doubt they had gained a new respect for the English aristocracy, of which they believed him to be a member.

He started walking, but the ground beneath him tipped. He must have taken too many blows, lost too much blood from the gash on his arm. Shaking his head, he tried to think. He staggered, then grabbed for one of the many barrels stacked along the alley. He squinted at the dark corridor, wondering how he had gotten there.

He scanned the narrow hutch-lined lane in confusion, then in the distance glimpsed a flickering glow. He weaved his way toward the light and saw a small, shiny black chaise. Odd place for a carriage, he thought, staring at the open conveyance and the beckoning comfort of its wine-colored seats. Perhaps he could hire it.

He passed a searching glance over the area for the driver, then attempted to step forward. But his legs would not work. His knees trembled, then buckled, and his hand grasped at thin air. He saw the street coming up to meet him. Then nothing. . . .

Collier watched the duke's long frame slip to the ground in an unconscious heap. From his hiding place behind a stack of barrels, he peeked out and smiled. He'd followed the man from the tavern, awaiting the opportunity to render him senseless and relieve him of his purse. But after seeing the way the duke had disposed of Dooley O'Ryan and his thugs, Collier had no wish to pursue that plan any further. A man *that* powerful was not someone to cross—at least not physically.

Moving slowly out of the shadows, Collier cautiously approached the inert man, eager to relieve the duke of his gold. But Collier's hopes were soon dashed. He found only a few shillings tucked into the satin-lined pockets. Bloody hell. It was hardly worth the effort.

Collier stood, placing his hands on his hips in disgust. One would expect a man of stature to carry sufficient coin on his person. Of all the wretched luck.

Shaking his head in disappointment, he caught sight of a black chaise. At first he didn't recognize it. Then the light dawned: the Denwick chaise.

Surprised, he eyed his surroundings. What in the name of Providence was Uncle Richard doing in such an ungodly place at this time of night?

Ignoring the man on the ground for the moment, Collier edged closer to the chaise, then toward a light flickering through the window of a shabby hovel behind it.

Curious, he sneaked up to the open window and cautiously peered over the sill. A burlap covering impeded his view.

Swearing inwardly, he lifted a gloved finger and ever so slowly inched the corner of the coarse fabric aside.

Paddington McDaniels and Victoria sat at a broken-down old table playing cards. *Ria.* Collier's eyes widened, and he backed away from the window.

Paddy McDaniels. Of course! Ria had always adored the lowly bastard. Collier should have known she would come to him. But the few times Collier had seen the man while en route to the tavern had never given him pause. Bloody hell, he thought. Imagine the chit calling on her old groom. His brow shot up. She didn't even perceive the danger to her person. Her reputation. For bloody sakes, she hadn't even considered how she'd compromised herself.

Collier froze, then suddenly swung to face the duke still lying on the ground. Compromised? A low rumble rose from his chest. No, she wasn't compromised, not yet. But she soon would be. He would see to it. It was perfect. If Ria and the duke were found in an indelicate situation, they'd be forced to marry. And quickly.

Collier could have clapped his hands in delight. The duke's unlimited funds would become Victoria's, and of course she would most graciously share them with her favorite cousin. "Perfect. It's bloody well perfect!"

He hesitated when he thought of how this plan would end his own chances to marry Ria. But with all that money he wouldn't need vows. He'd simply make her his mistress.

Satisfied with the alternative, he quickly returned to the duke's side, grasped the larger man under the arms, then pulled him closer to the chaise. Opening the half door, he dragged the limp form up onto the seat, then tugged the duke into a slumped sitting position.

He jumped down and started for the shanty, then noticed the stain of blood on his gloves. A slow, evil smile stretched across his mouth.

"Ria!" Collier pounded furiously on the hutch door. "Come quickly, Ria. A man's been injured!"

The door flew open to reveal a wide-eyed Victoria Townsend, her mouth agape. "Collier? What are you doing here?

How did you know I— *What man?*" She spied Collier's hands and paled. "Oh, God. What happened?" Her gaze flew to the chaise. "And how did *he* get there?"

Collier hid a burst of satisfaction with an airy wave of his hand. "I put him there. I found him on the street. The chap's obviously been set upon by thugs. A stroke of luck that I spotted your conveyance here." He sent her a reproachful look. "A matter we shall discuss at length later." He gestured toward the duke. "In the meantime this man needs a physician, quickly. Come now. We'll take him to an inn, then fetch Arthur Polk." He glared at McDaniels before directing another disapproving look at Ria. "Then I'll see you safely home."

McDaniels stepped toward the chaise. "Who is he?"

Collier scowled at the shabbily dressed man. "I haven't the foggiest notion. He's obviously in no condition to introduce himself." Turning back to Ria, he grasped her arm. "Come along. We must make haste."

Victoria's thoughts whirled with the swiftness of everything that had happened. One moment she was happily losing the last of her coin in a game of cribbage, and the next she was being hustled into her chaise to sit beside a large man who looked as if he'd been trampled by a team of horses. "Collier, I don't believe this is such a good—"

"Don't worry, love, he won't harm you. Now, just relax. There's an inn 'round the next corner."

The chaise leaned to one side as Collier took the curve with more speed than Victoria felt was necessary. The man beside her slid in her direction until he had her pinned against the side, his hand landing in a most embarrassing place on her person. She shoved the offending paw from her lap, then attempted to shoulder his heavy weight a respectable distance away. She couldn't budge him. "Collier, I—"

"Almost there, love."

Victoria sighed.

The chaise rolled to a stop before a ramshackle building that looked as if it should be abandoned. Weathered boards nailed diagonally across broken windows and steps with missing slats belied the structure as a place of business. Only the overhead sign, one side swinging free, gave evidence that this decaying edifice truly *was* an inn: the Dockside Inn.

"Stay here," Collier ordered as he leapt from the driver's seat and raced inside.

"Stay here," Victoria mimicked, knowing she couldn't have moved if she'd wanted to—which she most definitely did. "You might at least have pulled the beast off me first," she mumbled into the darkness.

Squirming against the man's weight, Victoria became uncomfortably aware of his not so pleasant scent. He smelled of ale, stale tobacco, and another odor—blood.

Warily she turned her head to see the man more clearly—and nearly swooned. Mere inches separated her lips from his. She tried to pull back, to look away, but neither feat seemed possible. Unwillingly her gaze wandered over his battered features, from the silky black hair, still caught in a queue, to the bruises distorting a strong square jaw and a straight though slightly puffy nose. She inspected the twin fans of thick black eyelashes resting against high swollen cheekbones before allowing her gaze to drift lower, to the firm line of his mouth, which had somehow escaped damage. His lips were beautifully formed, gently arched on top, fuller at the bottom—very sensuous yet slightly cruel.

An unfamiliar sensation fluttered through her breast. She pulled her gaze away, directing it toward the dilapidated building. Who was this man? She could tell by the quality of his clothing that he obviously ranked high among those of stature, but she was certain she'd never seen him before. At least she didn't *think* she had. With his face all battered, it really was hard to tell.

The inn door swung open, and Collier strode toward her, followed by a huge man in a crookedly buttoned shirt and baggy woolen breeches. The man was monstrous. He dwarfed her six-foot cousin by half a foot or more. And those arms. Heavens, they were the size of tree trunks.

"This way—Jonas, isn't it? Help me get the du—man inside."

"Atwood ain't gonna like this, Mr. Parks. If the man ain't got no coin, like ya said, he ain't gonna let him stay."

Collier waved a dismissing hand. "You let me worry about Atwood, old chap. You just cart the poor soul to a room."

Shaking his massive head, the gargantuan fellow walked around the chaise and opened the door opposite Victoria. As if the man beside her were a mere child, Jonas lifted him in his arms and lumbered toward the inn.

"Come on," Collier commanded Victoria. "Let's see him settled. Then I'll fetch the physician."

Eyeing the dingy establishment, she shook her head. "I'll wait here."

"No! Um . . . I mean, don't be absurd. I'm not going to leave you out here alone. Gad, Ria, there's no telling what kind of wastrels might be about." He glanced toward the inn. "Perhaps even the same ones who attacked that poor gent."

Victoria didn't point out that he hadn't been concerned a moment ago when he left her alone, pinned beneath that same poor gent. "Very well, but let's do hurry. I must return home before I'm found out."

A sudden twinkle in Collier's eye gave her a decidedly uncomfortable feeling before it quickly disappeared.

"Of course, love. We shan't waste a moment." His hands closed around her waist, and he lifted her from the conveyance.

As Victoria followed Collier through the door, she came to an abrupt halt.

The giant, still cradling the injured man, stood before a thin balding man of indeterminable age whose voice rose in a high shriek. "I said, take the bastard out!" He flailed a skinny hand toward the door. "No coin, no room!"

Collier stepped forward. "Mr. Atwood, the proprietor, I presume?"

The skeletal man turned watery bloodshot eyes on her cousin. "And just who might you be?"

"Collier Parks, nephew to the earl of Denwick." He dipped his blond head regally. "And you would do me a great service, sir, if you'd allow your man here to take the gentleman to a room."

The light of recognition lit Mr. Atwood's eyes, and his mouth twisted into a tight smile. "Certainly, your highness. Soon as I see the color of your gold."

Collier's boyish features grew taut, and bright red stained his neck. "You'll get your damned fee on the morrow. My station alone should assure you of that, my good man. Now do as I say."

Mr. Atwood crossed his bony arms and lifted his chin stubbornly. "All the fancy titles in London don't pay the bills, your princeliness. I get my money this night, or you find other lodgings."

Collier clamped his jaw shut, and Victoria saw the warning signs of his impending anger—a terrible thing to see as she well remembered from her childhood. She swung her gaze toward the injured man, and something even more horrifying caught her attention. "He's *bleeding*."

Mr. Atwood looked stricken as he stared at the red puddle near Jonas's feet. "The devil haunt you! Get him out of here!"

Collier blocked the way as Jonas started for the front door.

The big man stopped, his gaze flitting from the proprietor to Collier and back again.

Mr. Atwood glanced frantically at the trail of dribbling blood staining his worn but still serviceable floor covering. "Damn your eyes, you cockswains! All right. Get him upstairs. But you scurvy blighters'll pay for the carpet *and* the room."

Victoria hesitated, then forced herself to ignore the churning in her stomach and followed Collier and the giant man upstairs.

In the upper hall Jonas kicked open the door to a sparsely furnished room. After striding across the bare warped floor, he laid his unconscious burden on a coverlet adorning a narrow bed. Turning, he eyed first Collier, then Victoria, and a small smile curved his mouth. "I'd be wary of Atwood, if I were you." Nodding briefly, he left the room.

Collier stared at the closed door, then crossed the room and picked up the only chair. He placed it next to the bed, then motioned for Victoria to sit. "Watch over our patient while I fetch the physician."

"What are you saying? Have you lost your senses? I can't stay *here.*"

Collier sighed and took her hands. "Look, Ria. We've no choice. It's far too dangerous for you to go for Mr. Polk by yourself." He nodded at the bed. "And we can't leave a gent of his obvious station unguarded. Before we rounded the first corner, Atwood would have him out on the street. The gent'd have his throat slit for the clothes on his back before we returned. You simply must stay."

He scanned the room, his gaze coming to rest on a tin pitcher and bowl on a stand near the bed, then moving down to a pile of cloth on a lower shelf. Something flashed in his eyes that she couldn't interpret; then he turned. "And I suggest you attempt to stem the flow of blood while I'm gone. Wouldn't want the fellow to expire. I'll return as soon as I can." He kissed her lightly on the lips, then abruptly left the room.

Victoria blinked in disbelief. Her cousin had never taken the liberty of kissing her in such a familiar manner, nor, were he in his right mind, would he have considered leaving her alone in a room with a bleeding man. She nervously peeked at the injured fellow and felt a weakness claim her knees. The sight of blood wasn't her only problem. Her charge was about to *wake up*.

Chapter 3

Victoria stood frozen, her gaze locked on the man thrashing about on the bed. Her heart had nearly snapped its strings when his eyes fluttered open. Good heavens. She feared that she would die of fright if the man regained his senses before Collier returned.

She eyed the closed door. Perhaps she should wait in the hall. She could keep the innkeeper at bay, repress her fears, and at the same time maintain some thread of decorum. She took an anxious step toward the exit, but Collier's words came rushing back: "Stem the flow of blood." *Blood.* Collier knew very well what the mere mention of the word did to her.

She halted her stride and cast another wary glance at the injured man. Dark red soaked his left sleeve. She felt herself pale and looked quickly to his face. Which didn't help at all. He seemed so ill. She knew she couldn't leave him like that.

Glancing from the man to the door and back again, she released a long, resigned sigh and walked to the bed. "When you recover, sir, you'd best show great appreciation for the position I'm placing myself in on your behalf."

Uncertain how to proceed, she stared down at him for a moment, trying to decide what to do. "I know one thing for certain: his coat'll have to come off," she muttered.

Gingerly she tugged at the sleeve on his uninjured arm, trying to slip the brocade down over his hand as one might a child's. The material wouldn't budge.

She moved to the head of the bed and braced her knee against the straw tick, then pulled his arm up by holding on to his cuff and slipped the sleeve free.

He groaned and turned his head to one side.

Victoria dropped his hand and sprang back, her heart slamming against her chest. After a long fitful moment he settled again, and she relaxed.

Keeping one eye on the man's face, she walked around the bed, then cautiously inched the fabric from beneath him and off the other arm.

At the sight of the torn shirtsleeve wet with blood, bile rose at the back of her throat. She swallowed and reached out with shaky fingers, lifting the jagged edge of linen away from his flesh. Her stomach gave a warning lurch. His skin lay open across half the muscled expanse of his arm—*and it was covered with thick, oozing blood.*

Her vision wavered. Terror-filled memories flashed through her mind. She jerked her hand back. She couldn't do this.

But as the horrifying images faded, her senses cleared. Her own fears were in the past. This man needed help now, and she was the only one here.

Fighting back her panic, she boldly tore the sleeve away from his shoulder and gently eased it down. Then, averting her gaze, she rose and took a cloth from the bedside table. After dampening the poplin, she returned to lightly scrub at the wound.

The man's muscles contracted, and his breathing faltered. He arched his body as if in pain.

She stopped abruptly. The last thing she wanted to do was cause him further injury. Afraid that she might hurt him again, she folded the cloth into a pad and gently laid it over the gash. Relief filled her, but as she applied constant pressure, her bent, awkward position made itself known, and the muscles in her back stiffened into an ache.

She glanced at the chair on the other side of the bed, then at the bed itself, tempted to sit on it. But of course that was unthinkable.

Her gaze drifted back to the cloth, and she lifted her hand

for the briefest instant to examine the effects of the compress. Her ministrations seemed to have retarded the flow of blood, but she couldn't stoop over like this all night, for heaven's sake. Where was Collier with the physician?

Again she cautiously inspected the man's countenance. He appeared harmless enough. Though he was a big man, quite powerful looking, in repose he seemed rather young and defenseless, in an odd sort of way. Surely there could be no harm in merely sitting beside him.

Easing down on the bed, she made certain to keep a foot on the floor for easy flight, if necessary. Now much more comfortable, she relaxed against the worn quilt.

With nothing to look at in the sparsely furnished room, she allowed her gaze to wander back over the man, then immediately wished she hadn't. The front of his shirt gaped open to reveal a wide expanse of smooth muscled skin. Not a single hair marred the sculptured perfection.

Feeling heat sting her cheeks, she quickly averted her gaze again. What was the matter with her? She was behaving like a—a strumpet, for heaven's sake.

The arm beneath her hand moved, and a low moan rumbled in the silence.

Victoria gasped, poised to flee.

The man rolled his head, then burrowed his cheek into the pillow, mumbling something in a language she'd never heard before. And she barely heard it now, with the way her heart thundered in her ears.

Nervously she moved to take her hand away, but before she could, he reached up, trapping her fingers against his arm. Her startled gaze flew back to his face.

His eyes were open.

She inhaled sharply. Oh, dear God.

"Sam . . ." His voice sounded harsh and raspy as if he'd been struck in the throat. He stared uncomprehendingly, then blinked as if to bring his gaze into focus. Sadness suddenly etched itself on his strong features. "How my heart aches for you," he murmured before closing his eyes. "How I miss you, little outlaw."

Torn between sympathy and fear, she made another

attempt to pull her hand from his, but he wouldn't release it. Uneasiness rose inside her. Fleetingly she gave thought to Collier and how she'd like to flatten his nose for putting her in such a situation. Then, as the man's words penetrated her brain, dawning realization replaced dread, and she raised her eyebrows so far they nearly met her hairline. His heart ached for an outlaw named Sam? Another man? Her eyes sprang wide open. Oh, good heavens! He was *short-heeled!*

Unwittingly she let her gaze travel the length of his superb body. For the first time she became aware of the snug breeches he wore, of the powerful muscles that rippled beneath the satin. He appeared so totally male, it was hard to believe he would prefer those of his own sex.

She tugged once more to free her hand, but the man's grip would not loosen. "Please, sir," Victoria pleaded, hating the way her voice shook. "Let me go."

His eyes opened, then closed again. Still, he retained his hold, his thumb drawing tiny circles on the back of her hand. "You are forbidden to me," he whispered. "But that does not stay my desire."

Victoria's heart twisted painfully. How awful it must be to care for someone, yet fear displaying affection. She examined his swollen features and felt a wave of sympathy. How truly unhappy he must be.

Without thinking, she brought her other hand up to cover his caressing one. "I wish I could help you."

The man opened his eyes, for a moment seeming coherent, then lowered his gaze to the curve of her lips. "You can," he rasped softly. He eased his fingers out from between her hands, then lifted them and began threading them into her hair.

She drew in a stunned breath.

His fingers tightened for an instant, tangling in her reddish locks before he pulled her forward and daringly covered her mouth with his.

Her blood surged with panic, then iced over with terror. She pushed at his chest. But the man held her in his firm grasp, not hurting, but secure.

Pressing his mouth harder, more insistently, he traced her tightly closed lips with his tongue.

Victoria squirmed, then kicked out wildly, striking only air, her fists pummeling his immovable shoulders.

He rolled over, taking her with him, until she lay pinned beneath his length, his long body crushing her into the folds of the tick. Barely giving her a chance to breathe, he continued to ravage her mouth.

Shocked by his swift movement, she parted her lips on a gasp. He pressed his tongue between her teeth, and she felt a shudder pass through his body—and hers. His arm tightened around her back. He pulled her close, as if he wanted to make her a part of him.

Her senses whirled out of control. She tried to push his tongue away with her own. The contact was explosive. Recoiling, she attempted to free her hands from between their chests, to hit out at him, to make him stop.

Tremors spiraled through her arms and legs, and her mouth tingled where his tongue brushed against hers.

He raised his injured arm and placed his hand just below her breast. Slowly, tauntingly, he drew a thumb back and forth across its lower swell.

A blend of fear, excitement, and anticipation churned inside her. *This is wrong,* her mind screamed. But, God help her, she couldn't do anything to stop him. And as her pulse pounded insanely, she suddenly wasn't certain she wanted to.

She would regret this, hate herself when he finally released her. But for the barest instant she softened beneath him and allowed herself to savor the sensations he stirred in her.

Abruptly the chamber door burst open. "Victoria Ann Townsend!"

The man atop her pulled back and turned his head toward the open door.

Victoria's gaze flew in the same direction. *Oh, no.* Her vision faltered, but her eyes never left the red-faced figure standing in the door. "Father!"

Hawk blinked. *Father?* A low groan slipped past his lips,

and he glanced back at the woman beneath him. What had happened? One minute he had been standing on the docks; then he was dreaming of Samantha. The next instant this lovely dark-haired vision was saying she wished she could help him. Blood had gone straight from his head to his loins as he wolfishly thought of a way to grant her wish. He had not expected her to resist his kiss. In fact, he thought she meant to tease him. Perhaps if he had not consumed so much ale, he might have realized sooner that her struggles were genuine. He had been about to release her when she melted beneath him, destroying his good intentions.

Eyeing the woman warily, he edged out of the bed, grimacing in pain as he stood. He turned to face her father. Hawk could better deal with the man's anger than with his own confusion.

"What's the meaning of this?" the man bellowed, shaking a glossy black walking stick in Hawk's direction. "By God, I'll have you gutted!"

The girl stood up. "Father, please. You don't under—"

"Silence! You . . . you harlot," the man shouted at the wide-eyed girl. "How dare you speak to me when you stand before me half naked."

The woman gasped and glanced down. "Good heavens!"

Hawk followed the woman's gaze to her open bodice and fought a smile as she fumbled to restore her modesty. He always had been good at that.

The father advanced a pace. "Who are you? You debaucher! You defiler of children! I would know your name before I put an end to your miserable existence."

Feeling a sudden rise in his own temper, mostly because he was caught in a situation he did not understand, Hawk met the man's gaze steadily. "Do you challenge me?"

"After what you've done, you have the gall to ask? Of course I challenge you. You have destroyed my family's name and honor. I will be the talk of the *ton* because of what you and this—this whore have done."

Hawk stiffened. "What manner of father curses his daughter when he has yet to hear her explanation?"

The heavy-jowled face turned purple. "There's nothing to explain. Her actions—and yours—speak for themselves."

"Father, it's not what you think. I swear. I was—I was—"

"What's wrong, Victoria? Can't you conjure up a lie quickly enough?"

"He was injured, and I was taking care of him." She raised a shaking hand toward Hawk. "Can't you see his face? Collier went for the physician. I intended merely to stay until they returned."

"You expect me to believe that? Ha!" Her father's hands clenched around the cane. "If you're so bloody innocent, then tell me, Victoria, what were you doing sneaking out at this time of night?"

Hawk swung his gaze to the woman. Good question.

She flinched. "I—ah . . . I—"

"And to think I would have been blissfully unaware of your conduct if Col—er, a colleague hadn't witnessed you entering the inn and seen fit to fetch me." He turned back to Hawk. "And you, you rapscallion, I will have your name for your headstone."

A name for a grave? Hawk smiled, then flinched against a stab of pain in his jaw. "Adam Remington."

Both father and daughter seemed to freeze in place. Dead silence thickened the air in the room.

The man cleared his throat. "The duke of Silvercove?"

Hawk nodded slowly.

The girl dropped down onto the edge of the bed—or did she fall?

Hawk returned his attention to Townsend. A new light had entered the man's eyes. Wary now, Hawk watched him closely.

The older man straightened his shoulders and smoothed a wrinkle from the front of his yellow waistcoat. "Well . . . um, Your Grace, perhaps I was a bit hasty in challenging you. I'm certain that we, as gentlemen, can work this out both to your satisfaction and to mine." He cleared his throat again and glanced at the girl. "I'm sure you realize the ramifications of your actions and what they've done to the reputation of my only child. Under the circumstances, I know that you, as a gentleman of the realm, will want to do what is proper."

"And that is?"

The father flushed. "Why, marry her, of course."

Marry her? A white woman? "No."

"What?"

"No."

"You mean you *refuse* to marry her, even though you've debased her?"

"Yes." Hawk had no idea how he'd gotten here or where the woman had come from. But he had a fair idea someone had arranged this little scene. "I do not know this woman."

"She's a *child!*" the man screeched. "Damn it, man, she's only fifteen! And you were *ravaging* her. I saw you."

Hawk's gaze swung to Victoria. Fifteen? He lowered his eyes to the fullness of her breasts. *This* is a *child?*

Steeling himself, he turned back to the man whose name sounded vaguely familiar. "Her age—or lack of it—is of no importance. Nor is the simple kiss you witnessed. I will not marry her." He kept his gaze away from the girl, knowing if she revealed any sign of real distress he might be tempted to consider the absurd notion. His voice turned cold as he directed it to the father. "You wanted a challenge until you realized my position. Would that not still avenge your honor?"

The man swallowed and looked nervous.

Hawk mentally shook his head. Victoria's father had obviously heard of the savage duke and his many brawls. "Well?"

The man looked distraught, as if he'd just lost a fortune. He drew in a deep breath and nodded. "I will give you one day to set your affairs in order. Pistols at dawn. Day after tomorrow in Stuart's field. Bring your second." He grabbed Victoria by the arm and jerked her to her feet, then marched her out of the room.

When the door closed behind them, Hawk frowned. Had the girl planned this, hoping to force him into marriage?

Remembering how startled she had looked when her father arrived, he did not think so.

Hawk glanced again at the door, wondering if her father would harm her. His jaw clenched at the idea, but he quickly relaxed it. He was not responsible for her. Then another thought struck him. He needed to know the meaning of the word "second."

Turning to recover his coat and cape, he spied the bloody redingote on the floor but saw no sign of his black cloak. He frowned, trying to recall where he had left it, then hazily remembered using it as a shield against the dagger during O'Ryan's attack.

Memory of the battle reminded him of the pain slicing across his arm. He palmed the cut and was surprised to find his sleeve missing. Puzzled, he inspected the moon-shaped injury and decided it was only minor. He had suffered much worse.

Unconcerned with the missing sleeve, he crossed to a dressing mirror hanging over a plain bureau to see the damage done to his face. He groaned. His eyes were swollen, their gray color practically hidden behind puffy lids. A cut near his temple looked raw and angry. Along his left jaw harsh red scrapes rose into welts. Then he grinned. Not too bad, considering there had been four of them.

Still smiling, he ignored the bloody clothing and moved to the entrance. He would have to slip into the apartments without his mother's knowledge. If she saw him like this, she would demand an explanation, one he was not prepared to give. Shaking his head in disgust, he opened the door.

A thin, pointed-faced man who had been reaching for the latch jumped back as if he had been shot. "Bloody hell! You near startled a score o' years off my life. I thought you was out cold." Red suddenly tinted his cheeks, and he looked around anxiously. "I, er, saw the earl draggin' his daughter out o' here and was just comin' to check on you." He cleared his throat and straightened his shoulders. "An' now that I see there ain't no need for concern, that you're not ailing, I must insist that you spot the coin for your lodgin'."

"If you are asking me to pay for the room, then I might

remind you that, since I was unconscious when I arrived, *I* did not request to be brought in here." He narrowed his eyes on the smaller man. "How *did* I get here?"

"The Townsend gel and Collier Parks, her cousin, brung you in when you was bleedin' so bad. My man, Jonas, carried you up before leavin' for the night. To my way o' thinkin' they saved your life. And *you* owe the bill."

Not able to recall any of what the man described, yet knowing the demand was not unjustified, Hawk sighed. He would have to return with payment. He did not carry coin on him when he came to the docks because thievery was so common. Instead, he merely ran a tab at the tavern. "Your fee will be paid tomorrow."

The man opened his mouth to speak, but Hawk turned abruptly and strode down the hall.

He made his way back through the mist-filled streets, his stride still somewhat unsteady as he attempted to walk off the evening's vigorous effect on his body.

The grounds and house were quiet as Hawk slipped in through the great doors and stepped into the candlelit entry hall. Glancing about, he moved quietly toward the curving staircase. Just as his foot touched the bottom step, a door opened somewhere behind him.

"Adam?"

Hawk stiffened, but he did not turn. "I would rest now, madam. Save your questions for another time."

He heard her soft whoosh of breath. Then something rustled. "Very well. I just stayed up because I thought you might like to know the post delivered another letter from Jason Kincaid this afternoon. I didn't remember it until after you'd departed."

She lies, Hawk thought tiredly. She had waited up for him again. He turned around.

His mother gasped, her hand flying to her mouth. "Oh, my word! What's happened to your face?" Her gaze shot to the crescent-shaped cut on his bare arm. "Who did this?"

Swearing inwardly, Hawk held up his palm. "It is of my own doing. Where is the letter from my brother?"

"He's not your brother."

"He is more a brother to me than you are a mother." Seeing the pain in her eyes, Hawk instantly regretted his words, then steeled himself against feeling compassion for this woman. He would not feel pity. He would not feel anything.

Turning her back to him, she crossed the hall to a small, finely carved table near the door, lifted an envelope, and handed it to Hawk. Without meeting his eyes, and without a word, she moved to leave.

Remorse for his harsh words clawed through his conscience. "Madam?"

She stopped but did not turn, her head lowered. Candlelight glinted off her sand-colored hair, now sprinkled with gray. The blue velvet dressing gown she wore hugged her slim shoulders, revealing their slight quiver.

Hawk opened his mouth to apologize, but the words would not come. He glanced around, then focused again on her back. "What is a second?"

She tensed and whirled sharply. "Where did you hear that word?"

Hawk shrugged. "I am to bring one to—a meeting."

The woman clasped her hands tightly at her waist. "And will this *meeting* by chance take place at dawn?"

"The particulars are of no importance. Just the definition."

She uncurled her fingers and raised a shaky hand to her forehead. "A second is a man one might take with him as an alternate when challenged to a duel."

"Would this man have any special requirements?"

"No. But usually he's a friend."

Hawk considered her words. He had made no friends in England—at least no male friends. "I see."

His mother lowered her trembling hand. "No. I don't think you do. Dueling is not like the battles you've experienced. Give you a knife or a musket and there are few who could equal you. But pistols or swords? Have you ever even held one?"

At her skeptical glance, he raised his chin. "Yes." Well, he had *held* Jason's pistol. Inspected it quite closely, too.

"But you've never fired one, correct?" Without waiting for an answer, she turned toward the study. "What's the gentleman's name? It's time to make use of the money and power affiliated with the Remington title. I'm certain, whatever the cause, the fellow will see reason when his pockets are lined with gold."

"No."

She spun back.

"I will touch none of your father's money."

She opened her mouth, but he raised a silencing hand. "It is a matter of honor."

She looked stricken for a moment, fear clouding her eyes. Then, as if realizing words would not dissuade him, she dipped her head in a resigned nod. "I'll pray for you, son," she whispered softly, then quickly left the room. But something about her manner, her unnatural submission, made him wary. She would probably attempt to take care of this problem for him. *If* he allowed it. Which he would not.

Dismissing the thought, Hawk mounted the stairs to his room. As he entered, he noticed the candle flickering on the mantel over the fireplace. His mother again. Closing the door, he shook his head and tossed the envelope on his desk, then crossed to the bed. He would read Jason's letter later, when his eyelids were not so heavy.

Stretching out on the shimmering gold quilt, he folded his hands behind his head and closed his eyes. Immediately visions of the beautiful Samantha Kincaid rose to tease him. Her clear green eyes and silky black hair still haunted him. Though she was of the hated white race, she possessed the courage and daring of a Shawnee brave—and a heart as pure as a child's. His mouth tightened as the familiar pain of wanting this woman gripped him. *Go away, little outlaw. You are wife to my brother.*

As if by his bidding, her image faded only to be replaced by a vision of Victoria Townsend. Victoria Ann Townsend, a name he would not soon forget—if he lived. Her wide blue eyes reminded him of a spring sky, and all that soft dark hair gleamed like polished cherrywood. His brow creased. There was something about her that disturbed him. Something familiar. Was it her name or her face?

When Hawk next opened his eyes, it was late afternoon. He blinked toward the window at the darkening sky. Immediately memories of the night before returned. He bolted upright in the bed and winced against the pain. Ignoring the aches, he tossed back the coverlet. He needed to find a second.

After rising from the bed, he bathed as quickly as his sore limbs would allow, then donned the fresh yet constricting clothing of the white man and sighed, wishing again for his buckskins. Soon he would wear the soft leather. The moment this duel was behind him, if he survived, he would leave this cold, heartless land. He would arrange passage to Virginia. Casting off the twinge of homesickness, he selected another cape from the armoire and headed for the door.

As he left the house and strode toward the stables, his thoughts tumbled. Where could he go to find this second he required?

Visions of the tall, lusty blonde who serviced him came to mind. Cassandra? She had pleasured him many times, as he was certain she had several others. Perhaps she would know of a man he could use. Smiling wryly, he headed for the Remington chaise.

Half an hour later, when Hawk reached Cassandra's cottage in a small rural area, the door was answered by her thin elderly maid. Without greeting, she led him into the parlor, giving him, as usual, the impression that she did not approve of him, or perhaps of male callers in general.

He glanced around at the silk-covered furnishings. The parlor, she had called it. He still could not understand why the white man insisted on giving names to all the rooms in his house. Rooms for sitting, for studying, for sewing. Rooms for eating, dancing, cooking, and sleeping. And even one for drawing. The list went on and on.

His thoughts drifted to his cabin near Lynch's Ferry. It had only one room with a table, a fireplace, and a bed. But it was all he needed. All he wanted.

The rustle of skirts drew his attention to the doorway where his mistress stood in a green dress that matched her jade eyes. Her honey-blond hair hung loose in soft curls around her delicately drawn face.

Her eyes grew wide at the sight of him. "Good heavens! What happened? Are you all right?"

"Do not concern yourself," he roguishly reassured her. "The wounds affect only my appearance."

Her gaze traveled down his length, and a smile softened her pink mouth. "I'm glad to hear that." She walked forward, her well-shaped hips swinging to the rhythm of her gait. "Sit down. I'll have Lissette brew us a cup of tea."

"I did not come for tea."

A thin, pale brow climbed her forehead, and she stepped closer, laying her palm against his chest. Her voice dropped to a husky whisper. "Then what did you come for?"

He could smell the intoxicating scent of her skin. It reminded him of the nights he had come to her. Desire tightened his stomach, but he forced it aside until later. "I need a man."

Cassandra's eyes nearly bulged from her face. *"What?"*

"A man. A second. But I know no such person."

The blonde's expression relaxed, and she chuckled softly. "I see." She turned away and fingered a prism hanging from a crystal lamp. "So, my lord, you're going to fight a duel."

"I am."

"Why?"

"A misunderstanding."

She gave a throaty laugh. "Yes. They usually are." She turned to face him. "So tell me, who misunderstood you? And when and where will you meet him?"

Hawk shrugged. "He is called Townsend, and I meet him at dawn in Stuart's field."

"The earl? What kind of misunderstanding could you have possibly had with the earl of Denwick? I've never known you to gamble."

"He claims I have compromised his daughter."

"Victoria? But she's just a child." Cassandra's thin brows drew together. "Did you do it? Did you find the lovely infant so irresistible that you lost your head?"

Hawk did not like the tone of the woman's voice. "Where do I find a second?"

Cassandra looked as if she wanted to respond, but she said nothing more about the Townsend woman. "I'll make some inquiries and see if I can find someone suitable." She smiled invitingly. "Come back later tonight, Adam." Her heated gaze devoured his body. "That is, if you're up to it."

Ignoring her use of the hated white name, Hawk teasingly traced a finger along the low neckline of her bodice. "I will." He grinned slowly. "And I am."

After leaving the woman, Hawk returned home, fortunately without seeing his mother. He tore off the detestable redingote, then moved to the desk and sat down, his thoughts on the event to come. Near midnight, he would return to Cassandra's and hope she had located a second for him. Then he would find this Stuart's field.

Raising a hand to his neck, he winced against the soreness in his arm. He longed for the healing cohosh herb to ease the throbbing pain. Glancing toward the bureau, he saw the tin of salve his mother had brought to him after his first waterfront battle. It was not cohosh, but it would have to do.

As he started to rise, he noticed the unopened envelope lying on the mahogany desk. The letter from Jason. He had forgotten all about it.

Hawk picked it up, knowing what the letter contained. Jason would want to know if Hawk had learned anything more of his fifteen-year-old half sister.

Fifteen. Hawk fingered the parchment. The child would now be the age of Victoria Townsend. His hands stilled. That was why the earl's name had sounded so familiar. Townsend was one of the two remaining names on his list. He again conjured up an image of the young woman's silky dark hair and light blue eyes.

Light blue eyes. A slow clenching began in his chest, and

he remembered the familiar sensation he had felt when he first recalled Victoria Townsend's pale eyes.

He glanced warily back at Jason's letter, and a cold certainty grew. His brother, too, had dark hair and eyes the color of a spring sky.

Hawk felt as if he were suffocating. *Oh, Moneto, god of all things, do not do this to me.* He stared at the sealed envelope in his hand. "It has to be the other girl." His fingers curled around the parchment, crushing it. "This one *cannot* be Jason's sister!"

Chapter 4

Victoria sat before her dressing mirror, a silver brush clutched in her hand. The last rays of evening light slid through a part in the wine-colored drapes to accentuate the dark shadows under her eyes and the bruise along her jaw. She shuddered at the memory of her father's violent fury.

Glancing at the now locked bedroom door, she sighed with a mixture of disgust and frustration. He hadn't even cared that she'd been innocent of any wrongdoing. He had tried and convicted her without even listening to her defense.

He'd always been strict, that was true. But until Mama's passing, he'd never been unfair or unreasonable. Her death must have hit him hard. Stripped him of compassion. Of any understanding.

She set the brush aside and rose to pace the confines of her room. She hardly knew him anymore. And since the duke refused to wed her, Father's temperament had grown even worse. He now planned to marry her off to the first man who revealed an interest.

She leaned against the fireplace, resting her forehead on the mantel's smooth surface. He didn't care that she'd be doomed to a cold, loveless marriage because of one minor indiscretion. He didn't seem to care about anything anymore. She moved away from the mantel. But she cared. Her father had to come to his senses before the deed was done.

But what if he didn't? What if he forced her to marry someone like Stanford Peckwood? She crossed her arms, rubbing away a sudden chill. The mere thought of Stanford's fat, clammy hands on her body, or those bloated lips violating her own, made her flesh curl. She drew in a shaken breath. "Oh, Collier, why did you leave me alone in that wretched inn?"

At the thought of her irresponsible cousin, she snorted. *He* had caused this mess. As far as she knew, he had never even returned with the physician. The least he could do was help her now. Perhaps talk to Father and somehow convince him not to force her into an unwanted marriage. Collier considered himself a master in the art of persuasion. Indeed he practiced it on her often enough when he needed a loan.

But then, he didn't know that Victoria had no use for the allowance her father awarded her. Her needs were purchased on account. She rarely used coin for anything. So why not let Collier have it? Still, she'd made a game of it, allowing him to cajole and coax her into submission.

She tried not to think about the times he'd told her he was in love with her. She knew it was just another part of his ploy, but sometimes he seemed so sincere that she wished she could feel the same way about him. He was handsome and kind and attentive. He would make a fine husband. Truly, if Collier had a fault at all it was that he spent too much time at the gaming tables. But then, so did most young men. Yes. He would make a good husband . . . for someone else.

Victoria raised a hand to finger the pink silk canopy over her bed. Love. What an overrated emotion that was. Certainly not the blissful state her friends had spoken of at school. Too many times she had seen the volatile outbursts of temper between her parents. She wanted no part of it. Life was too short for such constant upheaval.

She remembered again that a man might die tomorrow— because of her. Either her own father or the duke. No, not her father. He would be the victor—as always, whether by fair means or foul. She could only hope that her father would shoot merely to wound the duke rather than kill him.

A sad smile touched her lips to think that Adam Remington was being forced into a duel over her—a female. It was almost laughable that a man who preferred those of his own sex should risk his life over the virtue of a woman.

A soft tap on the door drew Victoria's attention. "Yes?"

"It's me, Ria," Collier's quiet voice called from the other side. "May I come in?"

She wanted to throttle her cousin for all the trouble he'd caused, but knew he'd only sought to help an injured man. She went to the door and placed her cheek against the frame to speak to him through the panel. "The door's locked."

"I know. The maid told me."

She heard a low chuckle, then a scrape as he slid a key into the lock. Shaking her head, she stepped back. Maybe she had underestimated his powers of persuasion. She crossed her arms and waited for Collier to enter.

Sheepishly he peered into the room. "Is it safe?"

"That depends." She lifted what she hoped was a menacing eyebrow. "Why didn't you return last evening?"

Collier stepped inside, closing the door behind him. "I did. But too late. The physician wasn't home. I had to track him down at the other end of town." He ran slim fingers through his white-blond curls and turned away, refusing to meet her eyes. "Hell of a time for Mistress Ludwig to have her baby. By the time Polk and I got to the inn, everyone was gone." He lowered his gaze and shook his head in disgust. "Atwood was in such a hurry to relay the gruesome details of your plight to Polk and me that he nearly broke his scrawny neck rushing to meet us."

Heat burned her face. "Mr. Polk knows?" she asked weakly, realizing that by now all of London knew of the incident. Her reputation was well and truly ruined.

"I don't know how to apologize for this ghastly dilemma, Ria." Collier glanced up, his gaze searching her face as if for some sign of compassion. "It's all my fault. I should have left the duke to his own fate."

As much as she wanted to agree, to be angry with Collier, she couldn't. "No, Collier, you did the right thing. Without your efforts the duke of Silvercove might be dead now." She placed her hand over his. "Although your chivalry and this nightmarish situation may still be in vain after all."

His fingers clutched hers tightly. "What do you mean?"

Victoria winced at the harshness of his grip. "Father has challenged the duke of Silvercove to a duel at dawn tomorrow."

For a long time Collier remained silent, then suddenly released her hand and turned away. "He refused to marry you?"

"Yes."

"Why?" Collier swung back to face her, his voice low and husky. "Is the man blind? For bloody sake, Ria, you're beautiful and gentle and so damned kind. Any man would be proud to call you his own."

Embarrassment stung her cheeks as she quickly looked away.

"The duke is obviously a fool," her cousin continued, his voice hard, angry. "But I'll be damned if I'll allow him to get away with this. By gad, I'll see him myself. The bounder will marry you or die a slow, painful death by my own hand." He turned for the door.

Victoria felt a rush of panic. "No! Wait!" She grasped his coat sleeve. "I-I mean, it's no use. The duke made his position quite clear."

"Listen, Ria. The man should marry you—do right by you. And I, as your cousin, intend to make *my* position clear to him. I will not allow your name to be tarnished." He took both her hands in his and brushed them with his mouth.

"Oh, Collier." Tears threatened at his kindness. "I appreciate what you're trying to do, but believe me, it won't change anything. I *can't* marry him."

"The bloody bastard's already married?"

Victoria shook her head. "No, no. It's nothing like that. I . . . I . . . Well, I just can't, that's all."

"Damn it, Ria. You're not making any sense. What are you talking about?"

Victoria's hands trembled in her cousin's grasp, and she lowered her gaze to the buttons on his brown waistcoat. "It's just that he doesn't like . . . I mean, he's . . ." She hated herself for what she was about to say. But the alternative left her numb. "He prefers men."

Her cousin looked absolutely stunned. "You're daft. He doesn't. I would kno— I mean, did he tell you this?"

She nodded.

"No. It's not possible. He must have said it to keep from being coerced into marrying you."

"He said it in his sleep," Victoria muttered in a low voice, feeling like an assassin. "He said his heart ached for someone named Sam. An outlaw."

Collier went still. He didn't speak for a long moment. Then, taking a deep breath, he nodded absently. "It will still work. You will marry the duke, and *he* will marry you. Unless, of course, he wants his little secret known."

Her head snapped up. "Collier, no! Oh, please. Don't you dare repeat this to anyone."

Her cousin smiled, not a nice smile. "I won't, unless he forces me to. It's perfect. Can't you see that, Ria? With his wealth and your dowry, you would have unlimited funds. You would be at liberty to do as you please. Free of your father." He lowered his voice. "Free to love whom you choose. The duke obviously wouldn't have an interest in consummating the marriage. Not with his . . . inclinations. It would be a splendid match for you. And me."

He rubbed his thumbs over the backs of her hands. "With the duke's money, we—you would never want for anything." His gaze swept suggestively down her body. "I would see to it personally." His eyes gleamed. "Besides, Remington is that duke who came from America. He's not yet familiar with the ways of the *ton* and won't know that they could care less about his preferences. He will be easily swayed to our way of thinking."

Our way of thinking? "Collier, you're talking nonsense. Stop this immediately. I will not allow you to use what I've told you as a weapon. And if I married the man, I certainly would not agree to the despicable union you're suggesting."

He kissed her quickly on the lips. "That's what you say

now, love. But you're young yet. Tell me that again in a few years."

"If you do this, I'll never speak to you again. I'll never give you another shilling," she threatened in one last desperate attempt.

Collier only chuckled. "Yes you will, love. When you come to realize I've done this for you. And it will be done. I guarantee it. He will propose to you on the morrow." With another quick kiss, Collier left the room.

Hawk stared disbelievingly down at his white brother's crumpled, unread letter still clutched in his fist. If Victoria Townsend was truly Jason's sister, Hawk knew he could not allow her to face shame. He would not do that to his friend. Nor to one who shared Jason's blood.

Hating the guilt that invaded his conscience, Hawk tossed the envelope aside and rose. He had to find out the truth. He raked his fingers through his hair, trying to think who might know of the Townsends' history. He doubted Cassandra would know much more than tales that had been passed among the aristocracy.

Hawk walked to the window and absently brushed aside the pale orange draperies. Alaina's old servant, Bertha, might know—but perhaps from distorted gossip that might or might not be true.

That left only one other. He frowned and swung his gaze toward the door. His mother.

He strode quickly from the room and reached the upstairs landing just as the elderly housekeeper appeared at the top of the steps.

"Bertha, where is Lady Remington?"

Her kind brown eyes widened at the sight of him. "Merciful 'eavens, Your Grace. What 'appened?" Then her nearly invisible white eyebrows shot up. "You've been to them docks again."

"Lady Remington?" Hawk repeated.

Bertha's wrinkled lips puckered into a frown. "Your mum should take a strap to your backside. It'd teach you a thing

50

or two 'bout brawlin' in the streets like some commoner. Why, your grandfather would 'ave . . ."

Hawk released a disgusted breath, knowing she did not mean to offend. Her often brusque tone stemmed from concern for his mother. Too, realizing she could go on for hours, he moved past the woman to descend the stairs.

"She's in the study," the housekeeper said belatedly from behind him. "But if you ask me . . ."

Shaking his head, he made his way to the study. Without knocking, he walked into the room where he saw his mother seated at a large oak desk.

She glanced up, then set aside her quill. Turning over the paper on her desk, she tilted her jaw at a stubborn angle. "Did you want something?"

Hawk eyed the back of the parchment, wondering what she was up to. Probably penning a letter to an influential friend in hopes of learning the identity of the man he would duel, Hawk surmised. Annoyed, he returned his gaze to hers. He would make it easy for her. "Tell me about Victoria Townsend."

"The earl of Denwick's daughter?"

"Yes."

Her gaze fastened on his jaw, then narrowed. "She's the reason for the duel, isn't she?" His mother rose from her seat. She placed her hands on the desk and leaned forward. "You're the nobleman the servants were gossiping about this morning. The one who ravaged young Victoria at the Dockside Inn."

Hawk said nothing in his defense.

"Oh, Adam, what have you done? That poor child." Alaina straightened up. "How could you?"

"I merely want an answer to my question, madam."

His mother's face fell. She looked hurt as she turned her back to him, her shoulders slumped. "What do you want to know?"

"Where the girl was born."

Alaina spun back around, her expression puzzled. "What possible bearing could that have on this situation?"

"Perhaps none."

"Then why—" Alaina pressed her lips together and walked to the fireplace. She rested a hand against the mantel, her gentle features revealing defeat. "I wasn't here at the time, but as I recall from later stories, Victoria Ann was born in the colonies."

Hawk already knew that, but he had wanted her to deny it. Give him something—anything—to hold on to. Trying to ignore the way his pulse drummed, he asked the next question. "Did her parents live in the colonies?"

"No."

He bit back a foul word. "I would hear the tale."

His mother turned to him, studying him closely. "I don't know much. Just that Alexandra and Richard Townsend, Victoria's parents, journeyed to the colonies to visit Alexandra's sister. And everyone was surprised when they returned with a child. They had been trying for several years to have one."

She frowned, drawing her still smooth brow into a crease. "Come to think of it, I do recall mention of people counting on their fingers because Victoria came early. There was some speculation as to . . ." She lifted a dismissing shoulder. "I don't remember the exact details. But what does this have to do with you?"

"Everything," Hawk ground out through clenched teeth. Turning abruptly, he stormed from the study.

He had no doubt now that Victoria was Jason's sister. The suspicion surrounding her birth, the fact that the Townsends had been trying for several years to have a child, then miraculously returned with one, all added up to only one conclusion.

Hawk stopped at the foot of the staircase and kneaded his forehead. He had two choices now: he could allow the earl to kill him, or he could marry the girl. The *white* girl. He drew his hands into fists and started up the stairs. Death might be preferable. But as much as he might like to consider that option, he knew he would not. He would marry Victoria Townsend. *But that did not mean he had to live with her.*

"Your Grace?" Bertha called from behind him. "There's a gent 'ere to see you."

Frowning at the lateness of the hour, he turned to find the yellow-haired man from the Waterfront Tavern standing in the entry. What did *he* want? "Thank you, Bertha." Hawk nodded his dismissal, then looked again to the man. "Yes?"

"Your Grace, I wish a private word with you."

"I do not know you."

"No. But I come on a matter of great importance—to both of us."

Hawk realized by the determined set of the man's jaw that he would not be easily put off. Curious, Hawk stepped back and gestured to the room called the parlor. "In here."

The shorter man took a seat on one of the twin gold settees.

Hawk remained on his feet and moved to the fireplace, his arms folded across his chest. "What is this great matter you wish to discuss?"

The blond placed his palms on his knees, then rose to stand beside Hawk. A smug smile played about his lips. "I am Collier Parks, Victoria Townsend's cousin." He paused, obviously waiting to see Hawk's reaction.

Hawk kept his features clear of expression. He was not sure whether he wanted to thank the man for saving his life or kill him for destroying the balance of it.

Parks took a deep breath. "I understand you refused to marry Ria."

"Ria?"

"Victoria, then."

Hawk nodded. "I did."

"I can't understand your reasoning. Hell, man, she saved your bloody life. And destroyed her reputation in the process. Is this how you repay her?"

Hawk said nothing.

"By gad, Remington. It's not as if she's some withered old maid. She's beautiful, for Christ's sake."

"Yes." Hawk had to agree with that. "But her looks do not matter to me." *Except that she's white.*

Parks turned to face Hawk fully and sneered. "I know."

"What?" At first Hawk feared he had spoken his thoughts. Then he realized that Parks had responded to his words. And something in the man's tone warned Hawk that he was a dangerous foe. "What do you know?"

Parks's teeth flashed in the firelight. "Enough." He turned away. "Oh, not that I'd use my knowledge, of course—*if* we could perhaps come to some kind of an arrangement."

Angry awareness tightened Hawk's muscles. "And just what is this *knowledge* you would not use?" Hawk feared Parks might somehow have learned of his Indian heritage and wanted to use the information to his gain. Not that it mattered to Hawk. It did not. But, as much as he hated to admit it, he did not want to see his mother shunned. He directed his fiercest glare on the intruder.

The blond's eyes met his, then crinkled at the corners before slowly traveling down Hawk's length as if exploring a woman's body.

Hawk tensed.

The man lifted his gaze to Hawk's mouth and studied it. "I know of your *preferences,*" he said quietly. "As a matter of fact I myself have on occasion, um, shall we say, enjoyed a *different* kind of lover."

Hawk felt the blood leave his face. *A different kind of lover.* He eased back a pace.

Parks smiled. "I think it would be to your benefit, Lord Remington, to reconsider your decision about marrying Ria."

"Do you?" Hawk's fury was so great he barely got the words past his lips.

The younger man lifted a shoulder. "Marriage would protect you from gossip." He again inspected Hawk's frame, then grinned. "Harmful gossip that could destroy a man's reputation."

"Let me see if I understand your meaning," Hawk said tightly, understanding very well indeed. "If I marry the earl's daughter, then my own reputation will not suffer. No one will ever learn of my . . . preferences?"

"Correct."

How Hawk kept from striking the bastard, he did not know. "I see." Then another thought occurred to him. "Why have you come and not the earl?"

The man smiled shrewdly. "The earl knows nothing of this situation. He still plans on a duel in the morning. Ria and I decided this is the best course to take."

"She knows of this?"

Collier's smirk widened. "Of course she knows. She told me. Evidently you called out for someone named Sam while you were unconscious. The gentleman—or shall I say outlaw?—your *heart aches for?*"

"Sam?" Hawk clenched his jaw. *Samantha.* He had called for Jason's wife while unconscious, and the girl, Victoria, had misunderstood.

Dragging in a deep, angry breath, Hawk nodded at the first man whose scalp he would have liked to lift. "I understand." He opened the door. "And you may tell the earl and your cousin that I will call tomorrow afternoon with the proposal of marriage."

A superior grin curved Parks's mouth. "I thought you might. Good night, Your Grace." He started to leave, then glanced back over his shoulder, his smile now meaningful. "Perhaps we might get together ourselves one day soon?"

Hawk stared at the man's retreating back, the mere thought of what Parks suggested turning his stomach. Hawk should have beaten the man senseless. And he still might. Of all the insane, idiotic . . .

He ground his teeth together. He had allowed Parks to insult him when he should have castrated the bastard.

"Who was that man, Adam?" Alaina asked from behind him.

Hawk abruptly faced her. He studied his mother, remembering her desertion. Then he thought of Victoria Townsend, and his rage grew. All white women were alike. Self-centered bitches. He glared at Alaina. "The man hinted that he might prefer to share my bed someday."

Her mouth fell open.

Concealing the fury boiling within him, Hawk ignored his mother's sputter of shock and walked stiffly away. On the veranda, he stopped and lifted a hand to the back of his neck. He rubbed at the tense muscles. Never in his twenty-four years had his manhood been doubted, and he was unsure how to react. But one thing was for certain: He needed to keep his appointment with Cassandra. *Now.*

Chapter 5

Victoria paced the parlor, then dropped down into a chair. She still couldn't believe that Collier had accomplished the deed. The duke would call today with a marriage proposal. How could she face the man, especially after what Collier must have threatened?

"Oh, why did I ever open my mouth about the man being short-heeled?" Victoria moaned aloud. "Now not only will I have to marry him but I will have to endure his hostility as well." And he *would* be hostile, she had no doubt of that.

The only advantage to this whole situation was the fact that she would have a home of her own, away from her father's unexplained tyranny. But married to a short-heel? A man who would never . . .

She leaned back, closing her eyes. Her chances of someday having children of her own were about as great as capturing a bolt of lightning. Unless, of course, she took a lover, as Collier suggested. Which was utter nonsense.

Disturbed by the prospect of remaining childless, she shot out of the velvet seat and stomped to the fireplace. "It's not fair. Blast Father! He's ruining my life!"

Feeling close to tears, she swallowed back the welling tightness.

"Lady Victoria?"

Startled, Victoria spun around to see Tess, the young servant, standing in the doorway. "Yes?"

"Lord Remington has arrived."

Victoria clenched her suddenly unsteady hands and nodded to the maid. "Show him in."

The girl hurried out the door, then returned a minute later and led the tall duke into the parlor before nervously retreating.

And Victoria couldn't blame her for being nervous. The duke looked a sight with all those purple and black bruises distorting his face. For a moment she forgot her tension. "Oh, you poor man."

Realizing she'd spoken the words aloud, she blushed clear to her slippers. "Forgive me, I didn't mean . . ."

He studied her closely for a space of time, but didn't speak. Then his attention moved to her jaw.

Self-conscious, she raised a hand to cover the bruise resulting from her father's blow.

The duke looked away, but she saw a muscle twitch in his jaw. He casually inspected the parlor and seemed to find it lacking.

Following his line of vision, she found nothing to warrant disapproval. It wasn't a palace, of course, and obviously below his lofty standards, but it *was* attractive. Her mother's touch shone everywhere from the gold chintz draperies to the finest Oriental carpets. No fault could be found anywhere in the room.

She lifted her chin defiantly. "Is there something amiss, Your Grace?"

He glanced in her direction, his expression cold. "No."

Victoria shifted and straightened her skirt. Well. "Would you care for a cup of tea?"

"Is that always the customary greeting?"

"I don't know what you mean."

"Nothing. And, no, I would not care for tea. I have come to set behind me the task of offering for your hand."

The man didn't mince words. "I see."

He just stood there, waiting. "Well?"

"Well what?"

"What is your answer?"

"What was the question?"

"I am not amused with your games. I merely called on you

as a formality. Your cousin made it quite clear that you seek this arrangement, and obviously there is nothing I can do about it. So do not make the task more distasteful by portraying the innocent."

Stung by the falsehood, yet not quite able to deny it, she drew on her anger. "Why, you arrogant blackguard. How dare you!" She balled her fists and placed them on her hips to keep from punching his nose. "I wouldn't marry you for all the tea in England!"

He eyed her calmly. "Miss Townsend, you are not being offered tea, as you well know. You are being offered a way out of an unfortunate situation and, as I am certain you recall, a duke's fortune at your disposal."

Victoria felt her anger drain away as she grasped the meaning of his words: she was being offered a way out of an unfortunate situation. He was right. Besides, she had no choice. She was obliged to accept the proposal, if that was what it could be called. "Forgive me, Your Grace. You are quite correct and extremely generous, under the circumstances. And for the sake of formality I do accept your proposal, such as it is."

The man watched her intently, then dipped his dark head. "Of course." Without another word he left the room.

Victoria fought the urge to scream vile names at his retreating back. She would never be able to live with such a pompous ass.

Closing her eyes, she tried very hard to gain control of her temper. Well, at least she wouldn't have to worry about sharing the scoundrel's bed.

Lifting the hem of her skirts, she stomped toward the stairs and the serenity of her room. How she wished she had the courage to do something outrageous. Something wicked. Something the duke would not soon forget.

Victoria's hopes rose. So why couldn't she? Her spirits immediately plummeted. She wouldn't know where to begin, that was why. She had absolutely no experience in such matters. Heavens. The most daring thing she'd ever done in her life was sneak food to Paddy. And look how she'd blundered that.

Entering her room, she closed the door behind her and leaned against it. She was doomed to a hapless life with an arrogant prig.

Collier Parks shifted against the upholstered carriage seat. He felt wonderful. Things were working out just as he'd hoped. In five days' time, Ria would marry the *odd* duke and gain a fortune—one that Collier could well use. He'd have plenty of money to buy back his vouchers and live in high style, never again having to look over his shoulder.

The only obstacle that remained was the duke himself. And *that* would soon be taken care of quite nicely.

Ria claimed she'd never give him another shilling, but that didn't worry him, nor did he concern himself over her moral attitude. He had no doubt whatsoever that she could be persuaded to lend him the coin he needed—and eventually to become his mistress. Her nature was too passionate by half, and before long her natural female urges would take care of the problem for him.

He squirmed in discomfort. Just the thought of possessing her caused a tightness in his breeches. Perhaps he should visit his current mistress . . . or one of his *special* male friends.

He smiled as he glanced out the carriage window at the tall-masted ships rocking at anchor. Yes. He would see Bertram. But first he had another matter that needed attention. Leaning back against the seat, he folded his arms and chuckled.

Within a few minutes the driver pulled the coach up before the Waterfront Tavern, and Collier jumped down. He glanced around, wondering how much trouble he would have locating the man he sought at this time of day.

Entering the taproom, he stopped by the door and waited for his sight to adjust to the dimness. When it did, he looked over the patrons, but the fellow was not among them.

Collier crossed to the bar and leaned an elbow on the scarred surface. "Markworth, where's O'Ryan?"

"Ain't seen him since I tossed him out." The hefty

barkeep turned in Collier's direction. "Did you bring me money?"

"I told you the end of the month," Collier reminded him. "That hasn't changed in two days' time. Now, tell me, where can I find O'Ryan?"

The burly man harrumphed, then presented his back to Collier. "Try the *Friendly Maiden*. Captain Ross oughta know."

Glaring at the insolent man, Collier pushed away from the bar and stalked out of the tavern.

It didn't take him long to find the *Friendly Maiden* swaying in her berth beside several other heavily laden cargo schooners.

He boarded the ship, then spoke briefly with Captain Ross who, in turn, directed him belowdecks to the seamen's quarters.

When O'Ryan answered the door, Collier's eyes grew wide. "Egad." The man looked as if he'd fallen beneath a runaway freight wagon. "You look bloody awful."

Dooley O'Ryan twisted his mangled face into a grotesque scowl. "What do ye want this time, Parks? Got another pregnant mistress to sell?"

Collier grimaced. Did O'Ryan constantly have to remind him of that mistake? He sneered. "I came to offer you employment again. But of a different nature."

The man's bloated lips spread flat across brownish green teeth, his fleshy cheek folding up over the bottom of the black eye patch he wore. "Employment, is it? And just what other kind o' job would ye offer the likes o' me? 'Less ye be wantin' a body's throat slit?"

Collier shifted uneasily. "What would you charge for something like that?"

O'Ryan's mouth stretched wider. "More than ye could pay, matey. Who's the cully?"

Flicking a quick glance around, Collier leaned closer. "A duke. Adam Remington."

"Jesu! Now I know ye ain't got enough coin. I don't mess with them kind for no pittance."

"You just set the price and let me worry about the money."

O'Ryan rubbed his chin thoughtfully. "Oughta be worth at least a couple hundred pounds."

"That's robbery," Collier snapped.

"No, matey. It's killin'."

Knowing he had no other choice, Collier nodded grudgingly. "Two hundred pounds."

"Before the deed."

Collier clenched his hands. "I can't get the coin until after the duke is dead and his inheritance passes to his wife." He'd foreseen this and hence had worn the ruby ring that had been a gift from Aunt Alexandra, one of the few things of value he still possessed. He slipped it off his finger. "You can hold this until I bring the money."

The one-eyed seaman looked at the ring and laughed. "A fancy piece, but not worth no two hundred pounds."

"Damn it, man. It's all I have. You'll get your money; you have my word on it."

"I know I will, matey. Yer snivelin' life depends on it." He took the ring. "When do ye want it done?"

Ignoring yet another threat to his person, Collier shoved his hands into his pockets. "There'll be a wedding at Denwick, about a mile north of Regents Park, in five days' time. I want it done then, but not until *after* the nuptials. Follow the bride and groom to their lodgings. But don't do anything in front of the earl's daughter. Take the man away before you—"

"Aye, matey. I get the idea. Ye don't want her ladyship to see the blood."

"I don't want her to know anything whatsoever about this. And that's not all," Collier added as the man started to open the door. "You'll need several men."

O'Ryan puffed out his barrel chest. "I can take care o' the likes o' one paltry duke, Parks."

"You and your jackals didn't do such a fine job a few nights ago."

"What?" O'Ryan's eye blazed, then widened in understanding. "Ye mean the codger we scuffled with is the one ye want done in?"

"The same."

Dooley O'Ryan's hands curled into massive knots, and his arms shook. With a whoosh of breath, he slammed his fist against the bulkhead. "A quick death's too good for the likes o' that crafty cur! I'll see the bastard suffer the horrors o' hell for what he done to me and me men." He tightened his bruised lips until they nearly disappeared behind scraggly red whiskers. "Aye, I will. And he *will* suffer, matey. I'll see to it."

As Hawk stood in the large brick building that housed the Remingtons' solicitor waiting to be announced, he glanced around the spotless office with its blue-gray walls and azure furnishings. From his short acquaintance with Prine Baylor, Hawk knew the man was as stiff and cold as the room. Probably much like Hawk's illustrious grandfather.

Moving to the window, Hawk stared out, his thoughts on his bride-to-be. He could not help wondering how she would feel when she discovered that her bridegroom had left her. Probably relieved, a tiny voice prodded. His mood darkened, though he could not understand why. Too, he still battled with his conscience over leaving her. How would he explain his desertion to Jason?

But staying in England was out of the question. Nor would he force the girl to go to the colonies and live in his single-room cabin. No. He would marry this white woman because he could not bring shame to Jason's sister. He would give her everything she needed. But he could not live with her.

"Your Grace?"

Hawk swung around to the ruddy-faced woman who had gone to inform the solicitor of his presence.

"Mr. Baylor will see you now."

As Hawk was shown into an inner office, the paunchy, elegantly dressed solicitor rose and stepped out from behind his desk. He took in Hawk's battered face, then turned aside in distaste as he gestured a distant greeting with his hand. "Lord Remington. How may I be of service?"

Reaching inside his pocket, Hawk withdrew a sheet of paper and handed it to the man. "I leave on a journey soon. These instructions are to be followed after my departure."

Baylor opened the parchment and scanned the contents, then sucked in a sharp breath. "You can't mean this. I m-mean, this is highly unusual, Your Grace." He looked worried. "Do you think giving control of your entire fortune to your mother is wise?"

"It does not matter."

Baylor stared at the paper he held. "I realize you're from the colonies and not quite up to snuff on procedure, but the sum you've allotted your wife each month is outrageous! Why, it's unheard of to allow a mere woman to squander such vast amounts. Bloody preposterous."

Hawk did not allow his expression to reveal his true feelings for the little man. "Will the Remington finances not withstand the expenditure?"

Baylor flushed. "Well, of c-course, without burden. But that's not the poin—"

"Then do it." Without another word, Hawk left the room.

That task out of the way, he headed for the dressmaker's shop. Cassandra had told him a new bride must have a trousseau—whatever *that* was—and that he could purchase it at Madame Bovier's. Cassandra had also mentioned that the groom was expected to give a special gift to the bride. A wedding gift. He sneered. Apparently a duke's fortune was not gift enough.

Halting the carriage before the clothier, he gave serious thought to abandoning the whole idea, but knew he could not. It was a part of the marriage ritual, and though he cared little for Victoria and his mother, he would not see them shamed before their people.

As he entered the small shop, a bell tinkled above the door. Hawk stopped and looked around. Fabric of every color and texture lay folded on table tops and on shelves along the north side of the room. Drawings of women in various stages of dress lined the whole south wall, while others were stacked on a table in the center of the carpeted floor. He glanced to the rear and noticed that red draperies formed a partition in the back.

"Un moment," a voice called as the curtains parted to reveal a short, round woman of many years. Her silver hair was coiled at the top of her head and pulled so tight that it stretched the skin around her eyes and cheeks. A long pointed stick, similar to the instrument his mother used for knitting, protruded from the silver knot. A yellow tape was draped around the woman's fleshy neck, the ends dangling over her heavy, mature breasts.

"Bonjour, monsieur. I am Monet Bovier." She waved a chubby hand, indicating the interior of the shop. "Zee owner. 'Ow may I 'elp you?"

"I wish to see a trousseau. What colors do you have?"

"Colors?" The woman's warm hazel eyes widened briefly, then softened with humor. "I see. And ees dees trousseau for your bride-to-be?"

Hawk nodded.

"Ah." She bobbed her head up and down. "When ees zee wedding?"

"Five days."

The woman gasped. *"Cinq jours!* Oh, *monsieur,* eet ees not possible to 'ave zee trousseau ready so soon." Her hand fluttered to her bosom. "Monet would need at least a month. No less. Zee clothes cannot be made so quickly."

"Madam, I only want *one* trousseau."

"Monsieur, please. You must understand. What you ask ees impossible." Her hand rose to her throat. "Eet ees obvious that you do not know of zee magnitude of zee trousseau. Eet ees—"

"If the task is too much for you," Hawk interrupted, "I will go elsewhere. The duchess of Silvercove *will* have a trousseau."

The woman's entire manner suddenly changed. "Zee duchess! Oh, *mon Dieu.* You are His Grace, *le duc? Le duc* from zee colonies?"

Annoyed, Hawk started to leave.

"Non, wait! Oh, *monsieur,* I did not know. Monet will

make your bride's trousseau. *Oui*. Eet will take many 'elpers and much work, but eet will be done."

Hawk stared at the woman for a moment, marveling at how easily people were swayed by titles and money, then nodded. "Five days."

"Wait!"

Exasperated, Hawk swung back around.

"I must know her size."

Her size? How the hell was he supposed to know? He raised a hand, indicating Victoria's height to be just below his chin. "Short." He attempted to gesture the size of her waist, then clenched his hands in disgust. "Small."

"She is petite, no? Very nice." The woman's lips twitched. "But Monet needs measurements."

Hawk gnashed his teeth. "Madam, I do not carry the information in my pocket. You will have to ask the girl."

"Oh, *oui*." She rushed to the table of sketches and retrieved a quill and parchment. "What ees 'er name?"

"Lady Victoria Townsend."

"Little Ria? She ees but a child!" Red suddenly stained the woman's cheeks. "Forgive me, *monsieur*. That ees not my concern. And Monet 'as *mademoiselle*'s sizes. I make all her clothes." She arched a questioning brow. "Unless, of course, she 'as—um—gained weight?"

Hawk did not like the woman's insinuation, nor did he like the way his stomach tightened at the thought. Especially since he had never— "No. She has not." At least not to his knowledge. Once again, he turned for the door. "If you have more questions, ask the girl."

Leaving the shop, he tried to dismiss the woman's remark from his mind, but could not. Victoria would never have children as long as she was married to him. Unless she took a lover—or Hawk took her to the colonies with him.

Oddly disturbed by both ideas, Hawk climbed into the carriage and closed the door. He could not do this cruel thing to her. Nor would he destroy the life she knew by spiriting her away to America. Which left only one alternative. He would wait a respectable amount of time, then quietly give her a divorce so she could remarry. But even that thought did not comfort him. Disgusted, he snapped the reins. Enough. It was time to arrange his passage home. Past time. Smiling now, he made his way to the docks.

Aboard the *Sailor's Choice,* Hawk learned that the ship would not leave for the colonies until two days after he and Victoria were wed. Disappointed but not deterred, he decided to have his bags taken to the ship by the Remington servants; he would stay aboard the vessel after the ceremony.

From the docks he set out to meet with a well-known horse breeder from whom he purchased a powerful, well-trained bay, then had it sent to Silvercove. He did not know if Victoria Townsend rode or not, but it was the only gift he considered suitable.

Having accomplished his day's business, he made his way to the Dockside Inn. He still owed the innkeeper for that damned room.

If Atwood was surprised to see him, the proprietor gave no evidence as Hawk entered the common room and placed the price on the counter.

Atwood stared at the coins for a moment, then raised his head. "That'll be another crown, your worship. Had to hire a woman to come in and clean the carpet after you bled all over it like you did."

Hawk glanced at the faded spots on the floor covering and nodded, then added another coin.

Atwood's skeletal hand scooped up the gold. "Never thought you'd come back. You bein' a friend o' Collier Parks an all. The cock's not exactly known for payin' his debts 'round these parts, 'less a body holds him at gunpoint."

"We are not friends."

Atwood blinked. "Ah, I see. You're another one o' that little lady's cronies."

Hawk tried not to reveal his surprise. "Another?"

Atwood laughed. "What's the matter, your godliness? Did you think you were the chit's only gent?" He folded his bony arms on the counter and leaned forward, his expression smug. "I could tell you all about the gel—if the price was right."

Hawk restrained himself from reaching for the bastard's neck. Withdrawing several more coins, he tossed them on the countertop. "Speak."

"Well, now," Atwood said, rubbing his chin. "Seems to me the doxy's been coming down here for the past six months or so, meeting up with some comely older fellow that lives in the alley behind me inn. I seen the pair o' 'em meself a time or two, hugging and all afore he leads her inside his shack. And she always brings a bundle. No doubt a change o' clothes."

He winked a watery eye. "Heard tell the blighter was her groom till her papa crippled him and tossed him out." Atwood grinned, showing gaps between his crooked teeth. "I figure her papa probably caught 'em dallyin' in the hay and tried to kill the cur." Atwood shrugged. "I hear tell McDaniels—that's the chap's name—suddenly comes into a goodly sum o' coin after she leaves. I figure the chit's either paying him for services or helping her lover out."

Hawk kept from revealing the boiling emotions raging inside him, but he did not know how. He turned without a word and left the inn. He could not believe the Townsend girl had fooled him so well. He would have sworn she was an innocent. But the news just reaffirmed his beliefs about white women.

She and her cousin, Collier Parks, *had* arranged the whole thing—Parks obviously for money. But he doubted that Victoria Townsend would risk her life to come to the wharfs for a mere bed partner. No. She came to help out her lover. And with the Remington fortune, she could set him up for life.

Enraged, Hawk stormed down the steps. The woman had made a fool of him, and her cousin had insulted his manhood.

For a moment he considered returning to the solicitor and dressmaker to cancel his instructions, then decided against it. He was not concerned about the money or what the woman did with it. She and her lover could bathe in it for all he cared.

He wanted to kill them both, slowly, torturously. Yet he

knew he would not. He could not harm Jason's sister. Nor, when he returned to Virginia, would he tell his friend of her treachery. He would not see Jason hurt.

But Jason would find out about the wedding later on, when he wrote to his half sister. So how would Hawk explain returning without his bride?

Suddenly an idea struck him, and he relaxed against the carriage seat. There would be no need to explain anything if Hawk took Victoria with him. What better way to punish the lying whore than to remove her from the life she obviously loved? Deprive her of the parties, theaters, and balls of London and force her to live in the rugged Virginia mountains?

A slow smiled curved his mouth. What a surprise wedding present for his little bride.

Chapter 6

May 22, 1775, the day of Victoria's wedding, dawned crisp and cool, the chill of spring rearing its head. That it was her sixteenth birthday, no one seemed to remember, and she tried not to let the lapse affect her as the household hummed with activity. But it did.

Knowing this wretched day would be even worse if she allowed feelings of self-pity to surface, Victoria focused on the upcoming ceremony. She had considered herself fortunate so far. Father had passed along a story that explained the scandal. He claimed that she'd had an argument with him that resulted in her running away. Then, adding credibility to the lie, he had professed that Collier had gone after her, and together she and her cousin had found the duke on their way back home. Further embellishing, he vowed that after she saved the duke's life, Remington fell madly in love with her—hence the wedding.

Victoria smiled at the outrageous tale. Very few people would believe that.

The bedroom door opened, and Victoria's maid hurried in. Behind her stood several other servants with buckets of water to fill the brass tub that sat on the other side of her dressing screen.

Sighing, Victoria gave herself up to their ministrations.

For the rest of the day the pace was hectic. The domestics bustled about frantically cleaning the house and airing the bedding while the cook railed over the short notice and the extensive menu.

By the time Victoria was draped in her mother's wedding dress and ready to go to the chapel, she felt thoroughly exhausted. Not to mention naked. The maid insisted she wear only her petticoats beneath the gown—and nothing more. Victoria couldn't spoil the woman's romantic notions by informing her that *this* wedding night wouldn't be— Victoria's nerves coiled. She didn't want to do this!

Knowing there was no way out, she pasted on a smile and attempted to hide her nervousness. But her stomach twisted into painful knots as she climbed into the carriage for the short ride to the church.

When the driver slowed before the white chapel on a small knoll near the edge of Denwick grounds, Victoria felt the first surge of genuine alarm. *She couldn't go through with it.*

She panicked and fully intended to escape when the coachman pulled open the door. But in that instant her father emerged from the building, his eyes narrowed as if he suspected her purpose. He raised his ever-present cane in a gesture that dared her to defy him.

Drawing in a ragged breath, she cast one last forlorn glance at the freedom of the distant hills and warily resigned herself to her fate.

"Smart girl," her father murmured low enough so that only she could hear as he stepped up beside the carriage and looped her arm through his. Then, louder, he added, "Come, dear child, let's not keep your bridegroom waiting."

Victoria didn't point out that the duke could wait until the sea evaporated for all she cared. Gathering her courage, she lifted her chin and fixed her gaze on the arched double doors of the church.

From the corner of her eye, she caught sight of the Remingtons' somber black coach with the Silvercove crest etched on its doors. Terror stiffened her limbs as the magnitude of what she was about to do struck her. She was going to marry a man she'd seen only twice in her entire life!

Her step faltered.

Richard Townsend tightened his hold on her arm.

She winced, then continued forward, grasping the only reassurance that she had—the duke, since he was short-heeled, obviously would not claim his husbandly rights. She gave thought to never having children, but at sixteen she wasn't overly concerned. One never knew what might happen in the future. Squaring her shoulders, her thoughts and fears on the moment at hand, she marched toward her bridegroom.

Inside the chapel Hawk stood rigid before the white-clad man of the church and watched the last of the guests he did not know arrive and take their seats. He felt like a captive on display. Why did they not just get on with it?

Behind him the arched doors swung wide. What he saw nearly stopped his heart.

Victoria Townsend stood beside her father, her head bowed beneath a net of misty gold. The matching dress she wore dipped low in front to reveal the gentle swell of her upturned breasts, then tightened around her tiny waist before flaring out in lacy ruffles to the floor.

Through the gold veil, he could make out her delicate features surrounded by silky cherrywood-colored hair, and for a moment he remembered its soft texture. Hawk gripped the customary ring he held, the one he would soon give to her, and cursed her for being so beautiful—and so young.

Then, recalling his battered appearance, he turned back to the man in white. He did not want her to look upon his mangled face. Let her think of the money she sought instead.

He smelled her sweet, flowery scent long before she stopped beside him, but he did not turn. He would not look upon her again until she was his.

Victoria felt overwhelming rejection when the duke looked at her, then turned his back as if the mere sight of her repulsed him. Tears stung her eyes. This was her wedding day . . . and her birthday. It should have been the happiest day of her life.

She took her place beside the man who would be her husband, but she barely heard the priest's words when he began the ceremony. Her thoughts clouded, then dulled. Yet somehow, during the long service, she managed to make the appropriate responses, and shortly heard herself pronounced the wife of Lord Adam Remington, fifteenth duke of Silvercove.

It was done. For the rest of her life she would belong to this man. Swallowing with difficulty, she turned to face her husband but lost her nerve and lowered her head.

He lifted her veil, then placed a finger beneath her chin. As he raised her lips to meet his, she closed her eyes and prayed he would not be a cruel man.

In answer to her silent plea, he kissed her gently, almost reverently. Victoria allowed herself to enjoy the incredible warmth of his mouth and the feel of his body as he pulled her against his masculine length.

Masculine? She went rigid.

Obviously sensing the change in her, he released her and stepped back.

Embarrassed, she glanced away, unable to meet Adam's gaze, knowing it would be cold and filled with loathing.

The few well-wishers applauded boisterously. Then there was nothing for her to do but accept the rounds of congratulations and hugs from her friends and the smattering of distant relatives.

From the church, the wedding party and the guests retired quickly to the main house for supper and the mandatory festivities, though Victoria had never felt less like celebrating. But there was little else she could do. Forcing a smile, she willed herself to appear the enamored bride.

And she managed quite well through most of the evening, except when Collier shot her a bold wink or her father impaled her with a satisfied smirk.

Lady Remington was Victoria's only salvation. Alaina seemed to be the only person in the room who understood Victoria's frightening position.

When the musicians began a lilting minuet, Victoria's gaze darted to Adam. Her nerves clenched. The bride and groom were expected to lead the first dance.

The duke's mother was speaking quietly to him, obviously telling him something he didn't want to hear, if the way he scowled was anything to go by. He shot a disapproving look at Victoria, then glanced toward the musicians, and his mouth drew into a deep frown.

He didn't want to dance with her. Any imbecile could see that. But he walked in her direction nonetheless.

Desperately trying to hold on to her composure, Victoria met his gaze, calmly waiting for him to escort her to the center of the floor. But her facade crumbled when he reached out, grabbed her upper arm, and marched her out the front door.

"Wh-what are you doing?"

The duke didn't look at her. "Leaving."

Good heavens. Was the mere thought of dancing with her that distasteful? "You can't do this," she whispered breathlessly, her feet barely touching the ground as he pulled her along.

"I already have." He stopped and lifted her into his waiting carriage.

Sliding onto the seat, Victoria twisted the unfamiliar gold band on her finger in anxious frustration. She didn't want to leave yet. With *him*. They should have stayed for hours, but the wretched man acted as if he had no sense of propriety at all. Her husband was truly an unprincipled rogue.

Husband. What a strange sound that word had to it. Edging as far away from the duke as possible, she straightened the skirt of her wedding gown and folded her hands.

Adam Remington seemed to find her presence boring. He completely ignored her, just sat there holding aside the edge of the drawn curtain, staring out the window. They rode in silence for so long that Victoria began to feel invisible, and she felt dreadfully naked without her undergarments. Blast the maid, anyway. Finally she could stand the deafening silence no longer. "Where are we going?"

He didn't turn away from the window. "To our lodgings."

"The ones you share with your mother?"

"No."

Victoria sighed. The man had a lot to learn about conversing. "Your Grace, are we to spend our entire married life in complete silence?"

"Apparently not," he said dryly.

She felt her anger stir and crossed her arms, then leaned back, clamping her lips together. Fine, she thought. You don't want to talk? Then we won't talk. Pompous fool.

An eternity later, when the carriage at last pulled to a stop, Victoria brushed aside the window curtain and glanced out. Shocked, she stared at the sign announcing the name of a hostelry: The Dockside Inn.

If she'd had any doubt before, she didn't now. Her reluctant husband was well and thoroughly furious over being forced to wed her. With blinding clarity she realized that, even though she wouldn't share his bed, being married to the sulky duke was going to be a trial in itself. Thank goodness she didn't have anything else to contend with.

Inside the stark common room, Mr. Atwood grinned as he motioned for the hulking Jonas to take Victoria's portmanteau. "The room at the top o' the stairs."

Realizing that Mr. Atwood meant the same room that she'd been in the night of the scandal, Victoria was torn between outrage and humor. Humor finally won out. Turning to her husband, she feigned pleasure. "Oh, wonderful. That's my favorite room."

She could have sworn she saw his lips twitch before he dipped his head. "I am glad you approve." He gestured toward the stairs. "After you."

In the room Jonas set the bag down, then offered her a slight smile before he left them.

Glancing about, she noticed that only one change had been made in the furnishings. The single narrow bed had been replaced by a larger one. Quickly forcing aside a rush of wariness, she mentally surmised that Mr. Atwood had arranged that, thinking she and the duke would share the bed.

The mere thought of sleeping with Adam Remington sent a skitter of nervousness down her spine. She tore her gaze away from the bed, only to have it land on a large stack of boxes in one corner of the bare room. At first she thought the rest of her luggage had been brought in from the back of the carriage, then realized it couldn't have been, since they just arrived. "What are those?" she asked, pointing.

"I am told they are a trousseau."

Victoria couldn't hide her surprise. "For me?"

"I did not purchase them for the maid."

She ignored the remark and allowed a surge of happiness to swell inside her. Her husband had given her a birthday present, however unwittingly. Tears stung her eyes, and she lowered her gaze, not wanting him to see how his kindness affected her. "Thank you, Your Grace." After gaining control, she glanced up through still damp lashes. "Do you mind if I wait until we get home before I take the garments out of the boxes?" She felt her cheeks sting. "I— It's just that this room is so . . . I'm afraid they might get . . . soiled."

He frowned and looked around the room as if seeing it for the first time. His expression turned grim, and he nodded.

Relieved, Victoria sneaked another curious peek at the boxes, wondering how her husband's taste ran in women's apparel. He really couldn't have had much practice.

"Turn around," Adam said softly. "I will unfasten your gown."

Victoria's heart hit her throat. "What?"

"Does your hearing fail?"

"N-no. Of course not." Her cheeks flamed. "I just didn't expect—"

"That I would assist you?"

A slight tremor shook her body at the thought of his hands on her flesh. Besides, because of her maid, she wore no substantial undergarments. Victoria quickly admonished herself. The man isn't in the least interested in . . . "No. I, um, just thought we might dine first."

He stepped behind her and reached for the row of pearl buttons down the back of her dress. "You thought wrong." He moved closer, his warm breath caressing her ear. "But then, you are wrong about a lot of things."

Something tripped across her belly. What was *that* supposed to mean? Struggling to keep the shivers at bay, she waited for him to finish the task. Unfortunately, when he did, he slipped the sleeves of the gown off her shoulders.

She grasped the front to keep from exposing herself. "I can manage the rest, thank you."

He turned her to face him, holding her gently but firmly by the shoulders. "And deny your bridegroom the pleasure?"

Her breath caught. "You're not going to—"

He leaned closer, his eyes smoldering. "Yes."

She blurted out a reply without thinking: "But you don't like women!"

His jaw tightened for just an instant; then he smiled and lowered his gaze to her nearly bare breasts. "You are not a woman . . . yet."

"That's not what I mean and you know it. You prefer *other* entertainment."

He dug his fingers into her shoulders as if he were restraining himself. "I do? And just what might that be?"

Victoria swallowed a lump. Oh, heavens. Something about his very masculine, very dangerous manner gave her pause. She'd better not have been wrong about him. "I, um . . ."

He released her shoulders, and she nearly sighed aloud with relief, until she felt the bodice of her dress being wrenched from her hands, exposing her bare breasts. Before she could move to cover herself, he jerked her to him, and his mouth captured hers.

Fear trembled through her body. The angry urgency in his kiss revealed not only passion but fierce, savage domination. Oh, God. She *had* been wrong about his preferences!

She tried to pull away, but he held her fast. A loud drumming thundered in her ears, and she realized it was her own heart. Again she sought freedom by kicking at his shins, only to have him tangle his leg around hers and tumble her onto the bed.

Nearly hysterical with fright, she pounded and shoved at his massive frame. Nothing affected him. His kiss became more demanding, more explosive.

She twisted her head from side to side, trying to avoid his kiss.

Adam pressed her down with his body, so hard she could barely breathe. His hands tangled in her hair. He ground his lips against hers, uncaring of the damage he did to her tender mouth. Uncontrollable fear quaked through her. Never had she dreamed he'd want to hurt her—that he'd attempt *this*.

"No!" she cried softly.

The duke's hold tightened. "Yes, *wife.*"

Oh, dear God, he was going to force her. "Please don't."

He lowered one hand from her hair and covered her breast, his fingers hard, bruising.

The destructive power in that hand infused her with terror. "No! Stop!"

His mouth moved down her throat until it covered the peak of her breast jutting between his thumb and forefinger.

At first incredible warmth spread through her; then she felt his smooth teeth brush her nipple. Nearly insane with fear, she arched her back and screamed.

He bit her gently, warningly.

A choked sob escaped her heaving chest. "Please, please don't do this to me."

He raised his head, and his eyes blazed savagely; then he released her abruptly and rose from the bed. "You play the simpering virgin well, but we both know the truth about your purity."

Victoria was too relieved to be free of him to immediately grasp the meaning of his words. By the time she did, he was gone.

As he stormed along the upstairs landing, Hawk felt sickened by what he had nearly done. He had not meant to frighten the child or to kiss her—or to lose himself in her. But when he had seen her naked back, he could not control the leap of desire that singed his flesh. He had never known such a fierce urge to possess, to conquer, as he had at that moment.

And then for her to beg. *Beg.* Something a Shawnee

woman would never do, even under torture. He shook his head. Victoria might be Jason's sister, but she displayed none of his courage or honor.

"Honor!" Hawk spat the word aloud. She had displayed as much honor as *he* had. Not only had he almost raped her, he had intended to exact his revenge by taking her to the colonies. *Had? He still* intended to.

Disgusted with himself, yet strangely unwilling to change his plans, Hawk bounded down the stairs and through the common room, thankful that, for once, Atwood was not about. The innkeeper, assuming the newly wed couple would not wish to be disturbed, would not be aware that Hawk had left his bride. Though Hawk did not know why he should care. It would not matter if word got out. Victoria would not be here. All the same, unreasonably, he was pleased that her reputation would not suffer yet another blow.

As he neared the door, he thought again of the long wedding and the celebration that had followed. The gathering had been small. Had it been a proper ceremony with the posting of the banns and the usual waiting period, the guests surely would have been numerous.

He had actually been enjoying himself throughout the later festivities, watching Victoria. With pride he had noted the graceful way she moved, the way she tilted her head at a slight angle when she spoke or raised a slim hand when emphasizing a word. Her smile had been genuine then, parting her lips to reveal small straight white teeth. Then he had seen her cousin wink at her conspiratorially.

Hawk gripped the door latch, vowing to someday plant his fist in Collier Parks's smirking face.

The thought easing his anger somewhat, he remembered how shocked he had been when his mother whispered that he and Victoria were to lead the dance. Dance! He did not know how. And though his wife had been embarrassed when he led her away, it would have been much worse for both of them had he made the attempt.

As he opened the door leading to the street, another thought occurred to him, and he felt a pinch of guilt. The girl had been so pleased over the trousseau. He would not like for her to learn that he had not thought of it himself. Then he remembered his other gift, and he could not wait to see the expression on her face when she saw the stallion.

His spirits lighter now, he passed through the door, anxious to get to the ship and make certain the cabin was ready, then unload Victoria's luggage from the back of the carriage. Then he would send for the horse. Until today he had kept his plans from his bride, but in a few hours . . . Stepping out onto the boardwalk, he started down the rickety steps, his smile growing.

A sound thudded behind him.

Instinctively he turned.

Something hard slammed against his temple.

He blinked and tried to focus, then staggered as everything faded into whirling blackness. . . .

Chapter 7

Silvercove
March 8, 1782

Victoria inhaled the crisp salty scent of the ocean as she walked toward her horse, away from the village. She also pretended not to notice the little shadow that followed her. The same one that always trailed her when she brought food to the townships under Silvercove's protection. Nigel. An eight-year-old scamp who had stolen her heart the first time she visited the hamlet seven years ago—and she knew what he wanted.

She smiled when she thought of the remaining sugar biscuits in a satchel tied to her saddle. Though she'd given all the children one, Nigel always came back for another— and she always gave it to him—but not because he was crippled and not because she wanted a child so desperately, she assured herself.

Resentment toward her husband rose, and for the hundredth time, she cursed him for leaving her, for denying her the thing she wanted above all else. A child. Not that she'd wanted one when they married. She hadn't. She'd been too young to care then. She'd been completely content to assume her role as mistress of her own house and to enjoy freedoms she'd never before experienced. But later, as the years slipped away from her, she began noticing an emptiness in her life. Something missing.

She had watched her friends marry, rejoiced at the birth of their babes, and attended numerous christenings. But being a godmother wasn't enough. Something inside her ached with the need to hold her own child to her breast. A need that couldn't be satisfied as long as she remained married to a man who pretended she didn't exist. A man who hadn't made an appearance since their wedding night.

Oh, how naive she'd been back then. The days following Adam's disappearance had been torture for her. Her mother-in-law had insisted Victoria stay with her at Silvercove, on the ocean near Brighton, and not concern herself with Adam's disappearance. But Victoria felt certain he'd been waylaid somewhere and possibly killed. Finally, after a week with no word from him, she'd gone to Adam's mother with her fears—and plans to investigate.

Alaina had gently told her of Adam's intent to return to the colonies. Still not fully mollified, Victoria checked with the servants and found that the domestics had indeed taken his luggage aboard a ship the day before the wedding.

Victoria had been infuriated by his desertion and refused to waste another thought on the unprincipled rogue. Of course, that hadn't come to pass. She was reminded of his cruel desertion by the sly smirks sent her way by members of the *ton*, by the pitying looks she received from the servants, by the sadness in Alaina's eyes each time she posted another letter to the Kincaids' plantation in Lynch's Ferry, Virginia, knowing his friend Jason would see that he got it. But Adam hadn't answered a single one, nor had he contacted Victoria.

Alaina, ever patient, merely told Victoria not to concern herself with his failure to reply, that it had taken Adam fourteen years to respond the last time.

Victoria had taken her mother-in-law's advice and firmly put the blackguard out of her mind—and her life. Until now.

Brandy, Victoria's stallion, nickered beside her, pulling her from her musings. He slapped his shiny black tail, swiping it across his glistening sable-colored rump.

Victoria stroked his sleek neck. "We're about ready, boy." She looked back over her shoulder at the thin barefoot child who had followed her. With unevenly cropped red hair and a small round face splattered with freckles, and wearing only a pair of baggy breeches, he resembled a street urchin from London.

Her gaze drifted down to his twisted right leg as she recalled the day his drunken father had run over him with a cart. She looked at his face, at the expectant look in those big green eyes.

Warmth filled her. "Did I forget to give you a biscuit again, Nigel?" She tried desperately not to smile when the boy shifted uncomfortably.

He stared at the satchel on her horse, then back at her, obviously torn between his desire to tell the truth and his fear of not receiving another treat.

Guilt stung her for putting him in such a position. "Well, it doesn't matter. I've brought a few extra." She knelt down and touched his smudged cheek. "Would you like one?"

A dimpled grin brightened his face, revealing a space where his two front teeth used to be. "Yeth, yer ladythip."

She smiled as fondness for the boy enveloped her, and she had to check the urge to pull him into her arms, to cuddle him as she would her own child someday. Her smile faded. If her marital situation didn't change soon, there wouldn't be a someday. At nearly three and twenty, her childbearing years were becoming quite limited.

Oh, why had she waited so long to consider the course she was about to take? Certainly at first it had been quite enthralling, being her own mistress and not having to answer to anyone over an occasional lapse in behavior. But with the war and all, the years had slipped away from her. Too many of them.

Trying not to reveal her despair to the boy, she rose and retrieved a biscuit from the satchel and handed it to him. "Make certain the other children don't see this. There aren't enough biscuits for all of them."

Nigel nodded vigorously. Then with a grand smile and a shy thank-you he darted off into the sparse forest.

Victoria watched sadly as the child hobbled from tree to tree on his mangled leg, wishing again that his father would allow her to take him to London to see a physician. But he wouldn't, and she feared pursuing the matter further. If she asserted her authority, the father might turn his wrath against her toward the boy. But maybe someday . . .

She gritted her teeth. "That word again." With a sigh, she rested her head against Brandy's neck. She stroked the muscled jaw, enjoying the scent of leather and hay that clung to his smooth coat. At least she still had the stallion.

"Have I told you today how much I love you?" She nuzzled him. "I do, you know. More than anything. You're the one good thing that came out of my wretched marriage. And if I ever see my cretinous husband again, I'll thank him for *you*, if for nothing else."

The bay sidestepped and snorted as if he understood.

Lifting her head, Victoria stared across the meadow bordering the village, toward the towering fortress that sat on a cliff edge. Silvercove. Impressive and regal-looking with its imposing gray walls and staggered turrets, it dominated the craggy landscape above the ocean.

She shuddered at the memory of her first sight of the fortress seven years ago when she and Alaina had arrived here shortly after Adam's desertion. Victoria had assumed by his manner that the duke was cold and hard, *among other things*, but she'd never expected his harshness to overflow into the home she would have been expected to share.

No, they would not have shared it even if he hadn't disappeared. According to his mother, Adam had never stayed at Silvercove—had in fact refused to set foot in his grandfather's home. Fleetingly Victoria wondered where they might have lived if he hadn't deserted her. It certainly couldn't have been drearier than Silvercove.

Thank Providence that Alaina had agreed to remain with her in this dismal place, to help her redecorate at least a few of the hundred rooms. Back then Victoria's beautiful mother-in-law had been the only wisp of breath in this lifeless citadel created by a line of cold Remington dukes.

Chills pricked her skin when she thought of the last man who'd ruled the menacing structure. Although Lady Remington hadn't said as much, Victoria had inferred that Alaina's father, Walter Remington, was a cruel, merciless man. Victoria had often wondered if Adam was anything like his grandfather.

She smiled suddenly, recalling how she'd at first thought her husband short-heeled. Later she was thoroughly stunned when her mother-in-law told her of Adam's somewhat scandalous reputation among the women of the *ton*—and of his heritage. At sixteen, the mere thought of being married to a lustful "savage" Indian had nearly given her apoplexy. And to think that her mother-in-law had actually lived among them—*in the woods!* She shivered even now at the thought of living within the terrifying confines of a forest.

A few years later, when she'd finally accepted her husband's ancestry, she had actually laughed—especially when she recalled the evening of their wedding when she and Adam had been expected to lead the dance. How affronted she'd been at the time, when he'd snatched her away, ignoring propriety. Now, of course, she realized he probably hadn't known the complex steps of the minuet—or of any dance, for that matter, unless it was a war dance.

Once she'd become accustomed to being married to a Shawnee brave—one who was definitely not short-heeled— Victoria's natural inquisitiveness had taken over. For weeks she'd assailed her mother-in-law with questions about Adam's people, their ways, their beliefs.

With amused tolerance, the woman had told Victoria of the peaceful Shawnee village, of Adam's Indian father, Flaming Wing, and of Alaina's tranquil life there. But Victoria still felt that her mother-in-law had left a few details unexplained. Vital ones—like why she had left the village and people she obviously loved. But Victoria hadn't pressed the older woman for more than she wanted to give.

Brandy whinnied.

Victoria glanced up, then groaned when she saw her cousin Collier weaving his way down the cliff path toward her. For six and a half years, she'd lived in peace with him away in the war. But in the months since he returned to take up residence at Denwick, he'd made annoying her his life's work.

As she listened to waves crash into a small cove on her left and watched his tall frame negotiate the last of the rocks, Victoria noted the changes that had taken place over the years. He had filled out; his shoulders were a little broader, his stance a bit straighter, his white-blond hair now light gold. But there was more—a new ruthlessness to him, a dangerous mien that hadn't been there before he joined the king's navy and fought in the colonies.

"Ria, love," Collier called, strolling up to her. "The maid told me you had ridden to the village again, so I waited. But you were gone so long, I began to fear for your safety." He lifted her hands and pulled her forward, brushing her lips with his. "I was concerned that something might have happened to you."

Victoria made a valiant effort to look contrite. "I didn't mean to worry anyone. I guess I lost track of time."

He slipped an arm around her waist, pulling her against him. "Speaking of time, isn't it about time you stopped this foolish maidenly game?"

It's not a game, Victoria wanted to rail at him as she strained against his hold. "Collier, please, I've told you a hundred times: *I will not be your mistress.*"

"Damn it, Ria, you're wasting your life—and mine!" He tightened his hold, his smoky cigar scent invading the clean sea air. "It isn't right for you to deny yourself like this. You're twenty-two years old, for bloody sake, nearly twenty-three, and you've yet to know a man's touch."

She bristled. "You don't know that."

"The hell I don't. It's the talk of the *ton.* All of London knows that bastard husband of yours left you on your wedding night. Atwood saw to that when he brought your supper tray and found the duke gone. Bloody hell, Ria. Haven't you ever noticed the way a room suddenly goes quiet when you enter?"

How could she help but notice? Victoria thought angrily.

His voice rose against the roar of another wave as it rumbled into the cove below. "Everyone snickers behind your back. They call you frigid." He stepped away. "It's even been rumored that your husband left you because you were unacceptable, because you refused to let him bed you."

He tossed a dismissing hand. "Of course we know it's not so, but that doesn't prevent the hordes from gossiping."

She clamped down on her rising irritation. She knew what everyone believed, but what could she do about it? Too, she couldn't help wondering if there might be a grain of truth to the tale. After all, she *had* fought him.

"It isn't right," Collier continued. "Damn it, love, I *need* you." He jerked her up against him. "Even before I went away to that damnable war I wanted to make you mine. In every way possible. Can't you see that?"

Victoria drew in a shaky breath. "Yes. I can see what you're trying to do, but I won't allow it." She met his heated gaze, then immediately regretted it.

Collier's eyes flashed, and his grasp on her waist tightened. He kissed her hard, his mouth hot and bruising. "Damn you," he murmured heavily. "Don't you realize what you're doing to me? Gad, Ria, I can't go on like this. I can't sleep, I can't eat, I can't think of anything but having you."

Victoria felt his hard maleness rub against her belly through the folds of her skirt and was appalled by her own reaction to the manly embrace. How she dreamed of someone to hold her like this. To whisper words of love. To give her children.

She pushed the images aside, praying the unholy feelings would pass quickly. "Don't, Collier. Please, just go."

He continued to press her against him. Then finally, with obvious reluctance, he released her. "I'll go . . . for now," he vowed meaningfully. "But I'll be back. You can be sure of it. And you'll soon come to see things my way." He lowered his voice seductively. "You can't resist the urges of your own body forever."

As much as Victoria wanted to deny that, she knew it was very likely true. With every kiss, every touch, her resolve slipped another notch.

She watched her cousin's lanky frame disappear up the winding path, then raised a trembling hand to her forehead. "Curse you, Adam Remington, for leaving me to this fate." It wasn't fair. The duke had no right to do this. She whirled toward Brandy. Her mother-in-law would be in the study working on the household accounts—another matter Adam hadn't bothered to concern himself with—and Victoria needed to see her. It was time to put a stop to this marital nonsense once and for all.

If Adam Remington wouldn't return to his responsibilities, then by all that was holy, she'd go find him. She would see that he freed her from this silken prison. He'd give her an annulment or return and take up his duty as her husband, the father of her children. She stumbled at that last thought, but quickly regained her balance. He wouldn't come back.

Reining Brandy toward the castle, she took the short sloping path up a green hillside to the stables.

Alaina glanced up as Victoria strode into the study. Closing the ledger she'd been writing in, she smiled warmly. "Good afternoon, dear."

Victoria stood motionless, gazing at her beautiful mother-in-law. The woman hadn't aged a day with the passing years. She was still absolutely stunning.

Fleetingly Victoria wondered if the duke favored his mother. On that thought followed another more startling one: Victoria wouldn't have recognized her own husband if he'd stood before her. She'd never even seen a miniature of him. And the way things were going, she would never know what lay beneath the puffy bruises she remembered. "Excuse me, My Lady. I don't mean to interrupt, but there's something I'd like to discuss with you."

Alaina frowned. "Victoria, why are you addressing me so formally? I thought we'd progressed beyond that years ago?"

"We have, but—" Unable to meet the woman's eyes, Victoria lowered her gaze to the thick carpet depicting a scene from the hunt. "It's just that—that—"

Her mother-in-law muttered something under her breath and, as she often did when agitated, picked up the pure white eagle feather that always lay on her desk. She slid her fingers along its softness and studied it, then carefully replaced it. "Collier's been here again."

"How did you know? Did he disturb you?"

"No. And I didn't have to see him to know he'd been here. Only after he visits are you so unsettled. What was it this time? Has he already started badgering you for money again?"

Victoria fidgeted with the material of her skirt. The woman was too perceptive by half. "No. He hasn't mentioned money since he returned. Besides, he couldn't have gone through Father's entire estate in a mere seven years."

Alaina's expression turned bitter.

Victoria could sense the woman's disapproval of what Richard Townsend had done, even beyond the grave. But it hadn't mattered to Victoria that he had changed his will and left everything to Collier. She had no need of his fortune.

Besides, she still remembered how desperate her cousin had been for money right after her wedding. He claimed his life had been threatened over gambling vouchers. Victoria had finally given in. At Paddy's suggestion, however, and before she released the funds, she had insisted that Collier use a portion of the money to buy a commission in the king's navy. She'd wanted him to learn responsibility and make something of himself. And he had. As a naval supply officer, he'd made an extraordinary amount of money, or so he boasted.

"I will never understand why your father left you out of his will. You *are* his only child."

Victoria felt a stab of pain, recalling how her father had died just two days after her wedding. "It doesn't matter. I didn't need his money then, and I don't now."

Alaina inspected the length of Victoria's modest coral gown. "Obviously you do. You won't spend my son's wealth. If you had your father's, you might at least have some more elaborate gowns made." She rose and moved to stand before Victoria. "Child, I don't approve of what my son has done to you, but he did at least léave you a generous allowance. Why won't you use it?"

"I have used some of the duke's money."

"Yes. For the villagers and to send Paddington McDaniels to the healing waters at Bath. But except for a few paltry coins for repairs to the castle and the purchase of Collier's commission years ago, you've barely spent a pittance on yourself."

"There's no need."

"There's every need," Alaina countered in exasperation. "Just look at yourself. You look more like a pauper than a duchess. You've purchased only the barest necessities since Adam bought your trousseau."

Victoria lifted her chin stubbornly. "I'm sorry if my attire offends you."

Alaina's gaze softened. "Victoria, there's nothing you could do to offend me. You know that. I love you as if you were my own daughter. I just hate to see you being so inflexible about this." She returned to the desk, then traced a finger along the spine of the white feather. "And since the direction of this conversation is obviously upsetting you, why don't we change the subject, hmm?" She met Victoria's gaze. "Now, tell me the reason for Collier's visit."

Unable to restrain her frustration, Victoria blurted out a reply: "He wants to become my lover."

"What?"

Victoria plopped down in a wing chair. *"That's* what he's been nagging me about ever since his return."

Alaina stood deathly still. When she finally spoke, her voice came out in a strained whisper. "What did you tell him?"

Surprised by the intensity in her mother-in-law's quiet query, Victoria glanced up. "I was tempted to say yes." She hid her true feelings of uncertainty behind a carefree facade. "After all, I imagine it would be considered acceptable, or at the very least *expected*, under the circumstances." She offered a weak grin. "But I refused."

A look of relief smoothed the older woman's features. "Thank heavens."

"At least for now," Victoria continued. "Alaina, you don't realize what I've gone through. Every day I expect Adam to reappear. But he never does. He has left me in a most awkward position. I'm neither married nor free. And the truth is, I'm quite tempted to take a lover"—she waved a hand—"whether it's Collier or someone else. It goes against all my beliefs, but what else am I to do? I can't continue like this. I've got to do something. I'm *going* to do something."

Alaina sank into her brown leather chair. "What?"

"I'm going to find my husband. If he doesn't want a wife, and obviously he doesn't, then I want my freedom. If he refuses, for whatever unearthly reason, then . . . well, I guess the life of a tainted woman is better than no life at all."

Alaina picked up the feather from her desk and studied it with a faraway look. When she at last looked at Victoria, there was a new light in her gray eyes. "You're right, child. It is time for Adam to accept his due." She twirled the feather, then nuzzled it with her nose. "In fact, a trip to the colonies might do us both good."

Water lapped at the sides of the freighter's hull. The rancid smell of filth and stench rose from the damp floor of a cargo hold. Hawk wrinkled his nose, then took a shallow breath and prayed for the cover of darkness to come quickly. He wanted out. He needed to feel the sweetness of fresh air filling his lungs. But he could not chance going above in the light. The schooner's captain was not noted for his compassion toward stowaways.

Hawk glanced at a tiny beam of sunshine slipping in under the door at the top of the steps. For several weeks now that had been his only source of light. That and the moonlight during his nightly excursions in search of food and water.

Hatred for the one who had done this to him flamed. Seven years. For seven long years he had been beaten and starved, forced to work unending days beneath the scorching Algerian sun. As the other slaves in the salt mines dropped around him, only two things had kept him alive— Victoria . . . and revenge.

His wife. Even the title burned his tongue. That she was Jason's sister no longer mattered. Hawk's honor, even toward his blood brother, had been stripped away by the whip and hunger . . . and bitterness.

Even now, after all this time, he could still feel the searing pain of disbelief and the fury he had known on the night of his wedding. The fact that O'Ryan had been his captor and sold Hawk to the slave traders had not surprised him. But that the one-eyed seaman had maliciously bragged that Hawk's bride was responsible had left him stunned and strangely hollow.

But over the years the hollowness had been filled, inch by inch, with consuming, stomach-curling hatred. How had he ever thought her an innocent? His rage rose another degree. And he knew that at this moment if he could reach Victoria he would kill her with his bare hands.

He felt a surge of fury swell as he remembered the grueling months he had spent tediously carving out a cavity in the center of a block of salt deep in the mines, then formed a top to fit it precisely, risking discovery, even death, while he planned his escape. He had riddled the top with tiny pinholes to allow him to breathe, then waited for the right moment.

When several prisoners attempted to revolt, Hawk saw his chance. While the guards were busy, he shoved the salt cube in line with the others to be loaded on one of the wagons bound for Morocco, then sealed himself inside. From Morocco, it had only been a matter of stowing away aboard a ship headed for London.

A roar of shouts from the deck above startled Hawk.

"Land ho!" someone bellowed.

Hawk's feelings matched those of the men on deck. Within a matter of hours he would be free. Really free. The sound of thundering footsteps coming toward the cargo hold spurred him into action. The seamen would now ready the cargo for unloading.

Climbing back into the empty crate, his hiding place, he folded himself inside and pulled the lid across the top. Through tiny slits in the sides, he could see light fill the hold as the door burst open and two laughing men bounded down the steps.

For the next several hours Hawk barely breathed as the

sailors worked around him, stacking barrels, crates, and chests, all the while talking and jesting.

"So, 'arry? Ye goin' ta bed that sow-faced doxy at Tully's tonight?" the man leaning against Hawk's crate asked, his scratchy tone laced with amusement.

A more distant voice grunted, "The devil take me, Jamie, the way me britches is bulgin', I'd bed her scurvy grand-mother! Now hurry up, ye lazy blighter, the cap'n wants everythin' ready when we make dock."

The nearest man swore, then shifted his weight, causing the top to Hawk's carton to slip sideways.

Hawk's breath froze.

"Bloody hell," the man grated, his body so close Hawk could see the tobacco pouch hanging from his rope belt. "'Arry? Ye got an 'ammer an' nails? One o' the lids come loose."

"On the barrel by the steps."

The air slid from Hawk's lungs as the one called Jamie stepped away. That had been close. For a fleeting instant he gave thought to being nailed into the box, but dismissed it. It would not matter; with those slits in the sides of the crate, he could breathe, and when the crewmen carried him to the warehouse and returned to the ship for more crates, he would have plenty of time to escape.

Still, when Jamie returned and pounded nails into the wood, sealing it, Hawk could not contain a ripple of uneasiness.

After what seemed like an eternity, the men finally finished their task and left the hold. Hawk closed his eyes and tried to shift his cramped legs but could not move. Perhaps he should not wait to attempt escape.

Just as the thought formed, he felt the ship's sudden jolt—and the unmistakable sound of wood scraping against wood. Hawk closed his eyes and thanked the Great Spirit. The ship had docked.

When he heard the sounds of seamen scurrying about to unload the cargo, it was all he could do to keep from laughing.

Breathlessly he waited for the expected motion of his carton that would tell him it was being moved. When it happened and he felt himself being lifted, then saw daylight through the slits, he chuckled quietly to himself.

But the crate gave an unexpected lurch, then careened to one side.

"Ye blitherin' fools!" someone bellowed.

A wild falling sensation caused Hawk's stomach to heave. He heard a loud splash, then a sudden jolt slammed his face against the rough wood.

For a short span he felt a rocking movement, as if the crate were floating. But it was quickly replaced by an eerie sinking feeling and a rush of water in through the cracks in the sides.

The crate had fallen overboard. Hawk tried to kick at the end slats but had no room to lift his legs. Water gushed in, claiming his breath. He shoved on the snug lid. It did not budge. A wave of panic clenched his throat.

The wooden prison sank deeper.

With a strength born of terror, Hawk slammed his fist against the lid. The flesh across his knuckles tore. But the pain did not compare to the fire searing his chest. Again and again and again he struck the wood. And prayed.

Certain his lungs would burst, he increased the speed of his hammering blows.

With a wrenching squeak, the lid finally gave way.

Clawing frantically for the surface, Hawk pushed upward. His legs were useless. He had been in one position too long. They would not work. Drawing on every ounce of strength he possessed, he forced his numb hands and legs to respond to his will. Slowly, painfully, he felt himself move up through the water.

His lungs burned. Fear sliced through him. He willed himself not to suck in water. But it had been too long. His chest convulsed. Panic screamed through his veins. He felt his mouth open of its own accord. His senses whirled crazily. He could not think.

Water everywhere . . . so cool . . . so dark, almost soothing. He could taste it, feel it slipping down his throat. He stopped kicking and let his arms fall limp. He was tired of fighting . . . so tired.

He sucked in. It felt good. So clean, so fresh, almost like air. His eyes shot open. It *was* air! A strangled cough burst from his lungs. Then another, and another. When he at last caught his breath, he blinked to clear his eyes, amazed to find that he had truly broken the surface.

He shook the hair out of his eyes, expecting to look up into the faces of the ship's crew. Instead, he found himself staring at black slimy wood under the pier.

It took a moment for his brain to connect the fact that he was safe—*and free*. And when it did, he threw back his head and laughed, the half-winded sound lost in the swearing and yelps going on above him.

Relieved but not yet out of danger, Hawk maneuvered onto his back and floated to the closest piling, then relaxed against it. He would wait a moment to regain strength in his limbs, then swim away from the crowd and climb out.

Several minutes later Hawk at last slipped from the Thames and sagged onto the bank under Westminster Bridge, thankful that the hour was late and few people were about. Shivering and numb, he raced toward St. James's Park, anxious to avoid frequently traveled streets and reach his mother's apartments in Mayfair as quickly as possible.

Belatedly he wondered if his wife was there—or had she stayed at Silvercove? He hoped so. He did not wish to see her. Not yet. A bath, food, and warmth were his first priorities . . . then Victoria.

The old servant, Bertha, answered his knock, then took one look at Hawk and closed the door in his face.

Stunned, he stared at the oak barrier. His anger rose, then immediately plummeted. She did not recognize him. Wearing only breeches that hung in shreds, his body dirty and thin, he knew he must look like a beggar.

Sighing, he stepped back, lifted his leg, and slammed his foot against the door.

It crashed open.

A strangled cry burst from the wide-eyed servant as she sprang back.

"Bertha!" Hawk commanded harshly. "Prepare me a bath."

The old woman blinked and took a tentative step forward. "Your Grace?" Her breath caught. "Oh, sweet 'eavens!" She turned and ran, her voice echoing through the hall. "'E's 'ome! Come quickly! The duke is 'ome!"

Within minutes she had roused the entire household staff and, after a barrage of questions, had Hawk seated in a tub of steaming water with a chunk of bread in one hand and a hunk of cheese in the other. A tall glass of wine sat on the table beside him.

He smiled for the first time in a very long while. Perhaps there was something to be said for the white man's tastes after all.

It was then that he realized that he had not seen his mother. "Bertha, where is Lady Remington?"

The servant carried in a stack of fluffy towels and set them beside the tub. "Gone."

"Where?"

"Lookin' for you."

"Why?"

"To *find* you, o' course." Bertha looked at him as if his mind had suffered during his absence, then shrugged. "It weren't 'er idea, though. That young missus o' yours was the one set on goin' to them colonies."

Hawk felt numb. "My *neewa*—my wife—went to America?"

The servant nodded. "'Er an' your mama an' that crippled groom, Paddy McDaniels. Left yestaday, they did."

Confusion warred with anger as Hawk stood abruptly.

Bertha gasped and whirled around, presenting her back. "Good 'eavens, Your Grace!"

Having forgotten his nakedness, Hawk snatched a towel from the stack and secured it at his waist. "Where are my buckskins?"

The old woman peeked warily over her shoulder, then relaxed and faced him. She placed her hands on her hips, looking thoroughly disgusted. "Now, why would you be wantin' them? You just got 'ome." She eyed him suspicious-ly. "You ain't plannin' ta go off again, are you?"

Hawk's breath hissed through his teeth. "Yes."

"'Eaven's mercy. Your grandpapa's goin' ta climb out o' 'is grave, the way you're worryin' your poor mum." She shook her gray head. "It ain't right. No, sir, it ain't." Folding her fleshy arms over her sizable breasts, she stepped for-ward. "Just where do you think you're goin' this time?"

He forced himself not to snarl. "After my wife."

Chapter 8

Collier Parks tossed back the covers on the bed and cast a frown at the woman still lying between the sheets. "Who would be calling on me at this time of night at your house? Perhaps that old sour-faced maid of yours made a mistake."

Cassandra stretched lazily, her sleepy gaze leisurely exploring his naked form. "I doubt it."

Muttering beneath his breath, Collier jerked on his breeches. "Oh, yes, I forgot what a paragon the old bitch is." With a disgusted look at the beautiful blonde lying amid red satin, he tromped barefoot across the cool wood floor and slammed out the door.

When he saw Dooley O'Ryan standing in the middle of Cassandra's exotic parlor, Collier's temper rose another notch. "What the hell are you doing here? I thought we concluded our business last night."

"O'er that little accident ye wanted to happen, we did." The seaman glared out of his one eye. "Near got caught sawin' them axles on the carriage, though. Next time ye rough up some chit, ye can take care o' her pa yerself."

Collier checked the urge to bellow. "Fine! Now why are you here?"

"Don't be takin' that tone with the likes o' me, Parks. I wouldn't be here if I didn't have to be."

"What's so bloody important that makes you think you have to track me down at a whore's house at three in the morning?"

"The duke o' Silvercove."

The blood left Collier's face. "What?"

"The blighter's escaped."

"Escaped? What are you talking about?"

"I said, the duke," O'Ryan snapped, "he's escaped."

Collier felt his knees weaken. "Escaped from where? Damn you, O'Ryan. What are you saying? I paid you to *kill* him!"

The redhead scratched at his shaggy beard and shrugged a hefty shoulder. "An' I told *ye* I'd see the cully suffer the horrors o' hell. Sold him to a slaver for the salt mines in Algeria, I did. Figured he wouldn't last a fortnight. But he outlasted 'em all. An' now the bloody cock's run off. I figure he's headin' back here."

"*Son of a bitch.* You stupid imbecile!" Panic fused with anger. "Do you realize what you've done? He'll find out I'm behind this. I blackmailed him into marrying Ria. When he tallies up the pieces surrounding his abduction, he'll know I was involved—and he'll kill me!"

"He don't know 'bout ye." O'Ryan twisted his mouth into a grotesque smile. "I told him his wife done him in. Thought it might make his sufferin' a mite more painful, thinkin' his beloved betrayed him."

"What?" Collier didn't know whether to be comforted or even more furious. Relieved, certainly, that his own life was not in jeopardy. But what of Ria? The duke would probably kill her. If he could find her, a little voice reminded him. Collier's fear eased a bit when he remembered the note Ria had sent, informing him of her plans to travel to the colonies. Thank Providence for that much at least. Remington wouldn't find her before Collier had him eliminated—again. This time for good.

Scowling at the foul-smelling seaman, Collier gestured with a flick of his hand toward the entrance. "Get out of here, O'Ryan. Meet me at the Waterfront Tavern around noon. By then I'll have come up with a plan to correct your stupid mistake." He leered meaningfully. "One I won't pay for a second time."

O'Ryan squinted his eye, but he said nothing. He merely nodded and left the room.

Collier watched the burly man's retreating back, wondering whom he could hire to rid himself of that dirty bastard as well. He snorted and turned for the stairs. Hell, he might even slit the swine's throat himself. He'd had plenty of practice in the last few years.

Ria didn't realize what a service she'd done him by paying for his commission in the navy seven years ago. He had learned a lot about killing—and making money. As the supply officer, he'd had access to many valuable commodities. Commodities that he sold to the highest bidder, no matter what the color of his coat.

Yes. His beloved had definitely done him a favor. He'd been at his wit's end with all those creditors literally out for his blood. Recalling the full extent he'd gone to in an attempt to get the funds, he blanched.

The night of the wedding, after Ria and Remington left, Uncle Richard had summoned Collier to his study. There the older man had informed Collier of the change in his will—and the reason for it. At first Collier had been stunned by the earl's explanation, then elated. And with the new will, Collier was the earl's sole heir.

It had taken Collier only two days to arrange the earl's "accidental" death. Unfortunately the inheritance hadn't been dispersed soon enough to stay his creditors. Collier had still been forced to obtain the coin from Ria—at the price of joining the king's forces.

Thank God he'd had the foresight to choose the appropriate position. Through a little cunning—and after ridding himself of a few obstacles, like his righteous captain and first lieutenant—he'd managed to amass quite a goodly sum during those hellish years. Coins to buy himself the pleasures he'd never enjoyed before. His gaze drifted toward the upper floor. Funds enough to engage one of the most expensive whores in London.

He smiled as he mounted the stairs to Cassandra's bedchamber and opened the door. Glancing at the woman between the sheets, his smile broadened. Before his stint in the king's service, he could never have afforded her.

Crossing the room, he took off his breeches and climbed back into bed with the sultry harlot. Yes, he'd paid plenty for this bitch, and he intended to get his money's worth.

"Who was your visitor?"

Collier slid his hand up her side, then palmed a full breast. "No one important. Just some seaman." He squeezed her flesh, pinching the nipple.

She sucked in a pained breath. "Easy, love." Shifting to face him, she ran slim fingers through the blond hair on his chest. "What did he want?"

Collier bent to lap at the pink crest he held between his fingers, then bit it. "To tell me Adam Remington may return."

She cringed and tried to pull away. "Returned and left again, you mean."

Collier shoved her back. "What?"

"He returned and left again—according to my servant's gossip. Cook said she heard that the duke arrived yesterday then left this morning for the colonies."

"Bloody friggin' hell!" Collier shot up from the bed.

"What is it? What's wrong?"

"Nothing!" he spat, scrambling for his clothes. "I forgot an appointment, that's all."

Cassandra massaged her swollen red nipple, her expression relieved. "I'm sorry you have to go. But perhaps you can come back later."

Collier didn't miss the false ring to her offer—or the dread he sensed behind it. He almost smiled. "Yes, perhaps I can." The bitch would do anything for money, but she'd never been able to hide her revulsion at his style of lovemaking.

Casting aside thoughts of his pleasurable fetish, he jerked on the last of his garments, trying to control a tingle of anxiety. Remington had gone after Ria.

Collier's fingers stilled on his shirt buttons, and another burst of apprehension erupted. The bastard would kill her!

Grabbing his cloak, Collier stormed out of the room. He had to do *something*.

At the head of the stairs he stopped to still his pounding heart. He couldn't let Remington find Ria. If the bloody cock didn't kill her, he might just listen when she professed her innocence. Then where would the duke turn for revenge? To Dooley O'Ryan, that's who. And the scurvy coward wouldn't hesitate to point the finger at Collier to save his own fat neck.

Clenching his fists, Collier wanted to throttle the bungling fool, and he just might, once O'Ryan had helped finish the task he'd already been paid to do—a thing Collier would insist upon at their noon meeting.

He hesitated on the steps momentarily when he realized it meant traveling all the way to those hated colonies with the tagrag. But there was no help for it. They had to kill Adam Remington.

Molten heat poured over Hawk's back, the air so thick he could barely breathe. His muscles strained against the leaden weight of the pick, and he lowered it, resting it on a slab of salt. He licked his cracked lips and swallowed at the dryness clogging his throat.

A whip snapped.

Fiery pain sliced across his flesh. His body convulsed violently.

Another blow.

The burning lash nearly sent him to his knees. Sweat trailed down his spine, stinging as it mingled with blood. He trembled and tightened his grip on the pick as he fought to stay conscious.

"Back to work, filthy mongrel!" the taskmaster bellowed in Arabic.

For the first time in his life, Hawk wished for the soothing peace of death. He had watched many die over the years. It would be so easy. Then the vision of Victoria rose to taunt him, laughing, mocking. His resolve stiffened. He would not die. He would live to exact his revenge. Hatred for Victoria pumped through his veins, and though his hands shook from weakness, he lifted the pick and slammed it into the hard salt wall.

"Faster, lazy scum!"

The whip lashed again.

Hawk sucked in a sharp breath and blinked against the moisture stinging his eyes. Pain and heat stole his senses. Dizziness swirled. But he willed his limbs to move. Up . . . down. . . . *Victoria.* Up . . . down. . . . *Wife.* Up . . . down. . . . *You will pay.* Again. Again. Faster . . .

Hawk snapped awake as a burst of laughter erupted from downstairs. A sheen of perspiration coated his skin, and his hands shook as he battled the last fragments of the nightmare. No. Not a nightmare. A memory.

He curled up on his side and tried to still the clamoring in his chest. The coolness of the sheet beneath his bare flesh penetrated his hot skin, dragging him back to his surroundings, to the sleeping room over a public house in Yorktown, Virginia.

When his breathing slowed to an even rhythm, he sat up and raked his fingers through his hair. He did not know which was worse, reliving the day his mother deserted him or reliving the hell of the salt mines. He snorted. He knew which caused the torturous pain. *And his wife would pay for it.*

After rising, he strode across the worn wood floor to the window and glanced out at the night-darkened sky. By the set of the moon, he judged it to be past midnight, but still hours before dawn.

He turned away from the window and stared at the bed, but memories of his dream would not allow him to rest. Not this night.

He moved to a faded tapestry chair where he had tossed his clothes, picked up a pair of black linen breeches, then flung them aside. He would not wear the white man's clothes any longer.

His gaze darted about the sparsely furnished room until he found what he sought. The valise he had brought with him from London sat by a commode near the door.

From it he quickly withdrew his familiar garments. He

smiled as he slid the buckskins up over his hips. He had nearly forgotten how soft they would feel against his flesh. When he finished dressing, he glanced at his image in the clouded looking glass above the washstand and decided he more resembled a trapper than a Shawnee. He grinned. Good. He did not wish to reveal his heritage while still in the white man's town. But once he reached the forest, he would remove the cap and thong binding his hair, and when the time came to set his plan in motion, he would don the clothing of his people.

In the dark hall, boisterous laughter rose again from the taproom below. The smell of ale and sweat curdled the air like wine put to milk. His nose twitched at the offensive odors. Pulling his hat low over his brow, he headed for the stairs, anxious to leave the stifling confines of the building.

Once outside, he made his way toward the docks. Perhaps Victoria's ship would reach port today, and he could put his plan into motion. Although it was several hours before the sun would climb the heavens, he would wait. He had haunted the docks all day yesterday, from the time his ship arrived until long after dark when, exhausted, he finally found a room. He had been very careful during his vigil to keep himself concealed. When the trio arrived, it would not do for his mother to see his face. Not if he wanted his scheme to work.

So far everything had gone as intended. In London he had listened closely to old Bertha's tale of how Alaina had shared the secret of Hawk's Shawnee heritage with the astonished Victoria—and how horrified his wife had been. He would have liked to hear more, but the old woman had been interrupted then by some crisis in the kitchen. Still, he had learned enough to spawn an idea.

From the apartments he had gone straight to the docks and found that his mother and wife—and Victoria's lover —had taken passage on the *Molly Clay,* a ship scheduled for several stops along the English Channel. Hawk discovered he could arrive in the colonies before the trio if he took the faster cargo freighter, *Sea Master.*

He glanced out across the moonlit harbor toward several small ships at anchor near the pier. Others, larger ones sat motionless a good distance out, their longboats, some already loaded with cargo, bobbing alongside.

Soon Victoria's ship would join the others. He rubbed the back of his neck, rolling his head to ease the tension. He had grown tired of waiting over the years. Waiting for meals. Waiting for water. Waiting for the scorching sun to set. Waiting to escape. But to gain his revenge, he would endure it again.

He turned and headed for the vacant warehouse he had used earlier to observe the piers undetected. From the second story window, he could see the entire harbor and the passengers coming ashore.

The heavy door groaned as he shoved it open for enough to slip inside. Dust and mold mingled with rotting tobacco, turning the air rancid. Hawk frowned and shook his head, trying to avoid the smell as he made his way to the narrow wooden stairwell.

On the upper level he moved to a stack of empty crates near the window and sat down. Stretching out his long legs, he crossed them at the ankles, then folded his arms over his chest and leaned back. There was nothing left to do but wait. . . .

Victoria stared up at the *Molly Clay* rocking at anchor in the bustling Yorktown port, her stance shaky on the dock beneath her. Even so, it felt good to be on solid ground again. She still couldn't believe they had finally arrived.

After all the stops and the winter storm that had delayed their voyage for nearly a week, she had truly begun to wonder if she would ever touch soil again. To think if they'd left just a day later, they would have missed the storm entirely—or so the young man unloading their luggage had claimed.

"It's grown a mite since I seen Yorktown last," Paddy said quietly from beside her.

Victoria glanced over at her tall, attractive friend dressed in a smart coat and breeches of brown wool. "I didn't know you'd visited America before."

He explored the cluttered docks, alive with rowdy seamen and bellowing merchants. A sadness filled his azure eyes. "Aye, lass. Afore ye was born. The earl sent me ahead ta keep yer mama safe when she come ta visit her sister—the one that died 'bout ten years back." He looked down at her, a fond expression softening his features. "I was even here when ye come squallin' into this world."

Embarrassment stung her cheeks and she looked away. Something caught her eye—a movement—and she glanced toward the upper window of a warehouse, but saw nothing. Still, she could almost feel eyes watching her. Returning her attention to Paddy, she puzzled over his statement. "I thought Father traveled with my mother."

"He planned ta come along, but the king sent for him right when we was leavin'. Yer mama went on without him—accompanied by me an' that elderly maid, Louise. Yer papa came later."

Alaina joined them and brushed at a tendril of golden hair feathering her cheek, her confused gaze on Paddy. "How dreadful. Was the earl detained long?"

Paddy's eyes met the older woman's and for a moment seemed wary, then lowered. "I canna remember, yer ladyship. It were too long ago."

"My goodness. I didn't realize you'd been with the Townsends so many years," Alaina said, as if suddenly trying to lighten her tone.

"That's because ye never knew 'em personal-like afore ye met our lass, milady."

The older woman smiled gently but said nothing.

"Pardon me?"

Victoria spun sharply to see a snaggle-toothed young seaman wearing a stocking cap and a loose green shirt.

"Ya be Lady Remington?"

Surprised, she stepped back a pace. "Yes?"

"Good, good." He bobbed his head up and down. "I brung the carriage ya wanted."

"What?" Victoria blinked. "I didn't call for a phaeton." The hairs on the back of her neck prickled, and the eerie feeling returned. Unwittingly her gaze slid back to the dark second story window.

Alaina moved into her line of vision. *"I* did. I knew we'd need one, so I wrote ahead to have one constructed."

"But there hasn't been enough time."

Her mother-in-law smiled indulgently. "I posted the instructions and payment the day after our little talk. If you remember correctly, it was nearly two weeks after that before all the packing was done and the arrangements completed."

"But how did it get *here?"*

"Shortly before we docked I enlisted our first mate's assistance in fetching the conveyance. Obviously, Mr. Charles didn't waste any time."

Relieved, yet not knowing why, Victoria relaxed.

After handing a coin to the young man, Alaina gestured toward the carriage. "Would you be so kind as to load our luggage?"

"O' course, yer ladyship."

Paddy lifted the portmanteaus near his feet. "I'll help ye, lad."

Alaina watched the two men walk away, then turned back to Victoria. "It'll be good to reach Crystal Terrace, though it is some distance from here. Three days, I believe."

The tall, lanky Mr. Charles walked up at that moment, looking quite rugged in his snug brown breeches and dark blue jacket. "Did I hear you say Crystal Terrace?"

"Yes," Alaina confirmed.

"Are you sure that's the right place? The last I heard, no one's lived there since before the war."

"What about Jason Kincaid?"

The first mate's blond brows rose over deep green eyes. "Sorry, my lady, but I don't know him."

Alaina frowned. "Thank you, Mr. Charles. I'm certain you saved me a dreadful journey. I would have hated to make the trip all the way to Lynch's Ferry only to find

Crystal Terrace vacated. Though, in truth, I fear we're now going to have to travel the vast distance to Halcyon, Jason Kincaid's plantation in the Shenandoah Valley."

Victoria winced, praying there were no mountains between here and Shenandoah.

"You must, of course, have an escort familiar with mountainous terrain."

Victoria moaned.

"Oh, Mr. Charles, thank you so much," Alaina said. "But I wouldn't dream of taking you from your duties."

The first mate looked shocked, then chuckled. "I wasn't referring to myself, madam. I was thinking more of someone like a scout or a guide."

Victoria smiled weakly as she watched pink steal into her mother-in-law's cheeks.

"Oh, yes. Of course. How silly of me to presume—" Alaina cleared her throat. "Do you know of someone we might use?"

"Possibly." Mr. Charles tilted his head, his mouth compressed into a thoughtful line. "Well, there is this one fellow, Bragen Alexander. He's been known to hire out as a guide a time or two. A quite dependable sort, from what I've heard."

Alaina frowned. "But you don't know him?"

"Not personally. But he's got a fine reputation. I'm certain he's most reliable."

She cast a concerned glance at Victoria then back to the officer. "Perhaps if I met him. Tell me, Mr. Charles, how would I find this Mr. Alexander?"

"I'll see if I can find him for you. Where are you staying?"

"We haven't found accommodations yet," Alaina confessed.

"Might I suggest some, then?" He pointed down the road. "Turn left at the end of the street. There's an excellent boardinghouse 'round that corner. You can't miss it."

Alaina nodded gratefully. "I don't know how to thank you for all your help."

"My pleasure, madam. I'll see if Bragen's in town. And if he is, I'll send him over." Offering Victoria a charming smile as he had often done on deck, he nodded to both of them, then turned and sauntered off.

Victoria watched him for a moment, then glanced at her mother-in-law. "If Mr. Alexander is acceptable, how long will it take us to reach Halcyon?"

Alaina tapped her finger against her lips. "By the straightest route, over the mountains, nearly a fortnight. But it'll be worth it. If anyone would know of Adam's whereabouts, Jason Kincaid would."

"Haven't you written to this Jason since the war?"

"Not personally," Lady Remington said quietly. "It wouldn't have done any good. He wouldn't have answered. I'm afraid that Jason, like my son, has never forgiven me for leaving."

"Will he tell you where Adam is?"

Alaina lifted her chin. "If he doesn't, then we'll go to the old trapper, Jedediah Blackburn."

"Why don't we just go there first?" Victoria asked, becoming confused.

"It's a perilous journey I'd rather avoid, if possible." She shrugged. "I'll use it only as a last resort to find Adam."

Victoria shivered at the prospect of seeing her husband again after all these years, but quickly brushed the feeling aside. She wasn't in the least concerned. "Then Halcyon it is." She hesitated. "After a good meal, that is. And a comfortable night's sleep in a bed that doesn't move."

Alaina smiled as she laced her arm through Victoria's and guided her toward Paddy and the waiting carriage. "A splendid idea."

Victoria wasn't certain anymore that this was such a splendid idea. Back in England, finding and confronting her husband had seemed simple. But the closer she came to actually seeing him again . . . Another eerie prickling needled her spine. She looked back and instinctively lifted her gaze to the warehouse window.

But once again she saw nothing.

Hawk remained in the shadows near the window. After he'd endured a week's wait, they had arrived. Finally.

109

Through the dirty glass panes, he watched his mother and his wife climb into the carriage, obviously to be driven by McDaniels. Loathing gripped him as the crippled man who had shared Victoria's bed patted her hand before closing the door.

Allowing his gaze to slide back to the woman responsible for his years of torture, Hawk blinked against the haze of burning hatred clouding his vision. He studied the object of his revenge. Though her soul was that of a snake, he could not deny that outwardly his wife had become an achingly beautiful woman. More so than he ever thought possible.

Sunlight sparked off strands of her dark hair, turning them to fire. But that was to be expected of a she-devil. The blue dress she wore clung to her narrow waist, the swells of her breasts revealed by the low décolletage. The memory of how their softness had filled his hands flashed, and a knife of desire stabbed his loins. He shifted and again cursed himself for not having visited Cassandra before he left London. After seven years without a woman, even his whoring wife looked desirable.

He scoffed, and directed his gaze to the seaman who had spoken to the women.

The sailor waved to a tall, dark-haired man, and together they entered a tavern.

Hawk rose. He would know what Victoria and the seaman discussed.

As he left the secluded warehouse, Hawk decided to return to his room before speaking with the sailor. Quickening his pace, he hurried back and again dressed in the hated black linen. All he needed to know was Victoria's destination. Then he could set his plan in motion.

Chapter 9

As Victoria's bathwater grew tepid, she rose with a regretful sigh. She stepped out of the tub, then wrapped a thick towel around her dripping body, wishing for her maid, Clarise. Not that Victoria minded tending herself. But she missed the girl's company. Too, it seemed odd that Alaina had insisted the servants remain in England. It was almost as if she didn't plan to return. Which, of course, was an absurd notion.

Victoria walked to the bureau, one of the many elaborate furnishings in her room, and pulled on her pink wrapper. She picked up her hairbrush before moving to sit in front of a glowing fireplace.

Heavens. It seemed like an eternity since she'd enjoyed a decent bath. Slowly she drew the bristles through the fullness of her waist-length hair. On the ship, she'd rarely had the opportunity to enjoy a proper toilet.

She smiled to herself, remembering how Mr. Charles had so gallantly presented her with a bucket of rainwater one morning after a storm. He had thoughtfully set it out just so she'd be able to have a refreshing wash.

But then, Mr. Charles had done a lot of nice things for her during the voyage. He was quite a gentleman, and if it hadn't been for her wretched marriage vows, she might have enjoyed getting to know him better. Then again, perhaps not, she admitted truthfully. So far she hadn't met even one gentleman in the last few years who appealed to her beyond mild interest. They were either too priggish, too pompous, or, as in Mr. Charles's case, too malleable. None stirred anything within her but boredom.

This lack of emotion she possessed must be a curse. She doubted she would ever feel the spine-tingling desire she'd read about in a risqué novel one of her friends sent from Paris a few years ago.

A sudden spark of memory flashed, and she vividly recalled Adam's stimulating kisses. She had definitely felt something at those times. But *that* she attributed to youth. After all, she had been a child at the time, and she'd certainly never felt those racy sensations since.

Perhaps her feelings would change with the annulment of her marriage. At least she hoped so. Thinking of her hollow, childless marriage, her anger rose, and she pulled the brush through her hair, then winced when the bristles yanked at the now dry waves.

Tossing the curtain of reddish brown over her shoulders, she stood, then crossed to where her clothes lay on the bed. She wouldn't think of her marriage now. After seven weeks on that wretched ship, and soon to spend two more in a cramped carriage, tonight she wanted to relax and enjoy a leisurely meal with her companions.

Less than an hour later Victoria descended the stairs wearing a simple yet elegant green satin gown that hugged her shoulders and dipped wickedly low. Because of the lateness of the hour, she hadn't bothered to put her hair up, knowing it would only be a short time before she'd have to take it down again.

Clinking dishes and murmured voices rose from below as she neared the large common room. The appetizing aroma of baked bread and roast chicken wafted up to tease her gnawing stomach. When she reached the foot of the staircase, she glanced around and immediately spotted Paddy and Alaina seated at a long wooden table with a smattering of other patrons.

Paddy looked up, then smiled broadly. "Ria, love. Come.

Sit by me." He patted a space beside him near the end of the worn bench.

Alaina, seated at the end across from him, flashed a warm smile. "My, don't you look stunning. That gown is so becoming. But of course with that remarkable figure of yours, how else could it look, hmm?"

Victoria's cheeks flamed at her mother-in-law's praise. "Thank you."

Alaina chuckled, a low musical sound, then pointed to a platter of steaming chicken and new potatoes in the center of the table. "Have some, dear. It's delicious."

As Paddy lifted the platter and set it before Victoria, the door swung open.

A tall, very attractive man entered. He wore a gray linen shirt that clung to his wide shoulders and muscular arms. The partially unlaced front revealed a hint of dark curling hair on his chest. Tight brown breeches hugged his powerful thighs, then melded into black boots. Fleetingly, she thought of her husband's broad-shouldered frame and felt her heart give a tiny lurch.

The man crossed the room in long, graceful strides, then stopped to say something to the proprietor. He bent from his great height, his dark head tilted, as he obviously listened to the innkeeper's reply.

The man straightened, then looked around the room, his gaze coming to rest on Alaina. It remained there for a moment, then slid to Victoria.

The blatant appraisal in that stare brought heat to her cheeks. She quickly averted her gaze and focused on her plate. How dare he stare at her so. No proper gentleman would do such a thing. But then, this *was* the colonies, she reminded herself, a land full of ruffians and savages.

"Lady Remington?" a slow, deep voice drawled.

Victoria jumped and nearly tumbled from the bench at the sound of the man's voice so close. Good heavens. She hadn't even heard his approach. She opened her mouth to respond, then saw that he spoke to her mother-in-law.

"Yes?" Alaina looked up.

"I'm Bragen Alexander. Lester Charles said you wanted to see me?"

"Oh, Mr. Alexander, yes. Yes. Here." She motioned to the space at the end of the bench next to Victoria. "Please. Sit."

He didn't look at Victoria as he lowered his long frame down beside her. But his thigh brushed against hers when he leaned forward. "I understand you need a guide to the Shenandoah Valley."

"I believe so." She smiled warmly. "Tell me, Mr. Alexander, have you taken anyone over the Blue Ridge Mountains before?"

"Yes."

Victoria remained silent like Alaina and Paddy, waiting for him to elaborate. And waiting.

Paddy cleared his throat. "Did ye run inta problems?"

Mr. Alexander turned those black eyes on Paddy and studied him. "No."

Victoria fought the urge to gnash her teeth. This man must have taken lessons from her husband in conversing. "Mr. Alexander, if you want the position, you're going to have to give us a little more information. If you don't want it, then merely say so."

He simply stared down at her in a most unnerving fashion. Victoria clenched her fists in her lap. "Sir, we don't have time to dally. Either supply us with examples of your experience or decline so we can continue our search for a suitable guide." Victoria felt better for having voiced her position, yet she was still unsettled by the way he lazily followed the movement of her lips.

"What would you like to know? How many carriage wheels I had to change? How many Indians I killed? How many travelers I lost?" He shrugged. "The answer to all those questions is . . . none. And I assure you, I know my way to the Shenandoah Valley." He turned to Alaina. "What I don't understand is why you want to go through the mountains. Wouldn't it be easier to take a ship on up to Philadelphia, then over milder terrain to the valley?"

Alaina lifted a slim shoulder. "That may be a less arduous route, but it would take twice as long."

"Do you have supplies?"

"That we do, lad," Paddy answered. "I be gettin' 'em afore we left the docks a few hours back."

Bragen Alexander looked from one to the other, then to Victoria. He stood abruptly. "Be ready at dawn." Not bothering to wait for an acknowledgment or rejection, he turned and strode from the room.

"Dawn?" Victoria gasped. "Of all the arrogance. Just who does he think he is?" She turned back to Alaina.

Her mother-in-law was smiling. "He's our guide, dear."

"What?"

Paddy chuckled. "He's a mite abrupt, darlin'. But the lad's a smart one, I can tell ye that. He'll do."

"How can you possibly have come to that conclusion? Or did I miss part of the conversation?"

"That's just it, Ria. He doesna carry on with meanin'less words. He's a man o' action, that one."

Victoria looked at Alaina. "Is that what you thought, too?"

"More or less."

"I don't believe this." Victoria rose. "But if I'm going to have to climb out of bed before even God awakens, then I'd better get some sleep." Nodding briskly, she headed to her room, trying very hard not to stomp her feet. Had Alaina and Paddy lost their senses? Her thoughts darkened on Bragen Alexander. Colonial men! Obviously they were all overbearing, insolent beasts. And here she'd thought that rudeness was merely a unique trait of her brutish husband.

As she trudged along the upper hall toward her room, she felt an uneasy sensation snatch her from her vexation. Sensing a presence, she whirled around, but saw only a dark, empty corridor. Still, she couldn't shake the feeling that someone was watching her—and had been all day.

Dragging in a shallow breath, she unclenched her fists and turned back toward her room. How ridiculous. Goodness, she had never been so skittish. If this kept up, she'd be ready for confinement in a locked attic before she ever found her husband.

* * *

Hawk watched his wife through a tiny slit in the door to his room and smiled. She reminded him of a nervous prey who sensed a stalking predator. His grin deepened.

When she disappeared inside her room and closed the door, Hawk did the same. Fleetingly he recalled his conversation with the seaman. The man had given Hawk the information he sought, though grudgingly. It had not been difficult for Hawk to tell that the man was half in love with Victoria.

After learning not only of her ultimate destination but of her immediate one as well, it had been easy for Hawk to find his wife. He had watched through the window of the inn until Victoria and the others were shown to their rooms. Once upstairs, he had quickly gone inside and procured one of his own, not bothering to retrieve his belongings from the public house until later.

Hawk gave a disgusted snort when he remembered watching just now from the shadowy stairs as a tall, raven-haired man entered the common room. How the one called Alexander had stared at Victoria, even as she sat beside her current lover. Hawk's fingers curled. She was obviously a tantalizing piece to those naive bastards who had not been on the receiving end of her deceit.

A feeling Hawk suspected was jealousy slithered through him, and he turned away from the door. He was not jealous, only angry that his whoring wife flaunted herself before any man who possessed a willing shaft. Even that damnable gown had revealed her intent more than any words. It barely concealed the tips of her breasts. He could still see the way their firmness quivered when she walked, still feel himself grow hard at the provocative display.

He flung himself onto the bed. Oh, how she had played the innocent tonight, keeping her eyes lowered and acting uncomfortable in Alexander's presence. She had looked the perfect picture of shy purity. He could not blame them for believing her performance. At first Hawk, too, had been taken in by that pristine act. But no more. Now he knew her for what she was—and he hated her for it.

Lacing his fingers behind his head, he stared at the

scrolled ceiling. Her game would end soon, though. Within a fortnight she would know the bitter punishment for betrayal.

Victoria couldn't shake the feeling that someone was spying on her. Even after nine days in the suffocating confines of the phaeton, she still sensed it. Dreamed about it. Brushing back a strand of hair, she shifted against the hard horsehair seat, trying to find a more comfortable position. Last night, for the second time since the journey began, she'd dreamed of a man standing over her while she slept, staring at her, his shadowed features twisted with hatred.

The wheel struck a bump in the rutted road they were following.

She grabbed for the window frame to keep from slamming into the side as she had several times on the first day of this wretched trip. She didn't think they would ever reach Halcyon. Nor, when they did, would there be a spot left on her body that hadn't suffered a bruise.

Releasing a long sigh, she glanced across at Alaina. How her mother-in-law could sleep so soundly in this teeth-jarring conveyance Victoria could not imagine. But then, Alaina hadn't complained about sleeping on the hard pasture grounds for the last three days either, once the inns were behind them. Her mother-in-law didn't even mind eating that dreadful wild game Bragen Alexander managed to appropriate during his mysterious disappearances.

Victoria's gaze drifted back toward the window. How she envied Bragen. Every time he passed on that prancing dun stallion, she fought the urge to beg him for a ride. Anything to get out of this miserable carriage.

Knowing the man would never allow her such license, she turned away from the tempting sight and prayed their journey for the day would end soon.

As if in answer to her silent plea, the carriage began to slow, and Bragen Alexander rode up alongside it. "We'll stop just ahead."

Victoria's relief was so profound, she wanted to kiss his

boots. But she didn't respond. She didn't dare. Every time she had, he'd made her angry by making light of her discomfort, and one of these days, she feared he might return her ire and leave them stranded.

Leaning forward, she tapped Alaina's arm. "We're about to lay over for the evening."

Alaina yawned and stretched. "So soon?"

Resisting the urge to curse, Victoria merely nodded. "According to Mr. Alexander."

Lady Remington straightened her skirt and glanced out the window. Her eyebrows rose slightly. "I must have slept longer than I thought. We've already reached the foothills of the Blue Ridge Mountains."

"How much farther to the Kincaids'?" It was the only thing Victoria cared about at the moment.

"About four days, weather permitting. Halcyon lies in a beautiful valley between the Blue Ridge Mountains and the Alleghenies. It's not really a great distance, but it's the worst part of the journey. Climbing and descending that steep terrain is quite tedious."

Victoria's heart sank to her toes. The *worst* part of the journey? She'd never make it.

When the carriage drew to a stop, Paddy climbed down and opened the door. By the time he'd assisted Alaina to the ground, Bragen stood, palm extended, ready to aid Victoria.

She hesitated the barest instant. Not that she didn't want to touch him. If anything, just the opposite. The warm strength in his hands always made her think of her husband's stimulating touch—what she could remember of it. Perhaps Collier had been right after all. Her own womanly urges would eventually be her downfall. Curse Collier. Curse Adam Remington. Taking a tight breath, Victoria placed her hand in Bragen's. Curse *all* men.

His fingers closed gently around hers. "How are you holding up, Ria?"

Victoria bit back a scathing remark. Only Paddy and Collier called her that. "Oh, wonderful. Thank you."

His black eyes sparked with amusement. As usual, her subtle sarcasm had merely bounced off that broad chest.

"I'm glad to hear that. I was afraid the trip might be too difficult"—his leisurely gaze slid down her body—"for someone as delicate as you."

Heat rose to her cheeks, but she ignored the hint of truth in his words. "Well, as you can see, your fears were groundless. Now, if you'll let go of me, I'll join the others."

Bragen released her hand and flashed that beautiful smile. "Yes, Your Grace."

"I thought you colonists didn't believe in titles anymore."

His gaze explored the contours of her face, almost as if he were trying to understand her antagonism toward him. "I'm not a colonist."

"Wha—"

"Ria?" Paddy called from near a stand of spruce trees. "I'll be puttin' yer bedroll under here with her ladyship's." He gestured to a woolen blanket he'd draped over some spiky lower branches, forming a shelter.

Victoria froze. For the first time she became aware of the tall dense pines surrounding them. They were in the forest! Oh, merciful God. She felt her knees wobble as she clutched her stomach. The ground swayed and darkened.

"Victoria?" Bragen's voice sounded far away. "Damn it, Victoria. What is it?"

"Bloody hell!" she heard Paddy bellow. Her senses whirled. Distantly she heard the thudding of hobbled footsteps. Then arms surrounded her, and Paddy's familiar voice soothed her panic. "It's all right, Ria. Paddy's here. I'll nae let anythin' hurt ye, lass. Never again."

The muscles in Hawk's arms bunched instinctively when Victoria's crippled lover embraced her. Until now the man had kept his distance. For that reason alone Hawk had spared his life. Then something else struck him. The paternal way in which McDaniels held her. There was nothing loverlike in his actions. He looked more like a father soothing a frightened child.

Oddly confused, Hawk swung his gaze to the tall, raven-haired man. Something in his expression gave Hawk pause. He seemed puzzled.

Hawk's mother, too, appeared uneasy.

Thoughtfully he stared again at his wife, and for the first time noticed her paleness—and the fear marring her features. What had frightened her? He made a sweeping search of the area, but saw nothing. Frowning, he watched his *nikyah* step forward, then lead Victoria to the carriage and climb inside with her.

The two men spoke briefly. Then McDaniels limped back to where he had spread the blankets. Alexander frowned and stared at the carriage. Hawk was not close enough to hear what they spoke of, but he could tell that the tall one was not happy.

During the last few days, Hawk had gained little respect for Alexander, the guide, who could not detect Hawk's nightly visits to Victoria's side. He did not protect those entrusted to his care, and Hawk still wanted to kill the man. Hawk had seen him watching Victoria when she wasn't aware of him. He'd seen the way Alexander lusted after her, and he knew it was only a matter of time before the guide attempted to bed Victoria. Even though she had so far slept near Alaina, at a respectable distance from her crippled lover, Alexander's intent could not be denied.

Hawk felt a burst of anger at the thought, yet he could not understand this burning urge to hurt one who would touch her. He did not care what the men did to the woman. He loathed her. But the mere image of one of the others parting her white thighs and driving himself into her flesh robbed him of coherent thought. Shaking his head to banish the vision, he looked back to the carriage. He did not know what had frightened Victoria, but he would find out.

Very soon.

After completing their evening meal Paddy and Alaina set about gathering more firewood while Victoria watched in wonder. She couldn't believe the ease with which Alaina moved in and out of the trees. Didn't the woman know of the dangers?

Suppressing her uneasiness, Victoria scanned the other side of their meadow. Just beyond a stand of pines, a path led to a ribbon of water. She curled her fingers. She could feel the grease from the rabbit they'd eaten at supper clinging to her hands and knew she'd have to traverse that small stretch of woods to the creek.

She thought of asking Paddy or Bragen to go with her, but she'd already made a fool of herself once today. That was enough. Her only consolation was that if she could see the water from here, then from the stream she'd be able to see the camp. Besides, she wouldn't have to spend more than a few seconds in *there*.

Gathering all of her fortifying forces, Victoria stiffened her back and lifted her chin. It's just a bunch of trees, she assured herself. Clenching her fists to stop the nervous ripple of gooseflesh, she walked forward.

Woodsmoke and the scent of pine wafted on the evening breeze. Flickering shadows from the firelight danced eerily, forming grotesque shapes on the looming branches.

Doing her best to ignore them, she kept her eyes straight ahead, never once letting the water slip from her sight. As she reached the tiny creek bordered by a grassy bank, she tried to stifle her terror and concentrate on how pretty it looked all aglow in silver moonlight.

Kneeling on the spongy ground, she forced herself to relax and trailed her fingers through the cold shimmering ripples, but her ears were tuned to every sound. A breeze rustled the leaves of maple near the water's edge. A large bird flapped its wings overhead, while a coyote howled softly in the distance.

For no apparent reason that eerie, unsettling feeling she'd experienced so many times in the past days assailed her again. Snatching her fingers from the water, she brushed them nervously against her green woolen skirt. She glanced anxiously to one side. A branch snapped behind her. Startled, she sprang to her feet and whirled around.

"I didn't mean to frighten you," Bragen said quietly as he stepped out of the shadows. "I just wanted to talk to you alone for a moment."

Victoria clutched her pounding chest. "I don't think I'm up to another of your remarks about my shortcomings."

He closed the small distance between them. "Paddy told me what happened, Victoria. I wouldn't tease you about something like that." He bent down, bringing his gaze level with hers. "I want to talk about why you're so testy with me."

"I'm not testy," she replied vehemently, although she was not able to meet his eyes.

"Yes, you are." He shook her gently by the shoulders. "Look at me."

Stubbornly she kept her gaze lowered.

"Victoria, you've been snapping at me since we began this journey. Why?"

"I don't know," she answered honestly.

"Is it because there's a slight attraction between us?"

Victoria didn't know what to say that wouldn't get her into trouble.

"If it is, you can stop worrying," Bragen said sincerely. "You're married, and I'm . . . not available. But I want this constant bickering to stop. It's irritating as hell." He tapped her chin. "I want us to be friends."

So that's what he thought was the reason for all her snappish remarks. How pompous. Still, she felt relieved and offered a weak smile. "Anything else?"

He leaned forward and brushed his lips across the corner of her mouth. "That's it."

Stepping carefully back, she nodded. "Friends it is, then. And I apologize for my boorish behavior."

"No need for that. I'm just glad we finally understand each other. It'll make the trip a hell of a lot more pleasant." Flashing that easy smile, he released her and sauntered back in the direction of their camp.

Alone again, Victoria pondered their conversation. She couldn't understand what she'd done to give him the impression she was attracted to him. Then she recalled that Collier had often made similar accusations about the way she revealed her desire by the way she moved her body when she walked and by the breathless tone in her voice when she spoke. Good heavens. She couldn't help the way nature had put her together. Or the fact that gentlemen misinterpreted her actions.

Even her own husband had misunderstood. On their wedding night he had accused her of being *impure*. A tremor shook her when she remembered how brutal he'd been just before that. Yet somewhere in the deepest part of her she couldn't deny that his touch had inflamed her. Even now her stomach still fluttered at the mere thought.

Releasing a long sigh, she turned back to the stream. Perhaps Bragen wasn't so wrong about her after all. More uncertain about her own being than she'd ever been, she bent to finish her ablutions.

A hand clamped over her mouth from behind. Another banded her waist and jerked her to her feet. She froze in shock. *Oh, God.* Fear stiffened her body—then whipped it into terror-filled struggles. She kicked out. Clawed at the arm around her waist. She twisted wildly, biting at the hand covering her mouth.

The assailant yanked her hard against his solid chest, the arm around her ribs nearly cutting off her breath. "Do not fight me," a low, menacing voice commanded close to her ear.

Victoria stopped struggling instantly, her body shaking as she fought the terror crowding her throat.

"You play the whore's game well, *neewa.*" The breath hissed through her attacker's teeth. "Now you will play for me."

Chapter 10

Neewa? He thinks I'm someone else! Wild with fear, Victoria screamed against his hand and rammed an elbow into his stomach.

He grunted, then tightened his hold. "Do not make me hurt you."

His words only made her renew her efforts. She curled forward, then slammed her head back against his jaw.

He swore harshly.

She bit his palm and stabbed his shin with her heel. A violent quaking racked her, but she couldn't stop fighting—didn't dare. Viciously she dug her nails into his arm.

He muttered another oath, then whirled her around.

Pain shot through her chin like a burst of lightning. Everything spun crazily and dimmed into numbing emptiness.

"Damn it!" Hawk swore again as he eased his wife's limp form down onto the spongy grass, though he did not know why it had bothered him to strike her or why he had pulled his punch to keep from harming her. She deserved it. Deserved more.

He glanced down at her smooth white throat veiled in moonlight, and visions of Victoria kissing Alexander clouded his thoughts. Again he felt the stomach-jarring urge to kill her—and her new lover.

Afraid he might be tempted to end the game before it began, Hawk swung his attention to her perfect features.

Long silky lashes lay soft against her ivory skin. Her brows arched gently while her upturned nose looked almost too small above her full pink lips. Lips, now slightly parted, that begged for a man's possession. A jolt shook his loins, but he ignored it. How could anyone be so evil and so exquisite at the same time? And she *was* evil. He had the scars to prove it.

Rising, he quickly withdrew a leather strip from a bedroll on the back of the horse he had purchased in Yorktown. He tied her hands in front, then carried her to his horse and mounted. Nudging the stallion with his heels, he guided it quietly toward the thickly wooded mountainside. He would not think of desire. Only of punishment.

Bragen Alexander glanced worriedly at Alaina and Paddy, then knelt at the spot where he'd last seen Victoria and lowered his flaring torch. The dewy grass, flat and twisted, in some places churned, confirmed his worst fears. There had been a struggle.

Bragen cursed himself for the hundredth time. The Indian had done this. He knew that as surely as he knew the sun would set—and it was all Bragen's fault.

His thoughts drifted back to the night he'd seen the brave enter their camp. Everyone had been asleep, including Bragen. But a sixth sense, keenly honed after years of living among the Shawnee, had awakened him, warned him of a presence.

Bragen had slid his knife from his waistband and, under the pretense of sleep, shifted, preparing to attack. Through lowered lashes he had seen a Shawnee brother standing over Victoria's sleeping form, watching her—and Bragen recognized him! He had seen the man before—in Yorktown, standing in the shadows of the stairs at the hostelry on the night Bragen met with Alaina and hired on as a guide. But the Indian had been dressed as a gentleman then. Before Bragen could reason it out or move, the man left as silently as he had come.

Bragen hadn't known what to think. But something—an instinct, or perhaps that tortured look in the man's face—

had told him that the Shawnee cared for Victoria. God, how wrong he'd been!

Though Bragen hadn't mentioned their visitor to anyone, he had kept Victoria in sight at all times. Hell, that was one of the reasons he'd followed her to the stream. He hadn't wanted her to be alone.

His hand tightened on the torch as he rose to his feet. But he *had* left her alone. All because of that damned kiss. He had meant what he said about wanting to be her friend, but he'd never expected his body to react to a mere brushing of lips.

Bragen turned to see Alaina's pale face and Paddy's strained features.

"What happened?" Alaina asked frantically.

He lowered his gaze back to the grass. "From the signs, it looks as if she struggled with someone. I think a man dressed like an Indian took her."

"What man?" Paddy burst out.

Bragen couldn't meet his eyes. "The one I saw sneak into our camp the other night."

Paddy's hand shot out, gripping the front of Bragen's shirt. "What are ye sayin'?" The older man's eyes blazed with rage. "Are ye tellin' me ye knew o' the danger an' dinna warn us?" The hand at Bragen's throat shook. "Ye bloody crow! If anythin' happens to me lass, I'll tear yer black heart out with me bare hands."

Bragen looked at the fist knotting his shirt. If any other man had tried that, his arm would be broken by now. But he understood Paddy McDaniels's fears, and he couldn't blame him.

Alaina pushed her way between the two men, her back to McDaniels, her face anxious, intent on Bragen. "What did he look like?"

Startled, Bragen stared at her. "Like a white man dressed as a Shawnee Indian."

"What was he wearing?"

Bragen scowled at the woman. "What the hell does that matter? Just a square scrap of leather covering his . . ."

Damn. She had him blushing like an adolescent. "Listen. We're wasting time. You two stay here. I'm going after her."

"Wait!" Alaina clutched his arm and tightened her fingers as if to restrain him. "Did he have a crescent-shaped scar on his right arm?"

Bragen swung toward her. "You saw him?"

"No."

"Then how did you know about the scar? I barely caught a glimpse of it myself by firelight the other night."

"There *was* one!" Alaina's features relaxed, and she turned to Paddy. "He won't harm her."

Bragen had taken all he could. "What are you talking about?" He spun her back around. "You know this man? For God's sake, Alaina. Who is he?"

She smiled. "Her husband."

Victoria came slowly awake to the rolling gait of a horse beneath her and a throbbing ache in her jaw. Groggily she became aware of other things. Her hands were tied, and an arm banded her waist, holding her against an unyielding chest.

Memory exploded. He'd attacked her! She twisted recklessly, trying to jump from the horse. But as she lurched forward, bending almost double, her nose hit something solid . . . and naked. *Naked?* She tried to look past her nose to see what she'd hit. The smooth bare leg of a man came into focus. Aghast, she dived for the other side.

"No," a deep voice commanded. The arm around her waist tightened, hauling her upright.

"Wh-what do you want? Who are you?" She had barely gotten the words past her paralyzed throat when she realized his chest felt naked, too. Wasn't the man wearing *anything?*

His hand gripped the material of her jacket at the waist, but he didn't answer.

Swallowing her fear, she pressed on. She had to know his intentions. "Please. J-just tell me what you want."

Warm breath hissed near her ear. "You."

Victoria's heart jammed in her throat. *Oh, my God.* Why

didn't she swoon? If ever there was a time, this was it! "Why?"

He chuckled softly. Then the hand at her waist slid up over her breast.

This time she was certain she'd collapse. Her senses spun wildly. She opened her mouth to cry out, but as if he detected her intent, he dug his fingers painfully into her flesh.

"Do not make me hurt you again, *neewa.*"

"My name's not Neewa! It's Victoria. Please, you've made a mistake."

He stilled. "Neewa is not a woman's name."

Then what does it mean? Victoria wanted to shout. But terror froze her lips together, and she couldn't stop shaking. She closed her eyes and tried to dispel the horrible thoughts of what he might do to her. And she prayed.

But the word *neewa* kept creeping into her thoughts. What language was it? She hadn't seen his face, but he sounded almost like . . . Her heart jumped. Was her attacker an Indian? If he was, and if he knew she was the wife of a Shawnee, perhaps he wouldn't harm her.

Just as she started to tell him, he pulled back on the horse's reins and halted it, then slid down and pulled her with him. Without a word he marched her toward a small clearing and shoved her to the ground.

A jutting branch scraped her cheek, and pain sliced into her tender skin. For a moment she was too scared to move and just lay there. Then, fearing he might take her stillness as an invitation, she hastened to sit up. "You've got to listen to me," she began. "I'm married to a Shawnee brave. Hawk. The son of Chief Flaming Wing." Something wet and warm trickled down her jaw, but she ignored it and peeked at her abductor for the first time.

She strangled on a gasp. He wasn't wearing anything! Well, almost nothing. That tiny square scrap of leather covering his . . . well, it certainly couldn't be considered clothing.

He looked at her strangely, then shifted his gaze to her

cheek. Something unreadable troubled his eyes before he raised them to meet hers. "I know who you are."

How could he know? She'd never been in the colonies before. Fear warred with confusion as she tried to sort things out. No one had reason to harm her, not even Adam—Hawk. She'd never done anything to him. *Except force him to marry you,* a little voice reminded her.

Her suspicion grew. Had he somehow learned of her arrival and planned this to frighten her away? Had he sent his friend to terrorize her? She glanced at her captor where he knelt over the small fire he'd started. He certainly appeared fierce. With all those muscles he looked strong enough to mangle a bear, and the way his gleaming shoulder-length hair was tousled, he looked wild enough to do it. But that didn't explain Hawk's reasons.

Her captor's gaze caught hers over the low flame. In the flickering light his eyes reminded her of smoke. Of smoldering fury.

She opened her mouth, ready to plead, to beg him not to harm her. But then she recalled one of her many talks with Alaina about Adam's people. "Above all else," Alaina had said, "a Shawnee detests cowardice."

Snapping her teeth together, Victoria lifted her chin, though inside she shook with terror. "Hawk sent you, didn't he?"

The man's features tightened. "Do not play games, *neewa.*"

"No, please," she rushed on. "I know he's unhappy about our forced marriage, but I never thought he'd want to hurt me because of it. It wasn't my fault."

His expression closed up, his eyes hard.

Victoria pressed on. "A-are you his friend?"

He stood abruptly, placing his hands on his hips. The action flexed the muscles in his arms and accentuated a small moon-shaped scar on his right arm. His gaze remained intent, harsh. A slow, not very nice smile slanted his mouth. "I am not Hawk's friend."

"You *do* know him!" Victoria exclaimed, then swallowed

her excitement. *He's not Hawk's friend.* A new surge of fear gushed through her. Oh, merciful heavens.

He walked up to her, towering over her in his spread-legged stance, the small square of leather waving slightly. He considered her for a moment, then turned abruptly.

"My God!"

He whirled around.

"Your back. The scars. What happened?" Heat raced to her cheeks. "I-I'm sorry. I shouldn't have said that. It's none of my business."

"Oh, but it is your business," he said so softly she barely heard him. He grabbed her by the arm and jerked her to her feet. *"Very much so."*

His fingers bit into her skin, and his other hand shot up to close around her throat. He squeezed, then shook as if restraining the urge to kill her. His eyes blazed with inhuman fierceness.

Panic held her immobile.

With a vicious snarl, he shoved her away from him.

Victoria stumbled to the side, then fell to her hands and knees, frantically sucking oxygen into her lungs. God, why was he doing this? When she could breathe normally again, she looked up to see him standing with his back to her, his own breathing rapid.

As if he'd felt her watching him, he turned. She was struck by his incredible handsomeness, the raw power in his regal stance . . . and the cruel determination in those silver eyes.

He stared at her for a long time, holding her paralyzed by a look filled with searing hatred. Then something else flashed in his eyes, and he moved toward her. "Take off your clothes."

His words hit her with the force of a swinging ax. "No!" She scrambled backward. "Oh, please, don't."

In slow, menacing steps, he advanced, his voice deadly calm. "Take them off, *neewa.* Now."

Horrified, she edged farther away. This couldn't be happening!

He lunged. With the swiftness of a striking rattler, he grabbed her and hauled her to her feet.

She swung her bound hands wildly. "No!"

His vicious fingers shredded her bodice, then the blouse and chemise.

"Bastard!" She screamed and kicked out hysterically.

Hard fingers dug into her stomach as the waistband of her skirt snapped, then tore.

Blind with panic, she clawed and twisted, then fell beneath him. Her bare back hit the ground. Air whooshed from her lungs. White specks flashed, whirled, collided before her eyes.

Immediately he lifted his weight, and she felt her skirts and petticoats being yanked down her legs.

Then he was gone.

Her chest and eyes burned, and she curled up on her side, gasping, terrifyingly aware that she was totally naked.

"Do you take off your shoes or do I?" his crisp voice broke into her numbed senses. Unable to respond, she wrapped her arms tightly around her shaking body and pressed her cheek into the ground, tears of humiliation and fear burning her eyes.

She felt his hands working at the laces of her shoes, but she didn't move. What did it matter now? Baring her feet meant nothing compared to what she'd already suffered.

With harsh movements he yanked off her shoes and stockings, then grabbed her upper arm and pulled her to her feet.

Instinctively she lowered her hands to shield herself from his gaze, but it was a fruitless gesture. He didn't even look in her direction as he guided her toward his horse and removed a long length of leather from one of the saddlebags, then swiftly tied it to the strip already binding her hands.

He released her arm, but kept a firm hold on one end of the leather. As if she were an animal on a long leash, he walked toward a young birch, pulling her behind him.

Caught off guard by the sudden lurch, she stumbled and fell.

Obviously unconcerned with her plight, he continued to walk forward, dragging her across stinging pine needles and gouging pebbles.

When he reached the tree, he looped the opposite end of the leather around the base and tied it securely.

Victoria tried to hold back her tears. He was treating her like an animal! Through blurry vision, she watched him walk silently across the little clearing, then mount his horse and disappear into the woods.

She let out a shaky, relieved breath and shivered in the night breeze. A crazy trembling shook her and caused her teeth to chatter as she fearfully contemplated what he would do next—if he came back. Rape her? Kill her? Both? She pulled against the lengthy strip binding her to the tree. She had to get away.

She scrambled to her feet, then raced to the birch and tore frantically at the tight knot. Pain cut into her fingers as her nails broke beneath the pressure. Unable to free herself, tears of frustration streamed down her cheeks.

She assaulted the bindings at her wrists next, twisting, clawing, trying desperately, but in vain, to reach the knot between her hands. Helpless rage consumed her. "I hate you!" she yelled. "You filthy beast. Do you hear me? I *hate* you!"

Receiving no response, she shot a nervous look around. Dark, hideous silence screamed at her from the inky recesses of the forest.

She fearfully scanned the line of trees, shifting her gaze anxiously from shadow to shadow. Her legs grew weak, and she collapsed at the base of the tree, clasping her arms tightly around her updrawn knees.

For what seemed like hours she sat frozen, her muscles aching from being held so taut, her lower lip raw from where she'd gnawed it repeatedly at every sound.

Then she heard it.

A low snort rumbled out from behind a row of foliage. Victoria's heart exploded into frantic beats. She could almost see the creature coming. Feel it tearing into her flesh. Hysterically she sprang to her feet and jerked savagely at the ropes.

"No. Oh, nooo . . ."

Chapter 11

Hawk caught sight of his wife through the branches and paused. She looked terrified. Her eyes were wide and glazed, fixed on the shrub in front of him. Her body quaked as she pulled frantically against the bindings. Blue tinged her hands from lack of circulation. He quickly scanned the foliage for danger, then the area, but saw no threat.

He heard her low, childlike whimper and felt a consuming need to go to her, to assuage her fears, whatever they were. His hand tightened around the squirrel he had killed for supper as he fought the damning urge.

Disgusted by his lack of control, Hawk hardened his resolve and nudged the horse forward.

Victoria's gaze remained fastened on the spot where the underbrush had moved. Her insides quivered with terror. Again she twisted against the bindings. *Dear God in heaven, not again.*

Suddenly the brush parted to reveal the head of the horse her captor rode, and Victoria thought she'd swoon from sheer relief. Or was she relieved?

Warily she watched him dismount and turn. His nearly naked body glowed bronze in the firelight, all smooth rippling muscles. Embarrassed by her own boldness, she tore her gaze away.

Then she saw the knife.

Panic choked her. She could see light spark off the blade as he moved in her direction. A low moan slid past her lips, and she pressed into the tree. He was going to kill her. Squeezing her eyes shut, she prayed it would end swiftly.

She could hear the muffled sound of his moccasined feet as he approached, hear the soft rasp of his breath, smell his woodsy male scent. These were the memories she'd carry to her grave. Memories of him.

Something touched her hands. Fear churned inside her. She was going to be sick. Unable to breathe, she waited for the stab that would end her life. But it didn't come. Instead, the rope between her wrists grew taut, then fell away.

Victoria's eyes shot open.

Her captor had turned his back on her. In his hand he carried something furry—and *headless*. He tossed it near the fire, then with a quick snap of his wrist sent the knife sailing into the air. It landed with a grating thud, its tip embedded securely in a stump next to the creature.

The man swung back around to face her, his features looking evil in the wavering light. "Come."

She hesitated.

"Come over here."

"Why?" She swallowed a lump of nausea as she rubbed her sore wrists, fearing what he might do next.

Muttering something low, he stalked up to her and tangled his fingers in her hair, forcing her toward the fire.

She winced and fought back tears.

He shoved her to her knees before the animal, which she now recognized as a squirrel. "Skin it."

Skin it? She didn't even want to *touch* it! "No. I—I mean, I can't." Her gaze skittered around. "P-please, whatever-your-name-is, I don't know how. And it's—it's *dead.*" She couldn't keep the revulsion from her voice.

"You would rather it be alive?"

"What? No!"

His voice, coming from somewhere close behind her, rasped meaningfully. "Then do it."

Afraid to touch the poor little thing, yet terrified not to, she pried the knife free and reached out a shaking hand toward the squirrel. Her stomach lurched. She couldn't do it. The knife slid from her fingers.

He clamped a hand over hers, forcing her to pick up the blade. "Please don't . . ."

Strong fingers tightened around hers, then guided the knife toward the mound of fur. Horrified, she watched as he slowly pressed the tip into the animal.

Blood spurted from the puncture.

Victoria's stomach rolled, then heaved violently.

She recoiled, her gaze fixed on the blood coating her fingers. Oh. *Oh.* She yanked her hand from beneath his and scrambled to her feet. Nausea stung her throat. Pressing the back of her wrist over her mouth, she ran to the edge of the glen, and dropped to her knees, barely making it before her insides convulsed.

Hawk stared in surprise at his wife's naked, shaking form all hunched over. Damn. He had not expected her to do that.

He went to the horse and unhooked a canteen before retrieving a piece of her shredded clothing. He lowered himself onto one knee beside her and gently touched her back. She whimpered in protest, but was forced to clutch her stomach again.

Guilt for the way he had treated her gnawed at his conscience, and before he could contain the urge, he dampened the fabric and pressed it against her forehead. Cursing his own lack of strength, he held it there until her retching passed.

When she finally settled, he cleaned her face and spoke to her in low, soothing tones, shocking even himself with his concern. After wiping her bloody hands, he tossed the garment aside, then raised the canteen to her lips. "Drink."

With a grateful nod, she took it and gulped thirstily.

"You have never skinned an animal," he said almost to himself.

She sputtered and coughed, fighting back another wave of nausea. "I've never so much as skinned a potato!"

"Peeled."

"What?"

He rose, pulling her to her feet. "Go sit by the fire. I will see what I can save of our morning meal."

"Morning?" She glanced up. A bright ring of yellow inched its way from behind the mountains. It *was* morning. They must have ridden all night. Averting her eyes from the dead animal, she rose. No wonder she was so exhausted.

Again becoming aware of her nakedness, she shielded herself as best she could, then edged toward the glowing warmth of the fire and sat down, fleetingly giving thought to her captor's gentleness of moments before. Unable to reason it out, she cast the thought aside and looked in the direction from which they'd come and prayed Paddy would rescue her.

An hour later the Indian brought her a steaming plate of squirrel cooked with wild carrots, onions, and horseradish. Unwilling to reach for it and expose her body again, or even consider eating the sickening fare, she tried to distract him. "How did you learn to cook like that?"

"All Shawnee warriors are taught to prepare food." He set the plate beside her. "We do not always take captives during a raid."

So he *was* a Shawnee. Victoria's thoughts flew to memories of her husband. "Does Hawk? I mean, does he go on raids?"

He didn't answer.

She wished he wouldn't stare at her like that. What did that look mean, anyway?

Standing abruptly, he tossed the remains on his plate toward the fire. "It is time to go."

"Go where? Why are you doing this? I don't understand what you want."

He didn't respond. Instead, he bound her hands again, then untied the length of leather from the tree and attached it to his own wrist and hers.

"Please, just take me back."

He cleared away signs of their presence in the glen.

Her nerves jumped at the determination in his silence as he walked to the horse and mounted, leaving her standing on the ground, but she wouldn't be swayed. "At least tell me where we're going."

"East." He nudged the horse forward. The leather between them tightened, then nearly jerked her off her feet. It was only then that she realized he intended for her to walk beside the horse—or to run, as the mood suited him. Dear God. She'd never live through this.

Collier Parks stiffened in the saddle and shot a glance at Dooley O'Ryan. "It's them." He returned his gaze to the black phaeton sitting in a small clearing. "Come on." He kicked his horse into a canter.

Dooley scowled and shifted his aching backside against the unfamiliar leather beneath him. "Slow down, ye cocky blighter. That fancy coach ain't goin' to get away from ye now. Not after ye've been trackin' it for near a fortnight."

Parks turned and glared at Dooley. "I know that, you fool. I'm merely anxious to see that Ria's safe. Now come on."

"Ye think I don't know how anxious ye are, matey? After gettin' me up in the middle o' the night like ye did?"

"It's not the middle of the night, *matey*. It's dawn."

"Now," Dooley returned, eyeing the man's back as he nudged the horse forward. After spending more than six weeks with Parks on that tub they called a ship, Dooley had had enough of the uppity gent. Not to mention that they had missed Parks's chit in Yorktown by more than a day. And now having to traipse through these bloody woods!

Dooley snorted and wondered once again if it wouldn't be better just to slit Parks's throat and be done with it.

Bragen Alexander folded his arms across his chest and glared down at Alaina Remington. "Even if you don't think your son intends to harm Victoria, *I* do. Damn it, My Lady, I saw the way he looked at her." Bragen turned toward his dun. "I'm going after her."

Alaina lifted her small chin. "Mr. Alexander, I believe I know Adam a great deal better than you do." She squared her shoulders. "He would not hurt a woman." Her gaze shifted to something behind Bragen, and she paled. "Oh, no."

He spun around to see two men riding toward them—a blond dressed in English finery and a bearded redheaded man wearing an eye patch and looking as though he'd never learned the purpose of bathwater. "Do you know them?"

She gave an unladylike snort. "The younger one is Victoria's cousin, Collier Parks," she answered in a disgusted tone. "The other's not familiar."

Bragen's gaze remained fixed on the men.

"Good morning, my good fellow," Parks greeted Bragen as he neared the coach. He nodded to Alaina. "Lady Remington." He glanced at McDaniels standing behind her, then sniffed and looked away.

Not acknowledging the man's greeting, Bragen waited.

Collier's lips thinned; then he shifted his gaze to the coach. "Ria? Are you in there, love?"

Alaina let out a breath. "No, Collier, she is not."

Parks looked surprised. "Then where the hell is she?"

"Gone."

The blond turned his confused gaze on Bragen. "What is she talking about?"

Bragen didn't trust this man. There was something in his eyes. "You heard Lady Remington. Victoria isn't here."

"That's quite obvious, my good fellow. But it does not answer my question. *Where is she?*"

Shrugging, Bragen turned toward the carriage. "With her husband."

Collier inhaled sharply. "My God, he'll kill her!"

"Who?" Alaina cried in alarm.

"Her husband."

Bragen tensed. "Explain yourself."

The cousin seemed near hysteria. He swung a glance at the one-eyed man. "I—I came after Ria when O'Ryan here told me what he heard at the docks. Go ahead, Dooley," he prompted the large man. "Tell them."

O'Ryan looked uncomfortable, then lowered his gaze to the buttons on Parks's waistcoat. "Word is that the duke got captured and sold into slavery a few years back."

Alaina clutched her throat.

Paddy placed a hand on her shoulder, his expression a mixture of fear and confusion.

"Now they're sayin' the bligh—um—man escaped and is

lookin' for his wife," O'Ryan continued, "'cause it were her who paid to have him done in."

A low groan sounded from Lady Remington.

McDaniels sucked in a sharp breath. "What are ye sayin'? Ria wouldna—"

"I've got to find her," Parks interrupted. "He'll kill her. I know he will."

"No!" Alaina cried. "He won't." Her gaze shot to Bragen. "Adam wouldn't do that."

Torn between the woman's faith and his own fear for Victoria, Bragen looked sharply at the one-eyed man. Something about O'Ryan's tale didn't ring true. It sounded almost as if someone had told him what to say. Bragen glanced at the cousin, then at Lady Remington. "Are you certain?"

"He won't kill her." She looked uneasy. "But if he believes what these men claim . . . I don't know what else he might do."

"Well, I *do* know," Parks snarled. "Damn it, if he doesn't kill her, he'll make her wish he had. I've got to find her."

"Do you know where this Adam might have taken her?" Bragen asked urgently. If the girl really was in danger, he damn sure wasn't just going to sit by and do nothing.

Alaina looked ready to crumble. "He might take her to his cabin or possibly to his father's village."

"Where are they?"

"The cabin's near Bedford County, in the mountains bordering on the east. The village, I believe, is still along the James River, at the point where the Blue Ridge and Alleghenies meet."

"Where the hell's that?" Parks scowled.

Bragen swung his gaze on the odious bastard. "Never mind. I'll go."

Collier raised his chin. "Not without me, you won't. She's *my* cousin. *My* responsibility."

McDaniels stepped forward. "I'll be goin' with ye, too, Bragen. I'll not leave me lass to the likes o' these two."

Bragen rolled his eyes. Christ! Anyone else? "Listen. This is ridiculous. We can't *all* go after her." He spoke to

McDaniels. "I know the area Lady Remington is talking about. You take her on to the Kincaids'." He pointed to the road. "Just follow it over the mountain until you reach the valley. I'm sure Lady Remington can find it from there." He glanced disgustedly toward O'Ryan and Parks. "I'll take them with me. And don't worry about Ria." He met the older man's gaze steadily. "I'll see to her safety."

As the horse cantered along the bank of a mountain stream, Hawk's mind churned with indecision. He could not decide what to do with Victoria. Certainly he wanted to see her suffer as he had. But why had he shown such weakness when she became ill? He snorted. He must have softened during his years in the salt mines.

His hand tightened around the leather, forcing his wife to keep pace with the horse. He knew what he would have liked to do. Taunting visions of him lowering Victoria to the grass and parting her thighs consumed him. The muscles in his stomach contracted. But *that* was hardly punishment.

Easing the horse into a slower gait, Hawk decided the first thing was to give his *neewa* one of the shirts in the saddlebag. He had sought to shame and punish her, not to distract himself from his purpose. Not wanting to think about how easy it would be to take her, he turned his thoughts to his mother.

Victoria's treachery had apparently gone undetected by his *nikyah*. His wife had obviously worked her wiles of deception well—even on his mother. Though it still did not explain their presence in Virginia.

Hawk focused on the ground passing beneath him. Victoria was no doubt clever, but he knew nothing else about her. What her fears were, her values—if any. If he could determine these . . .

Yes, he thought. He could do this. He would learn these things. Her weaknesses. What would *reach* her. And he would use this knowledge to hurt her as she had hurt him.

Pulling back on the reins, Hawk brought the horse to a stop and dismounted.

Victoria blinked up at him through red-rimmed eyes, but

she did not speak as he untied her hands and led her to a thatch of woods. "Relieve yourself."

She blushed clear to her fingers, then nodded. He watched with amusement as she looked around nervously, then cautiously slipped into the trees. For a brief instant he wondered if she would be fool enough to attempt escape.

Hawk smiled as he unsaddled the horse, then sat down. No, he decided. She would not run. She knew that she did not stand a chance of survival in the woods without a weapon and clothing.

A scream pierced the air.

Hawk sprang to his feet, grabbing the knife from one of his calf-high moccasins as he charged into the woods.

The scream echoed again, louder this time, from the left. He veered toward the sound. The foliage parted to reveal a small grassy clearing.

"Help!"

Hawk's gaze flew around in search of Victoria and the danger. When he saw it, he nearly burst out laughing.

Barely discernible, from an upper tree branch, he saw his wife's bare foot kicking frantically. Just below that, halfway up the trunk, a bear cub slapped at the exposed member.

"Help!" Victoria cried again, her voice hysterical.

Hawk briefly considered leaving her to suffer for a time, but the genuine terror in her tone stopped him. Too, seeing the way she kicked out at the cub, he feared she might slip from her perch. Easing toward the tree, he did not examine why that should trouble him.

He eyed the tree again, trying to decide the easiest course for rescue. It puzzled him how she had gotten so far out on that limb, but he did not ponder it. There was danger here. His gaze moved warily over the undergrowth lining the forest. He needed to know the location of the cub's mother.

Knowing the she-bear might appear at any moment, and realizing he might not have time to go up the tree after his wife, Hawk replaced the knife in his moccasin boot and stepped toward the overhanging branch. He stopped short. The shallow creek they had been following earlier ran just below the branch.

Cursing his luck, Hawk shook his head. Victoria would have to lunge toward him, and somehow he knew he was going to regret touching her naked body. Glancing up, he raised his hands. "Jump."

Victoria gasped and looked down. "Get it away from me. Please. Make the bear go away." Her voice sounded small and childlike.

"Jump now, *neewa.*"

She recoiled, then cast a desperate glance at the creek, then at the bear now making its way up the tree. Her eyes widened. She screamed. Then, without warning she vaulted.

Hawk lurched forward. He caught her by the waist, but the momentum of her fall pulled him off balance, and they both tumbled into the creek. With a chilling splash he landed on top of her.

Victoria cried out.

Hawk fought a groan as cold water surged over them. Damn it! Springing to his feet, he lifted his wife up out of the water.

She burrowed into his chest and clutched him tightly around the middle, her wet body trembling violently. Instinctively Hawk embraced her, then cursed the action.

After several moments, agonizing ones for him, she calmed and lifted her gaze. Damp red-brown curls clung to her cheeks. Clear blue eyes rimmed with dark wet lashes stared up at him. A drop of water slid down her cheek and touched the corner of her soft mouth. Warmth spread through his lower stomach.

At this close range, he could see only her beauty. Smell her womanly scent. Feel only what her body did to his. "Damn."

"What?"

He snapped to his senses. "Are you unharmed?"

"I think so." She glanced toward the tree and shivered. "Is it gone?"

Not trusting himself to look down at her wet body, he scanned the area. "Yes." Dragging his hands from her bare back, he gripped her arm and led her back to where he had left the horse. In a gesture of pure self-preservation, he removed the white shirt he had worn on the ship from England and thrust it into her hands. "Put it on."

Victoria looked stunned. "Where did you get this?"

"Put it on," he repeated through gritted teeth.

Dawning lit her eyes, and she snatched the garment, then in a belated gesture of modesty, she slipped behind a bush.

While fighting a smile at her ridiculous behavior and keeping an eye on the shrub, Hawk removed his loincloth, then pulled on his dry buckskins. He quickly saddled the horse and took up a relaxed position against a tree, waiting for his wife.

A few minutes later she stepped out from behind the hedge holding the bottom of the shirt out away from her wet body.

Hawk instantly realized he had made a mistake. She had taken her long hair down, allowing it to fall in damp waves to her waist and to curl temptingly at her cheeks. Somehow the sight of the silk shirt clinging to the moist upthrust of her breast was more enticing than complete nakedness, and he battled the desire to touch her. Hawk gnashed his teeth, but could not tear his gaze from the tight nipples straining against the fabric.

Obviously noticing where he directed his gaze, she clutched the silk together at the front and swallowed uneasily. "Um—thank you . . . ?"

Knowing she wanted his name, Hawk considered her thoughtfully before answering. Then, deciding against a complete lie, he settled for a half one. "I am called Shadow."

Victoria blinked up at the big man. Shadow? She traced the length of his straight midnight black hair brushing wide tanned shoulders, then looked up to his handsome, brooding features. Yes, she decided. The name suited him. Dark, elusive, mysterious. "Thank you, Shadow. For the shirt, I mean, and for rescuing me. I don't think I've ever been so frightened."

"The cub was harmless."

"Nothing in this place is harmless." She nervously searched the trees.

Hawk eyed her curiously. Did the woods bother her that

much? It was something to think on. Later. Anxious to remove her from his view, he quickly retied her hands and led her back to the horse. When he mounted, the stallion lurched forward, and she cried out as the leather cut into her wrists.

He steeled himself not to look back, not to feel compassion for this woman who had put him through hell. He would ride long, stopping only when necessary.

As the day wore on, his thoughts returned again and again to the child-woman stumbling along beside him—and the revenge he had planned. Seven years ago he had intended to take her to his cabin, and that hadn't changed. But instead of remaining there as his wife, she would now be his whore, his slave. It was fitting.

A low whimper sounded from the girl, and Hawk felt her cry touch his heart. Ridding himself of a disgusted breath, he reined the stallion carefully around a spruce, hoping by the time they reached the cabin, he could conquer this weakness. The woman did not merit his sympathy. After what he had suffered because of her, she deserved all the pain he could inflict . . . and more.

Chapter 12

Victoria knew she was going to die. She couldn't keep up this torturous pace any longer. For two days Shadow hadn't allowed her more than a few minutes' rest when he stopped to shove a piece of dried beef in her hand or give her a drink of water. Even when nature called, he had barely given her a chance to catch her breath before he mounted up again. Her arms were numb from the constant pull of the horse; her feet were bleeding. Twice she had fallen and been dragged several feet before Shadow managed to halt the stallion.

The weight of her hair clinging to her damp back and cheeks caused her to grow light-headed from the stifling heat and sweat of her own exhausted body. Her legs ached from the bruises she'd gotten when she ventured too near the horse's hooves.

About the only advantageous thing she could find in this whole situation was the fact that she didn't think about the forest so much anymore. She couldn't. All her efforts were concentrated on the sheer agony of just placing one foot in front of the other.

Yes. She was going to die . . . and she didn't care.

The horse's gait quickened, and Victoria stumbled, but she didn't fall. Thank heavens. The pain in her legs and back cut into her senses, and she tried to think of something else.

In her mind she conjured up a picture of Hawk and wondered how he would react to her being in the colonies once he found out. He would probably be furious because she'd invaded his privacy, she thought forsakenly.

She tried to drum up his image from their wedding, but recalled only his swollen features and powerful build—much like Shadow's. Obviously a Shawnee trait. The memory of Hawk's kiss flashed through her mind, and she felt a flicker of warmth. She gripped the leather binding and concentrated on his temperament—as well as she could remember it.

He hadn't wanted to marry her, that much was certain. But he hadn't been cruel to her, not really. He could have forced himself on her the night of their wedding, demanded his husbandly rights, but he hadn't. He could have left her without an allowance and at the mercy of her father, or his mother. But again, he hadn't.

The image of her stallion, Brandy, rose in her mind. No. Hawk might be heartless, but he wasn't a brutal man. She doubted he'd like the idea of her searching him out, but he wouldn't hurt her—if she lived long enough to see him.

But what about his people? Hawk's father controlled them. Flaming Wing might have been angered when he heard that his son was forced into marriage. The chief might even have decided to relieve his son of the burden by having her put to death.

She shivered at the thought and tried to recall what Alaina had told her about Flaming Wing, but the only words that came to mind were Alaina's declaration that her husband was extremely devoted to his family, and that he was on occasion a very brutal man.

Victoria stumbled again, and this time she fell. Hard. Pain cut into her flesh as her legs and thighs scraped over the rocky ground. The leather sliced into her wrists, tearing the tender skin. She managed a moan from her dry throat and nearly cried out in relief when Shadow at last managed to stop the horse.

"Please," she whimpered when he tried to make her stand. "I can't go on. Just kill me now and get it over with." She looked up and was surprised to see a flash of regret cross his strong features before he quickly masked it.

146

"We will rest tonight," he said, pulling her roughly to her feet. He led her to a small creek and pushed her down. "Clean yourself." With a look that warned her not to attempt escape, he rose and disappeared into the trees.

She almost laughed. He needn't have worried; she didn't have the strength to escape. She barely had the strength to wash.

Shadow returned a few minutes later clutching some odd-looking leaves in one strong hand and a skinned animal in the other. Victoria closed her eyes and thanked the stars that he hadn't forced her to clean it.

He tossed the leaves down by her knees. "Dampen them and rub them on your wrists and feet," he ordered brusquely. "After that, gather dry branches and start a fire."

Victoria dug her fingers into the pile of leaves and plunged a handful into the water, then slapped them on her wrists. "I hope you scald in hell," she muttered. But she had to admit, though grudgingly, that the wet herbs did indeed soothe her raw wrists. She repeated the process on her feet and legs and groaned in relief.

She peeked over at Shadow and saw that he was skewering the skinned animal on the pointed end of a green branch. Sighing, she knew she had to get up and build a fire. She staggered painfully to her feet, but fell with the first step.

Shadow said something ugly-sounding under his breath. "Useless woman." He gestured toward a grassy spot. "Sit."

Relieved, Victoria sank down.

After they had eaten, Hawk gave her a tin cup filled with water, then leaned back against a sapling. He studied his *neewa* silently. Perched on the grass, she sat with her knees firmly together, her hands in her lap, her slender fingers wrapped around the cup. Her lower thighs and long legs were visible beneath the hem of his shirt.

Seeing the cuts and bruises he had caused to mar the otherwise perfect flesh, and warring with the guilt building inside him, he forced his gaze upward. She stared into the fire, her eyes half closed in exhaustion, her mouth pressed into a tired line. Dark hair laced with threads of burnished red cloaked her back, its thickness glistening like glowing embers.

He looked away quickly but could not suppress a burst of pride at her endurance. Though he had deliberately driven her beyond tolerance, her spirit had not been broken.

Attempting to divert his thoughts from her suffering, he focused on the slow-moving stream beside him. But again his gaze drifted back to her drawn features, and he noticed that even though she was nearly numb with fatigue, she still searched the trees nervously.

"Why do you fear the forest?" he asked quietly.

She raised a trembling hand to her forehead. "It's not the woods. It's what's in them."

"The animals?"

"Bears."

"Like the one in the tree?" He shook his head. "They will not harm you unless you threaten one of their young or they are hungry." He surveyed the area, noting the dense, rich foliage. "Food is plentiful now. They are little threat."

He watched her throat work. Then she bent forward and set her cup down. As she did so, the hem of the shirt rose slightly. She immediately yanked it back into place—but not soon enough.

Staring, Hawk moved to stand before her, then knelt. He lifted her clenched hands away with one of his own and raised the hem of the shirt with the other. Four thin scars scored her silky flesh. How had he missed seeing those when she wore no clothing?

Then he realized that her right side had been next to the horse, and, too, he had avoided looking at her nakedness. He had wanted *her* to suffer, not *him.* "The cub was not your first encounter with a bear," he said gruffly, then met her anxious gaze. "I would hear the tale."

"Listen, Sh-shadow. It was a long time ag—"

"Now." He returned to his seat by the sapling, trying not to notice how distraught she had become.

She balled her small hands into fists as she gripped the bottom of the shirt. "When I was five"—she cleared her throat—"my family was on the way to a hunt in Sussex.

We stopped in the forest to rest and eat. I got lost in the woods."

At first he thought that was the extent of her story. Then her gaze drifted to the flames and seemed to take on a vacant, haunted look. Her voice trembled into a low rasp. "I wasn't frightened in the beginning. I knew my father or Paddy, our groom, would find me. It wasn't the first time I'd gotten lost on an outing. But they didn't come. And it grew darker . . . and colder."

Flames from the fire were reflected in her glazed eyes. "I heard some nearby brush rustle. I—I thought it was one of them, and I was so relieved. I ran toward the sound. But it wasn't a human. It was a bear cub." Her knuckles grew white. "I was so young and naive, and he was so sweet. I just wanted to pet him, let him keep me company until I was found."

Her face grew pale, and Hawk felt her terror.

"Then another bear, a big one, charged me." She shook violently, and tears filled her eyes. "I ran. Oh, God, how I ran. But I could hear it behind me, snarling, thrashing, clawing." She clutched her stomach. "Ahead of me I saw a dead tree trunk that looked hollow. My side and lungs hurt, but I knew I had to reach it. I had to. And I almost made it. . . ." She closed her eyes. The hand at her stomach twitched. "But the big bear was too quick. Just as I scrambled up the trunk and climbed inside, its claw caught my thigh."

Hawk struggled with waves of compassion. "Did the others come then?"

"I wish they had." She opened her eyes and blinked rapidly, as if trying to gain control of her emotions. "But they didn't. I spent the night there." She met his gaze. "I will never forget the blood. It was all over me—sticky, clammy, running down my leg. And the smell . . . the horrible odor of blood and rotting wood. I can't forget it." She lowered her voice. "Nor can I forget the terrifying sound of that bear, clawing and growling as it tried to get to me."

Hawk felt a rush of sympathy. He saw all the terror that small girl had suffered reflected in her misty gaze.

"Paddy found me. The next day." She smiled sadly. "It was the only time I ever saw him cry."

"You were fortunate not to have been killed," Hawk said, trying desperately to manage the battling emotions swirling through him. He ached for the child she had been, yet despised the deceitful woman she had become.

Gathering the reins on his resolve, he rose. He pulled her to her feet and led her to the spot where he had been sitting. Shoving her to the ground, he lifted her limp hands and secured them close to the base of the sapling. "You will sleep now," he instructed with a gesture for her to lie down, knowing it would be impossible for her to rest adequately while tied to a tree.

Her eyes grew wide as she stared up at him, but she did not argue.

Keeping his expression blank, he took a seat by the fire. He would not rest until after she fell asleep. He needed time to think on her tale—and on his revenge.

From the corner of his eye, he watched her squirm around, trying to find some small amount of comfort leaning against the tree. When that obviously did not work, she lowered one of her shoulders to the ground and placed her cheek against an upraised arm. Hawk flinched under the prick of his conscience, but refused to aid in her plight. Instead, he recalled the many torturous nights when he had tried to sleep with pain clawing at his flesh and the scent of salty dust burning his lungs.

By the time her breathing deepened to a steady rhythm, the flames had disappeared into flickering coals and the air had grown noticeably colder. He had begun to wonder if the woman would ever give in to exhaustion so *he* could.

Relieved that he could finally rest, he silently slipped beneath the wool covers he had spread out earlier, trying not to think about the woman's need for a blanket. Lacing his fingers behind his head, he stared up at the ebony sky dotted with specks of twinkling white. It was good to be home again. The familiar sound of an owl—a flutter of wings and a slight rustle of leaves—relaxed him. Truly at ease for the first time in years, he closed his eyes.

A pitiful whimper startled him out of the arms of slumber. He blinked and quickly scanned the camp. Nothing stirred. He glanced at his wife. She lay curled into a ball, one tearstained cheek pressed into her arm, her small body shaking.

Guilt nearly strangled him, and before he could control the impulse, he went to her. Cursing himself for his lack of strength, he untied her hands and carefully lifted her into his arms. A jolt passed through him when she clung to his neck but did not awaken.

He cursed himself for being a fool, for allowing her to affect him—and a bigger one for even considering taking her to the warmth of his mat. He could not trust his body. Not after seven years of celibacy. But his common sense drifted with the clouds as he lowered her to his bed.

She curled into him. "Blood. So much . . . Oh, please. Make it go away."

The agony in her voice touched his heart, and he enfolded her in his arms. He rocked her, felt her pain. How different his own life might have been if he'd experienced what she had. He looked over the top of her head at the shadowy pines silhouetted against the moonlit horizon and tried to imagine fearing the land he loved so much. But he could not.

"The bear is gone, Victoria," he whispered gently, hoping to banish her nightmare without awakening her—or his lust. "It is gone." After several minutes he felt her relax and knew he had succeeded. Yet for some unknown reason he could not let her go. Something about the feel of her pressed against him seemed so right.

He became aware of the soft brush of her breath against his neck, of her firm breasts molded to his chest, of his own palm resting at the base of her spine. His manhood stirred, and through the material of his buckskins he could feel the heat from her woman's mound nestled close to his loins.

Without thought to the consequences, he slid his hand down from her waist to explore the curve of her buttock. He swallowed a groan when his palm touched bare flesh. The shirt had ridden up and was bunched up above her hips.

He kneaded the gentle swell, enjoying the heady feel of the

satiny curve before slipping his hand under the material and gliding upward. The texture of her soft skin destroyed his reason. It had been so long. Too long.

He leaned back, giving himself better access to her smooth midsection, then higher.

He gently brushed his lips against her throat while easing his thumb upward until it touched her nipple under the silk shirt.

Her breathing quickened; then a low mewling sound vibrated in her throat.

Hawk felt his own strength drain away as he stroked the taut center.

She gave an odd little whimper and rolled her head against his shoulder.

The movement brought her ear close to his mouth, and he could not resist the temptation. He brushed his lips against it. When she did not protest, he grew bolder, tracing the lobe with his tongue, knowing the heat of his breath caused her shivers. His palm joined the siege on her breast, his fingers massaging the firm mound.

She moaned and turned her face to his.

His mouth slid from her ear, down across her cheek to taste her lips. They quivered, and he tauntingly outlined them with his tongue before penetrating the sweet barrier.

Her nipple tightened beneath his palm.

His body hardened in response, and he arched against her thighs, nearly blinded by need. Unable to control his trembling, he edged back. He had to touch her. He slid his hand ever so slowly down across her flat belly to her inner thigh. Inch by delicious inch, he worked his way toward the moistness he sought.

Her breathing grew rapid, and her legs parted willingly beneath his experienced strokes.

Hawk knew his own passion-starved body could not take much more. He was ready to explode. Forcing his hand away from her heat, he placed it over his throbbing shaft to halt the building pressure. When he regained control, he urgently pushed his breeches down until he at last freed himself.

Without thought to his actions, he rolled Victoria beneath

him and parted her thighs. With an urgency he had never known before, he raised her to receive him, his lips plundering hers while his fingers dug into her soft buttocks.

He felt her tense and realized she had awakened and come to her senses.

She turned her face away. "No! Oh, please don't."

Hawk stopped her protests with his mouth, filling her with his tongue. When she continued to fight him, he pushed her back down, then used one hand to hold her by the hair while his other forced her hips closer to his need.

He was vaguely aware of her frantic struggles, but he could not stop. Could not deny himself. He pressed against her opening.

"Stop! For the love of—"

His mouth crushed hers.

She twisted and kicked, but he was beyond rational thought. He was so close.

Out of the darkness something slammed hard against his head. Pain exploded like shattered glass. He blinked and tried to focus through a tunnel of rolling blackness. . . .

Victoria dropped the rock in her hand and took a deep, shuddering breath. Her heart pounded against her chest with such force she thought it would split. He had tried to rape her! She shoved the man's limp form off her and scrambled unsteadily to her feet.

But when she looked down, fear grabbed her. What if she'd killed him? Anxiously she eyed the trail of blood weaving a path from his temple to his jaw. The sight paralyzed her. *Blood.* Too, he looked so pale, so lifeless.

Shaking uncontrollably, she bent and placed her palm against his naked scarred back. A strong steady beat drummed beneath her fingers. Thank God.

She straightened, trying to ignore a wave of remorse, and headed for the horse. The blackguard deserved it.

Realizing she'd finally gotten her chance for escape, she quickened her pace and winced against the pain in her feet. But when she reached the horse, she stopped short. How could she mount it without help? Eyeing the saddleless beast, she drew on her determination. She knew there must be a way. After darting a nervous glance at her unconscious captor, she sent a hurried look around the area. A fallen log. If she could stand on that, perhaps she could swing her leg over. . . .

She snatched up the reins that held the animal tethered to a branch and led the horse to the log. Holding it steady, she climbed on the decaying wood and tried to position the horse so she could mount. But every time she tried to raise her bruised and battered leg, her muscles screamed in protest.

Several frustrating minutes passed before she gingerly stepped down. She sent another anxious peek at the prone man. He still lay face down on the blankets, his arms stretched upward and lying flat on the ground on either side of his head, his breeches draped low across his buttocks. Her belly fluttered. How close he had come to—

After taking a deep breath, she led the stallion to a line of trees, then dropped the reins and stepped behind it. If she couldn't ride the horse, then neither could her abductor. "Sorry, fella," she murmured as she drew her arm back then brought her hand down solidly on its firm rump.

The animal let out a shrill whinny, then bolted off into the woods.

Satisfied, Victoria grabbed up a spare blanket lying near the saddle and wrapped it around her shoulders. She sent a last glance at her kidnapper before dashing into the forest. If she could find the larger creek they'd followed earlier, she'd be able to find her way out of the mountains by going downstream.

Half running, half hopping over the rocky ground as quickly as she could with her sore feet, she raced frenziedly away from her kidnapper, fear gnawing at her as she rounded every shadowy bush. What if she encountered another bear?

Branches snagged her hair. Thorny bushes slashed at the tender bruised flesh of her arms and legs. The blanket caught again and again on spiky branches, and she finally tossed it aside. She didn't have time for more mishaps!

But the more she ran, the more she hurt. Her chest heaved as she fought for air. Sharp twigs dug into the soles of her feet, but she didn't dare stop. Not until she knew she was safe.

On and on she raced, her lungs burning, pain slicing into her side, her bleeding feet, her entire body.

At last, after what seemed like hours, a beam of moonlight slid from behind a cloud and sparkled off of something up ahead. The creek! It had to be. Gathering all her strength, she rushed toward it.

The ground suddenly turned to smooth moss-covered rock. Her feet slid out from under her; then the ground disappeared.

A scream tore from her throat as she hurtled downward, clutching at air. . . .

Chapter 13

Through a fog Victoria caught the scent of moldy soil and another odor she couldn't name. She blinked and sat up, vaguely registering the mound of fur and bone beneath her hand. She brushed her hair out of her eyes and glanced around at . . . utter blackness.

Twisting wildly, she looked up. Above, she saw a cluster of stars emerge from behind a gray cloud. She slumped in relief. "Thank heaven."

After taking a moment to still her thundering heart, she rose slowly, achingly, to her feet. Unable to see anything, she put her hands out. Granite walls met her fingertips on all sides. Her gaze flew upward again, and as her eyes adjusted to the darkness, she could see the outline of an upper rim. She was in a hole!

She pressed against the stone, trying to determine how she could get out. She stepped forward, and her toe bumped something furry. She squealed and jerked her foot back.

Palming her chest as if to keep her heart from leaping out, she took several calming gulps of air. An eternity seemed to pass before she gained control and convinced herself there was no danger. Gathering all her courage, she bent forward and touched the bulky mound with her fingers. The fur had little substance beneath it—mostly bone. A carcass? Uneasiness shook her, and she prayed there were not other animals in here with her. *Live* ones.

Swallowing against increasing terror, she straightened

and tried to peer into the darkness. Nothing. She again felt the confines of her surroundings. She hugged her middle, fighting back a surge of frightening panic. *"Help me. Some-one help me!"*

The raspy timbre of her own voice jolted her back to her senses. Taking a deep breath, she lifted her chin. "Get hold of yourself, Victoria. Calm down. Think."

It took several minutes before her brain finally decided to cooperate. Not that it helped much when it did. All she could grasp was the fact that she was trapped in a hole with no way out—and with a dead animal she couldn't name. "God, please, let it be a deer."

Hawk came slowly awake to the vicious pounding in his head. He groaned and clutched his temple. Something wet and sticky clung to his fingers. Opening his eyes, he squinted and looked down. Blood. "Damn her!"

He angrily wiped the back of his hand across the cut under his hairline, barely noticing the smear across his knuckles. He looked around, but saw no sign of his wife.

He jumped to his feet. Pain blinded him, and he grabbed his head again. *"Damn."* Slowly he became aware of his loose breeches. He stared down at the buckskin. It hung low on his hips.

A groan of pure frustration rumbled through his chest. *He had tried to rape his own wife.*

Guilt stung his conscience as he righted his clothing. Trying to ignore the sensation, he again scanned the area still aglow by yellow embers. Through an opening between the trees, he saw his horse meandering toward the light. Victoria had not taken it. Why? The stupid little fool did not know these woods. She feared them.

An urgency gripped him, and, though he did not under-stand it, he could not disregard the feeling. His *neewa* needed him. Now.

Quickly searching the ground, he found small footprints in the grassy soil that told him which direction his wife had taken. Silently thanking Moneto for the ability to track, Hawk followed the prints across the clearing, then came to a stop before a gnarly thicket. A piece of wool hung from a thorny limb. Recognizing it as a part of his blanket, he reached out to shove the brush aside.

"Hold fast," a threatening voice commanded.

Shocked, Hawk stiffened, then turned slowly. Before him stood Alexander, the man who had led Victoria's party. He held a pistol pointed at Hawk's chest.

Behind the guide Hawk was stunned to see a face out of the past—Collier Parks, Victoria's cousin, the man who had tried to blackmail him. Hawk's muscles flexed involuntarily.

He shifted his gaze to the man next to the cousin, and a surge of hatred nearly stole his breath. It was the one-eyed seaman who had sold Hawk into slavery. His fists curled. Hawk had waited a long time to see this one again.

"Where is she?"

The vehemence in the guide's voice demanded Hawk's attention. He composed his features and met the man's midnight eyes. "Who?"

"Kill him, Alexander!" Parks shouted. "He's murdered Ria! We all know it. Damn it, man. You saw her bloody clothes. And look at the blood on his hands. Kill him now!"

Alexander's mouth drew into a harsh line, and his cold gaze raked Hawk. "Let me rephrase the question, Remington. Where did you hide Victoria's body?"

Hawk stared at the man facing him. "The girl is not dead."

"We didn't expect ye to admit it," the seaman sneered.

"Shut up, O'Ryan. I told both you and Parks I'd handle this. So stay out of it." He turned back to Hawk. "Where is she?"

"She escaped."

"You bloody liar!" the cousin snapped. "Ria's terrified of the woods. She'd never take off on her own."

"Let me have a go at him, matey." O'Ryan uncoiled a black whip from his belt and stepped forward. "The blighter'll talk soon enough under the bite o' the lash."

Hawk's stomach cringed. He could almost feel the fiery pain cut across his back again, as it had so many times before. Something inside him closed up. He did not speak. He could not force words past his numb throat.

"Put that away," the leader ordered. He pressed the barrel of his pistol to the underside of Hawk's chin. "We'll find Victoria, Remington. And if you've hurt her, I'll use that whip on you myself."

The man spoke the truth. Hawk could see it in his steady glare.

"Now, put your hands behind your back." Over his shoulder, he commanded Parks, "Tie him."

Collier Parks moved hesitantly toward the edge of the clearing, then returned leading three horses. From one of the saddlebags, he withdrew a leather strip and a length of rope. A smirk curled his lip as he stepped behind Hawk.

Parks cinched the binding so tight it sliced into his wrists.

As the cousin completed the task, Hawk felt something wet drop on the top of his head. Then again. And again. Uneasiness flooded his midsection. Rain.

Hawk studied Alexander as he watched the rain splatter against a boulder, then glanced up. Something unreadable flashed in the dark-haired one's eyes. "Bind him to that tree," he directed, pointing to a birch.

Surprised, Hawk stared at the branchless stump of the tree. He would not be sheltered from the rain, which would wet the leather binding his hands. Did Alexander know the leather would stretch, enabling Hawk to escape? He narrowed his gaze. Of course he did. Alexander *wanted* Hawk to escape—no doubt so that he could lead Alexander and the others to Victoria.

He almost smiled at that. The guide did not know he could only follow Hawk as long as Hawk allowed it. Though Alexander had done a fair job so far, Hawk knew he himself was to blame. He had been careless, his thoughts too full of Victoria.

The guide continued issuing commands. "O'Ryan, spread blankets over those branches to make a shelter. I'll gather some firewood while it's still dry."

Parks gripped Hawk's arm and roughly shoved his back

against the trunk of the birch and tied him. "You're a dead man, Lord Remington," he vowed softly before joining O'Ryan.

Hawk watched the men scramble for more branches, then disappear beneath the woolen refuge. A few minutes later a stream of smoke rose out of a gap between two of the covers.

While he stood motionless, rain pelting his head, he allowed his mind to conjure up a suitable torture to bestow on O'Ryan. Someday soon.

Then thoughts of Victoria, terrified and alone in the forest, seeped in, and Hawk felt a surge of revulsion toward himself. It was his fault she was out there by herself. She had been so frightened of him. Yet he'd never dreamed she would brave the dangers of the forest alone. But then, he had never thought to lose control and force himself upon her, either.

He blinked against the rain coming down in heavy torrents and twisted his hands as water ran down his arms. Why had she dreaded his possession so much? As experienced as she was, she must have known he would not harm her.

Another feeling of foreboding gripped him. Victoria was in danger. He could sense it. He had to get free—had to find her. And he could not wait for the leather to stretch.

Spreading his legs, he pressed all his weight back against the tree, then lifted one foot and arched it back toward his hands. If he could just reach the knife in his moccasin boot.

Straining in the awkward position, he forced his leg higher, ignoring the pain screaming through his muscles. His fingers touched the soft leather. He worked them toward the top edge, feeling the outline of the knife beneath the tips of his fingers, then at last, the smooth handle.

Victoria huddled against a wall of the pit, shivering with cold and terror. Icy rain streamed into the hole and down her back, then pooled around her feet. But she didn't dare move and risk touching the animal carcass again. She felt as if her sanity hung on a thread as fragile as a cobweb, and even though he might finish what he'd started, she prayed for Shadow to find her. Besides, who else was there?

Water sloshed around her ankles. Even rape might be preferable to drowning in a pit with a dead animal. Drowning. Merciful heavens, she *would* drown if the hole kept filling up. God, how she wished she'd learned to swim.

She pressed her hands against the smooth sides of the pit and winced against the pain in her fingertips. It reminded her of how she'd clawed so furiously trying to get out earlier. And all for nothing. The pit was at least seven feet deep, she'd discovered, with no branches or rocks sturdy enough to help her escape.

Suddenly a flare of lightning shot across the sky, illuminating her dark prison and the mound of fur lying within. It lasted a mere second, but that was long enough for Victoria to identify the dead animal lying at the bottom of the pit.

She fought mind-numbing hysteria.

A bear.

Hawk didn't wait to catch his breath once he had freed himself. Sheathing his knife, he cast one last hate-filled glance at the woolen shelter harboring the men, torn between his desire to avenge himself and his need to find Victoria. Vowing to return the moment he knew she was safe, he hurried into the woods. Safe, hell! He would kill her for putting him through this.

He felt another wave of uneasiness. She was in danger. Very real danger. He could *feel* it. Fighting down his own rising apprehension, he pushed his way through the thicket and searched quickly for another sign of Victoria's path. With the rain falling, he could no longer follow her footprints.

Thunder rumbled, followed by a flash of light. It did not last a full second, but it was enough for Hawk to see another scrap of blanket hanging from a bush.

With every slosh of the water around her knees, Victoria felt the skin of the bear flutter against her calves. Too numb to move and too hoarse to cry out, she clung to the slimy wall of the pit, her insides shaking violently—and she prayed.

She prayed for her sanity, for Paddy to come, for the rain to stop, for the darkness to end . . . and for Shadow. He would save her from the bear—and from drowning. He *had* to. She was his chief's daughter-in-law.

"Oh, Mama," she whispered hoarsely to the darkness. "How awful it must have been for you that day at the lake." Water slapped her thighs. "How you must have suffered. How Father must have suffered when he found you." No wonder he had changed so after Alexandra's death.

Would Shadow change when he found Victoria's body? She shuddered and sucked in a shaky breath. Probably not. She could almost envision him shrugging those wide shoulders, then mounting up in search of another captive. The insensitive cur.

Anger simmered inside her, and she welcomed it. Anything to take her mind off the pit. And the bear.

She thought again of the brutal way he'd hit her when he first captured her, of the way he'd viciously torn her clothing off, of the way he'd dragged her behind that horse, attempted to make her skin that squirrel.

Her anger ebbed when she remembered the way he'd comforted her when she became ill. He had stroked her brow, cleaned her hands and face, spoken to her in that low, soothing voice, given her herbs for her cuts. She recalled how understanding he'd been tonight when she told him about her fear of the forest and of bears. Then he had let her sleep.

But sleep had only resurrected memories of the bear, the blood, the horrified five-year-old she'd been. She could have sworn she felt him lift her, heard him soothing her, talking gently, telling her everything was all right. And she'd believed him. She had felt safe.

For a long time she'd had the most erotic dream. Shadow was kissing her the way Hawk had, touching her, setting fire to her blood, until . . .

Something brushed against her buttocks, and she gasped,

surprised at the sensitivity of that particular area. Heavens, it was almost as if Shadow's hand had touched her in that private region. But it wasn't Shadow's hand.

It was the bear.

Hawk cursed for the thousandth time as he brushed the dripping hair out of his eyes. Damn her. Where had she gone? He had not seen any sign of her passage through this area since he found the discarded blanket.

He kicked a rock with his moccasined foot, sending it sailing down the grassy hill that led to the creek. Creek. He narrowed his gaze, trying to penetrate the darkness. She had stared at it several times during their journey. Would she think to follow it back the way they had come? Very likely.

He started down the slope. A bolt of lightning lit the sky, spilling a yellow glow over the slick, mossy granite embankment that led to the river below. The water had risen nearly to the edge of one of the many natural pits in this area.

Victoria would not be stupid enough to walk down the center of the creek. Surely she would know that the water coming down from the higher mountains would turn it into a gushing torrent.

Not as certain as he would have liked to be, he skirted the slippery granite shelf and walked closer to the raging water, searching for evidence downstream. Nothing.

Frustration rose, and a chill swept over him. He clutched the dripping blanket. He was wet and cold and miserable—and a damn fool for standing out here in the elements, when he knew full well his *neewa* had eluded him. At least for now.

Glancing around, he saw a large recess in one of the mounds of boulders. Another much bigger rock formed a roof over the hollow, fashioning a fairly dry cocoon. Knowing that dawn was not far away, Hawk decided to wait for first light. Turning his back to the fast-moving creek, he wrung out the blanket, then crawled into the welcome haven.

Once inside, he swiped the hair away from his face and leaned back, trying to relax. But though his body attempted to rest, his mind would not. He could still see Victoria's fearful expression when she told him of her experience in the forest; he still felt her terror.

He tried to convince himself that she was getting what she deserved. He wanted to see her suffer for what she did to him, wanted to see her cry out in horror and pain.

Something ugly wiggled through his conscience, and shame attacked him, quickly followed by a gripping sense of fear for his wife.

He closed his eyes, trying to shut out the anxiety. Unbidden, a tiny thought intruded. What if Victoria had not been responsible for his imprisonment?

He snapped into a straight-backed posture. Of course she was! Then why was she so shocked by the scars on your back? a little voice asked. Why did she ask you how you got them? "It was a ploy," he argued aloud. It had to be. She was the queen of deception and an excellent actress.

He folded his arms across his chest and once again leaned back, closing his eyes. But visions of his wife's beautiful face wavered before him again and again. The horror he had seen in her eyes when he told her to skin the squirrel. The way she had become ill at the sight of blood. Not exactly what one would expect of a cold witch who had paid to have her husband abducted.

He thought back to the day he proposed to her. She was shocked by the sight of his beaten face, and revealed her compassion before she thought. Not exactly the reaction of a heartless girl.

He frowned at the thought of her age back then. She had been a fifteen-year-old child. A very enticing one, but a child nonetheless. She would not have even known the one-eyed seaman, much less hired him.

He opened his eyes to glare into the dark. What about her lover, McDaniels? Again his conscience intruded. McDaniels had rescued her from the forest. He was old enough to be her father. He had been a servant to her family for many years. He was a friend.

Hawk tried to remember the innkeeper's words. Atwood claimed that the girl's father had thrown the crippled man out, that Victoria went to see him often, always carrying a bundle, and that after she left, McDaniels always had money. A sudden uneasiness lodged in Hawk's chest. Was the girl merely helping an unfortunate friend who was not her lover?

He shifted uncomfortably. He would speak again to Victoria. He peered out of his shelter. *If he ever found her.*

Water began to pour into her prison from a new source, from the other side . . . and much faster.

Victoria's panic rose as quickly as the water, and she tried to claw her way to the top. Pain ripped through her fingers as they curled into a small niche in the granite wall. Water sloshed against her shoulders, and she trembled. "Help me! God, *please.*"

Lightning speared the sky. Thunder roared. Water slapped her cheek, then something else. The bear fur. A scream rose in her throat, but she never released it. Something snapped inside her. Vaguely she heard a woman's high-pitched hysterical wail. Over and over it rang out like the cry of a demented, tortured soul. Who was she? Why wouldn't she stop?

Something cool tickled Victoria's lips and filled her mouth. A warmth stole over her, and the night grew quiet. So quiet. She could rest now, and nothing would hurt her again. Her upstretched arms relaxed against the granite, and she loosened her fingers. Then her body began to glide slowly, ever so slowly, downward. . . .

Chapter 14

Hawk heard a faint cry, nearly muffled by the pelting rain and bursts of thunder. Victoria! It had to be. He scrambled out from beneath the overhang, trying to see through the murky darkness.

Another chest-splitting scream, louder this time, just below him.

Lightning flashed, and in the glow he could see nothing but the pit he had noticed earlier. He scanned the area again and frowned. Had he only imagined the screams? Warily, his gaze returned to the pit.

"Damn!" He charged forward, slipping on the wet smooth rock in his haste. When he reached the edge of the recess, he leaned over, desperately trying to see inside. Only thick blackness met his anxious gaze.

Thunder rumbled, then another flash of light from the heavens.

The lightning revealed the rising water in the hole, and Victoria . . . slipping beneath the deadly surface, her hands sliding down the side of the pit.

Hawk did not stop to think of his own safety. He threw himself belly-down on the ground and grabbed for his wife's hands.

He caught one wrist, but the other dropped away from him. *No.* He tightened his grip, barely aware of the way he trembled. With every ounce of strength he possessed, he pulled.

166

He started to slip forward into the pit and wildly clutched at the granite. His fingers dug through the moss and touched a small groove. He grasped the niche savagely. It stopped his descent, but Victoria remained submerged. He yanked hard. "Damn it, *neewa,* pull!"

She shot up out of the water, coughing and sputtering, clawing madly at the hand wrapped around hers.

"Help me," she coughed out weakly. "I don't want to die."

"You are safe, *neewa.*" He attempted to soothe her fears. "Nothing will hurt you now. Hold on to me."

He felt her hands shake, then her fingernails cut into his flesh.

With agonizing slowness, Hawk scooted backward on the slick ground. Inch by torturous inch, he pulled his wife from the flooding pit.

The instant her knees touched the slimy surface, she scrambled toward him, then lunged into his arms. She trembled crazily, her arms a vise around his neck. "Oh, God, I thought I was going to die!" She hugged him tighter, her body quaking uncontrollably. "Thank you." She kissed his cheek, his brow. "Oh, thank you." She kissed his nose, his other cheek, his jaw.

His own emotions ragged, Hawk closed his arms around her. He had come so close to losing her. He crushed her against him. If he had not heard her screams . . . His heart pounded savagely. Desperately his mouth sought hers.

Victoria responded viciously, gripping his hair, drawing his tongue deep into her mouth as if to devour him.

Hawk realized that she had lost control, that her terror sought another outlet . . . passion. For an instant he thought to break the contact, but when she pressed her thighs hard against his manhood, his own control slipped. He opened his mouth over hers, filling her with his tongue as he wanted to fill her with his body.

She shivered and ground her lips against his, the movement causing their wet lips and tongues to glide erotically.

In that moment Hawk knew he was lost. He had spent too many years without the feel of a woman's body next to his, around his. He plunged his tongue deep into her mouth. Nothing, not even Moneto himself, could have stopped Hawk from possessing this woman. He rolled with her in a frenzy of clinging arms and melding lips until they reached the grass. He crushed her down on the soft earth and covered her body with his.

Cool rain plundered his back, yet nothing mattered but the feel of Victoria writhing beneath him, the taste of her sweet mouth, the frantic thrust of her hips as her body cried out its need.

Forcing himself to go slowly, Hawk eased up.

"No! Oh, please, don't leave me!"

"Shh. Easy, little one. I will not leave you. Not now." He pulled her to her knees to face him.

Lightning lit the sky, bathing Victoria in its golden glow.

Hawk caught his breath. The silk shirt she wore was wet and nearly transparent, revealing the full thrust of her coral-tipped breasts and the deep shadowy V at the juncture of her thighs.

He tightened unbearably. His hands shook like a young boy's when he raised them to unbutton the shirt and open it. The veiled image of her beauty was nothing compared to the reality.

Slowly, savoring the moment, he slid the shirt down her arms and let it drop to the ground.

The heavens burst with fire, and Hawk stared at the sight of the naked beauty he had not allowed himself to enjoy earlier. Her head was thrown back, her throat arched. Water glistened with each flash of lightning revealing the tiny riverlets cascading over her skin. Her dark, wet cherrywood-colored hair spilled around her shoulders and clung to her skin. Her lips were parted, her small pink tongue tracing the bottom one.

Minor explosions erupted in his lower stomach. He could almost feel that tongue gliding over his, their bodies merging. . . . Then that was all he *could* think of.

He stared down at her.

Her arms hung loose at her sides, her eyes were closed,

water slid down her smooth flesh in streams. Mesmerized, he followed its path through the valley between her breasts and down over the flat surface of her taut belly until it disappeared into the silky nest between her legs.

Hawk fought the urge to kiss that spot, but how he wanted to. Instead, he ordered hoarsely, "Touch me, *neewa.*"

She opened her dazed eyes and met his, then lowered them to the bulging thrust of his desire.

He expected her to recoil at the sight, but she did not. She seemed entranced as she lifted her hands to place them in his.

His pulse soared, and he gripped them, pressing them flat against his chest. His heart drummed savagely beneath her cool fingers as he slowly, torturously, guided them down his body. "Feel what you do to me," he said shakily, pressing her hands lower.

She gasped, then moaned and closed her eyes when her palms met his throbbing shaft.

Hawk's stomach twisted painfully, but he fought to hold himself in check and savor the feel of her hands on him. He helped her lower his breeches, then curled her fingers around his manhood. Gently, slowly, he eased her hand up and down. Rain made the movement slick and sensuous, and his body shook brutally.

Gripping her by the hair, he ground his mouth on hers as she continued to stroke him, her fingers a flutter of velvet against his pounding shaft.

He could not breathe, could not think, could do nothing but feel what she did to him. His body was alive with sensations, the smell of damp earth and pine, the roaring sound of water gushing into the pit. His sensitized frame tingled as a breeze tickled his flesh. Even the rain gliding down his stomach seemed as erotic as a caress.

Hawk's control shattered.

Easing away from her, he bent, then pressed her down onto the grass.

He kissed her savagely, then slid his mouth around to her ear. "I will show you what your touch does to me." Holding

Sue Rich

her hands pinned down on either side of her head, he
pressed his mouth to her neck, hungrily tasting the sweet,
water-slick flesh down to her shoulder.

He felt her shiver and moved lower still, flicking his
tongue over a silky breast until he reached the swollen
nipple. His lips closed around it, and he heard her gasp of
pleasure.

His own body flamed in response. He drew greedily,
worshiping the softness he had not sampled for so long. So
damned long.

He nibbled a path to her rib cage, her stomach, stopping
for a moment to delve into its tiny recess before continuing
on.

His hands moved down her arms to caress her full breasts
while he hungrily kissed his way lower. When she moaned
and shivered, he grew braver. He slid his tongue over the
sensitive area of her inner thighs, then up to gently ease into
her nest of curls.

She cried out and pushed wildly against him, her fingers
gripping his hair.

Hawk's own body had reached explosive proportions. He
grasped her hips and plunged his tongue deep into her
warmth. She shuddered and tightened her hold. Water
trickled between her legs, and Hawk drank thirstily, swirling
his tongue in slow circles over the tiny bud that stiffened
beneath his attention.

He felt her quiver against him, then arch savagely. He
covered her fully with his mouth and quickened the pace.
She tensed. He thrust his tongue against her. Faster. Faster.
She screamed into the night as her body erupted into violent
shudders.

Hawk's own need had reached its peak. He rose and
pressed her back, then penetrated her with one swift stroke.
Her woman's barrier gave beneath his straining flesh. He
inhaled in sharp surprise, but he could not stop. His body
would not let him.

He drove himself into her again and again, his fingers in
her hair, holding her pinned to the ground, his mouth
hungrily taking hers.

170

Rain pounded his back. Hair clung to his cheeks, but he was aware only of the heat, the intense pressure. Building . . . building.

An explosion hit his entrails. He stiffened as burst after burst of pleasure shattered around him, through him. His body twisted primitively, plunging deeper and deeper, spewing forth seven years of restraint, anguish, and gut-wrenching need.

Victoria felt as if she were floating through tunnels, first of heat, then of ice. And the pain. Why wouldn't it go away? It gnawed at her. It wouldn't let her rest. Wouldn't let her sleep.

She felt something press against her forehead, and she shivered. Cold. So cold.

"Drink this," a voice commanded. She tried to open her eyes, but the lids were too heavy. Then she felt something touch her lips, and a foul liquid slid into her mouth. She tried not to swallow it. But she felt a hand on her neck, massaging, making it slither down her throat. "Slowly, *neewa*. Yes. Good."

Neewa? Who was that? The voice seemed to drift into the distance, then fade altogether as a swirling mass of black warmth enveloped her.

Hawk watched her breathing deepen again, and sat back on his heels. It had been three days since he pulled her from that flooding pit and felt her passion. He closed his eyes, still shaken as he remembered her fear and the way she had clung to him, loved him until she lost consciousness. Then later, when the fever took her, how he had used every herb, every ritual, and every prayer he had ever learned trying to bring her back.

And not once had she been coherent. Her fever still raged. He had long ago ceased to wonder why he cared if she lived or died. He could not explain that. It only mattered that she *did* live. He would let no one take her from him—not even the Great Spirit.

She shivered pitifully, and he glanced down at her small

form beneath the blanket he had finally managed to dry out. It was not enough protection. She needed more warmth.

Knowing he would regret it, he lifted the cover and lay beside her, his own body warmed by the midday sun. He gathered her close, then pulled the blanket around them both. For a long moment he remained rigid, fighting feelings of helplessness. She was so fragile, so young—much too young to walk with the spirits.

Instinctively, protectively, he tightened his hold on her. But as the moments passed, he became intensely aware of the feel of her sweet curves against his hardness, of the scent of her fevered flesh and silky hair. Thoughts of their mating the night of the storm rose to taunt him.

He tried to turn his face away, to rid himself of building desire, but it did not help. He could recall in vivid detail the way she had given herself to him so completely, with such unrestrained passion. And she had been a virgin.

His blood raced. Cursing his overactive ardor, Hawk shut his eyes in an attempt to block out the sensations playing havoc on his manhood. But closing his eyes only made it worse. Every breath she took echoed like a promising whisper in the small cave. Each time she moved, he could feel the erotic brush of her naked skin against his. And when she made that odd little whimpering sound, he could feel the low vibration clear to his heart.

Unable to bear any more of the exquisite torture, Hawk abruptly sat up and laced his fingers through his hair. He needed to get her out of this cave, to a place where he could distance himself from her. He lifted his gaze to the horizon and thought for a moment. His cabin was too far. Then another solution struck him, and he smiled. He knew just the place.

Jedediah Blackburn heard the faint sound of an approaching intruder. Moving slowly against the pain in his gout-inflamed joints, he lifted his musket from its mount over the fireplace and stepped out onto the rough plank porch fronting his secluded home.

Though he'd lived in these woods most of his sixty years,

he'd never stopped being as wary of intruders as he was of the wild animals who shared the forest.

Slipping into the shadow of a stack of firewood at one end of the porch, he waited for the trespasser to make an appearance.

When he saw the Indian walking toward him carrying a woman in his arms, at first Jed didn't recognize him. Then his eyes grew wide and he lowered the gun. "Hawk?"

The Indian's head whipped up, and clear gray eyes met Jed's hazel ones. "Well, old man, I see you still breathe. Do you intend to cheat the spirits forever?"

Jed chuckled roundly. "As long as I can, boy. As long as I can." He set his musket aside and approached the breed. "Whatcha got there?"

Hawk stared down at the woman. "Trouble."

Jed laughed. "Son, I ain't knowed a woman yet that weren't that." He studied her pretty face. "Who is she?"

Hawk shrugged and stepped up on the porch. "My wife."

Jedediah Blackburn, for the first time in his life, was shocked into silence. But only for a moment. "Hawk, she's *white.*"

"My eyes have not yet failed me, old man. Where can I put her? The woman is ill."

"What happened?" Jed opened the door so Hawk could carry the girl inside.

The half-breed laid her on a narrow cot near the west wall and covered her. "She nearly drowned in one of the pits near high valley during the storm. She shivers with fever."

Jed barely heard the man's words as he stared aghast at Hawk's scarred back. What the hell had happened? He opened his mouth to voice the question, but snapped it shut again. The boy wouldn't take kindly to Jed's meddling. He looked at the girl. "It's a wonder it didn't kill the child."

The Indian turned to face him, his expression unreadable, as usual. "She is no child."

Jed lowered his gaze to the full curve of her breasts molded by the gray blanket. "No. I guess she ain't at that." He hobbled to the cupboard and took down two tin cups, trying to figure a way to turn the conversation to Hawk's scars. "So where ya been all these years?" He faced the Indian.

Hawk's jaw tightened.

Jed realized instantly that he'd touched private ground where the breed was concerned. "Um, ya missed a hell of a battle here in the colonies."

"I have heard of it." He nodded, obviously relieved at the change in the subject. "It is good this land has gained her freedom from its unjust chiefs. A man should have the choice to make his own decisions."

"Have ya seen Jason or Nick yet?"

Hawk shook his head. "But I will soon. After my *neewa* recovers."

"Have ya heard 'bout Jason's boys? He had a set of mirror twins, jest like him and Nick. 'Bout six years ago. That purdy little wife of his was beside herself, she was so happy."

Hawk's features closed up, and Jed could have bitten off his tongue. Damnation. How could he have forgotten the way Hawk felt about Jason's wife?

Jed poured whiskey into the cups and handed one to the breed. "What's yer wife's name?"

"Victoria. But she does not yet know I am her husband."

Jed's hand holding his own cup stopped halfway to his mouth. "What?"

"She does not recognize me as the man she married many years ago." He shrugged. "I saw no reason to tell her. She thinks I am called only Shadow."

Jed stared at him. "For hell's sake, why didn't ya jest spit it out?"

"You ask many questions, old man."

Jed snorted and took a swig of his drink. "I don't believe ya. No woman forgets a man who beds her."

Hawk looked at the woman, and something cold flickered in his eyes. "I did not take that pleasure when we wed."

Jed sputtered as he choked on his whiskey. "What? You, the brave who always managed ta escape ta my place ta avoid the wrath of an irate husband, didn't bed your own wife?" He shook his head. "Not likely."

Hawk rose and, in a vulnerable gesture, rubbed the back of his neck. "At the time it only mattered that I marry her to save the reputation of the Kincaids' sister." He turned on Jed. "If not for that . . ."

"God A'mighty, Hawk, *she* ain't the twins' sister."

The Indian straightened his spine. Silence crowded the room.

"Hawk? What is it, boy?"

The look on the Shawnee's face when he turned nearly curled the toes of Jed's boots.

"Not their sister?" Hawk's voice sounded as if he'd been eating icicles.

For some reason Jed felt as if he'd made a big mistake.

"Not unless they got more'n one. Jason found her right afore the war. He sent ya a packet ta yer mama's, tellin' ya about Nichole Heatherton. Didn't ya get it?"

Hawk's teeth clamped into a straight line, and his words hissed out. "Yes, I did." He lifted his chin and breathed deeply as if trying to control himself. "But I neglected to read it."

Something in Hawk's voice and in his blazing storm-cloud eyes made Jed wary. He gulped down a drink from his cup. "Jason come by the day he sent ya the message. Said he an' Nick tracked the girl ta Sussex, over there in England. Everyone got a real surprise when they found out Nichole was a friend of Jason's wife. Met the little scamp myself a few months later." Jed grinned. "Looks like a silvery-haired angel, she does. But she's given her brothers more trouble'n a passel a hungry badgers."

Hawk's expression hadn't changed. If anything, he looked ready to slit someone's throat. Jed took another jolt, glad that Hawk's anger wasn't aimed at him. But that sweet thing on the cot looked to be in a whole lot of trouble. Hawk trouble. "Ya gonna eat that little gal for supper, breed?"

Hawk turned that tight expression on Jed. "Not yet," he said softly.

Jed studied the younger man for a long time. He'd known Hawk too long not to recognize that something was different about him. He looked knotted up enough to explode, and it sure was odd the way his eyes kept drifting back to his wife every few seconds. "Are ya in love with her, boy?"

The cords in Hawk's neck bulged. "No white woman can touch my heart."

"Samantha did."

Hawk's expression instantly hardened. "My brother's wife is not like this one."

"Ya didn't think so when ya first met Samantha. Ya thought she'd stabbed yer best friend."

"I did not know the true situation then."

Jed met his gaze steadily. "I don't know what yer problem is with that purdy little wife of yers, but ya might want ta learn from yer experiences. Ya didn't know the situation eight years ago, son, an ya might be makin' the same blunder again."

"There is no misunderstanding this time. I did err by not checking further into the identity of the Kincaids' sister," Hawk admitted. "But how can I mistake the last seven years I have spent in hell because of this woman?"

Jed tried to keep his eyes from bulging. The scars! She had something to do with his scars. He glanced at the sleeping girl. What had she done? And what did Hawk mean about seven years in hell? Jed sure wished the breed wasn't so closemouthed. Besides, the lady didn't look big enough to cause mischief. "Well, I still hope ya know what yer doin'. Remember, boy, thin's ain't always like they seem."

Hawk crossed his arms over his chest, his eyes turning icy. It was a gesture Jed was well familiar with. Hawk had just shut him out. There would be no more discussion on the matter.

Jed shook his gray head. He just hoped the boy knew what he was doing. Messing with a woman could be dangerous. And he'd hate to see the young brave hurt any more than he'd already been by his mother.

Chapter 15

Victoria felt as if she were climbing up through layers of cotton. She raised a shaky hand to her forehead and moaned, trying to remember what had happened to her.

She opened her eyes to stare blankly at a log- and mud-lined ceiling. Blinking, she turned her head to one side. She was in a small wood structure of some sort; it looked like someone's home. A rickety table was littered with metal dishes and cups. Near her feet a fire burned low inside a stone grate, with a black pot hanging above it. Steam rose from the kettle, filling the air with a tempting aroma.

Licking the dryness from her lips, she turned her attention toward the two chairs before the fireplace. They had obviously been put together by someone without much expertise in the art of furniture making. The legs were uneven, the backs crooked and covered with a rough tan material.

A thump outside drew her attention to the door just as it opened.

Shadow, tall and regal-looking, entered carrying an armload of wood. He met her eyes and hesitated briefly, then set the logs on the hearth.

Shadow! Panic grabbed her by the throat. He'd found her. Caught her. Oh, God, what would he do to her now? She tried to sit up, but a pain ripped through her shoulder and she eased back down. "How did you find me? What happened? Where are we?"

"You do not remember?"

She edged back on the cot, wary, her thoughts spinning as she tried to recall. Suddenly her eyes widened. "The bear! The *pit*. It was filling with water—I was drowning." Her breath caught. *"You* saved me, didn't you?"

"I heard your screams."

Her heart thudded heavily. He'd saved her. He wouldn't have done that if he truly intended to harm her, would he? She began to relax, then remembered their last encounter. Guilt flamed in her cheeks. "I wouldn't have blamed you if you'd left me to die after I hit you with that rock—even if you did deserve it."

For the first time he smiled, a slow, beautiful smile that revealed an ivory row of straight teeth. "I considered it."

Victoria eyed him nervously. Was he jesting? Why was he grinning like that? "Fortunate for me you didn't." She glanced around. "Where are we?"

"In a cabin."

"I can see that. Are we trespassing?"

"It belongs to a friend. He allows us to use it."

"How thoughtful." She studied the small room. "Where do you and your friend sleep?"

Shadow shrugged. "Jed is on the other side of the ridge. He sleeps with his traps."

When he didn't answer the rest of her question, she swallowed. Perhaps she didn't want to know where Shadow slept. "Are we alone here?" Heavens. How silly and prim that sounded, considering all the time they'd spent together.

Obviously he, too, thought the inane remark didn't deserve comment. He walked to the table and picked up a half-full bottle. "Are you in need of a drink?"

Attempting to ignore the heat stinging her neck, she concentrated on the bottle. "What is it?"

"Whiskey."

At her skeptical look, he lifted a tin cup from the table and filled it. Then, handing it to her, he said lazily, "It will not harm you."

She stared at the whiskey. Slowly, cautiously, she took a swallow. Fire burned a path down her throat. She buckled forward, eyes burning as she tried not to strangle when she coughed and gasped. "Aghhh. That's horrible."

"Sip it a little at a time, *neewa*. It will relax you."

She hesitated, not sure at all that that was what she really wanted to do. Then, deciding not to chance angering him, she took a deep breath and did as he instructed. Strangely enough, the whiskey wasn't quite so bad the second time around, although it did take a moment before she could speak. "How long have we been here?"

"Here, only two days. Three days before that we stayed in a cave."

"Five days! I don't remember any of them. Why was I in a cave?"

His eyes met hers and held them. They seemed to be searching for something. "Do you recall the night of the storm? Being in the pit? Your illness?"

She rubbed a spot between her brows with a finger. "I remember the pit and you helping me." She lowered her hands and clenched them in the folds of the blanket. "After that, everything is blank."

He set his cup down and moved to stand before her in a very imposing manner. "It is difficult to believe that you do not recall our lovemaking. It is not something I will soon forget."

"What?" If he'd slapped her she couldn't have been more shocked. Lovemaking. He couldn't be serious. "That's not the least bit humorous."

His voice dropped to a husky ripple. "It was not meant to be."

There was no way she would believe him. She'd know if something like that had happened. Especially with *him.* Certain in her own mind that he had to be lying, for whatever reason, she changed the subject. "Where are you taking me?"

"You will see." Shadow turned abruptly, as if he, too, wanted their uncomfortable conversation to end. He motioned toward the simmering kettle. "I have made stew."

Food? Heavens. She felt as if she could eat an entire carriage team. Yet she couldn't keep from recalling his shocking declaration. What if she *had* made love to him? Stop it, she admonished herself. He's just trying to unnerve you. She looked at the pot of bubbling liquid. "What kind?"

"Pthuthoi."

"What?"

"Buffalo."

"I've never tasted it." She sniffed appreciatively. "But it smells wonderful. And at the moment my stomach wouldn't care if it tasted like burned rocks."

Shadow moved to the sideboard for a plate and spoon. After dishing up some of the aromatic fare, he pulled a chair up beside her cot and sat down. Holding the bowl in one hand, he raised the full spoon in the other.

An uncomfortable chill raced up her spine at the thought of this man feeding her. There was something so *intimate* about that. And why this change in him? "I-I think perhaps I should feed myself."

He cocked his head to one side, and a lock of hair fell over his brow, giving him a young, rakish look. "Why? Do you fear my ability?"

"No. Oh, heaven's no. It's just . . ."

"Just?"

What could she say? She certainly couldn't tell him how approachable it made him seem. How sensitive. "Nothing." Then to halt any further questions on his part, she opened her mouth.

She could have sworn she heard him chuckle to himself as he slid the spoon between her lips. But she instantly forgot everything when she tasted the delicious stew. "That's marvelous! Did you make it yourself?"

"I had a little help from the animal."

"You're a remarkable cook. I could easily spend the rest of my life enjoying food such as this. Why, if I wasn't married to Hawk, I'd ignore all etiquette and attempt to lure you into my clutches."

His expression hardened.

"Shadow? I didn't mean to offend you. It was a jest."

"I am not amused." A muscle throbbed in his jaw. "Marriage is sacred—at least to the Shawnee."

Victoria felt as if she'd been struck. "It is to the white man, too. Very much so."

Something ugly flickered in the depths of his eyes for a moment before they faded into unreadable slits of cool gray. "How long have you been married?"

"Seven years."

"And in that time have you remained true to your vows? Have you stood by your husband in sickness and health?"

Embarrassment pinched her cheeks. "You know Hawk, so you must know that he left me on our wedding night. I didn't have the opportunity to exercise any of my vows. But I would have. If he hadn't deserted me."

"He did not desert you."

"Is that what he told you? Well, it's not true. He left me in some horrible room and just disappeared—after he nearly raped me! And when we questioned the servants, they admitted to having taken his luggage aboard a ship leaving for the colonies. If that's not desertion, I don't know what else you would call it."

Something like confusion darkened Shadow's eyes before he shoved the bowl into her hands and rose suddenly. "I will bring fresh water."

Hawk closed the door behind him and took a deep breath, his thoughts reeling. He was still shocked to have learned that Victoria was not Jason's sister, that this farce of a marriage had been for nothing. But it was his own fault. He should have delved further, read Jason's missive, checked the last name on the list. Heatherton.

Too, it certainly did not please him to know that he had been right in the beginning about Victoria's innocence. As long as he'd had doubts, he could justify the cruelty he had inflicted. Bitterly he realized how he had wronged her. The one-eyed seaman, O'Ryan, had obviously lied to him about Victoria's part in the abduction. He did not understand the man's reasoning, unless he had just wanted Hawk to endure the pain of betrayal as well as the lash. But because of it, Victoria had suffered. *And O'Ryan would die.*

Guilt overwhelmed him when he recalled the vicious

things he had done to his wife. Deeds that could never be forgiven. Stunned by a feeling of loss, he stepped away from the porch. He needed to think, to decide what to do. But one thing was certain: he would not take Victoria to his cabin.

From the cot, Victoria watched Shadow return to the cabin just before midday. He carried a full bucket of water and another animal Victoria couldn't identify. Lord, but this country housed a lot of strange creatures—she lifted her gaze to her captor—including the two-legged kind. "What is that?" She pointed to the furry thing he carried.

"An opossum."

Well, that certainly told her a lot. "It's ugly."

"It is known not for its beauty but for its taste."

"Taste? You mean you *eat* that? Good heavens. It looks like a big rat. I think I'd rather eat a corset stay."

He set the bucket on the table, then tossed the animal down beside it. Victoria couldn't help but notice the way his muscles rippled when he moved. "How do you feel?" he asked.

She had trouble concentrating on his words. Her mind was on the powerful golden beauty of his bare chest. "Um, fine, thank you." Heavens. Had he always looked so good? She'd never noticed those breeches fitting that tight before, or how they molded his form so magnificently.

He met her gaze, and she felt her face drain of color. He had seen where she was staring. "Wh-when will your friend return?"

A strange light flared in his silver eyes—a new warmth she hadn't seen before. "Not for many days."

She looked away and nervously inspected the confines of the cabin, not certain at all that it was a good idea to stay here. Alone. She fixed her attention on their meal. "Is th-there anything I can do to help?"

Shadow walked across the room until he stood before her bed. His eyes caught and held hers. "Be careful what you offer, little one."

Victoria nearly choked. "I m-meant with *dinner.*"

His mouth curved into a slow smile. "Not this time."

Turning back to the table, he picked up the opossum, then slid a knife from the top of his boot. He brought the blade up to the animal's throat but stopped suddenly and looked back at her over his shoulder. He frowned and lowered the hand holding the weapon. "I will take this outside."

Victoria breathed a sigh of relief when he disappeared through the door, and she felt pleased by his consideration.

As she lay listening to the sounds of Shadow moving around outside, she suddenly realized that she no longer feared him. As a matter of fact, when he did things like that for her, when he smiled at her so engagingly, she melted a little.

How she wished Adam—Hawk—had been like that. Visions of her husband, though somewhat distorted, rose before her. She could again picture the haunting color of his eyes. Gray—like Shadow's. He had been about the same size, too, but slimmer—and younger. Younger? She smiled at that. He was seven years older now, just like her.

Hazy images of their wedding came into focus. Under the circumstances of their forced marriage, Hawk truly had been considerate. And, a niggling little voice reminded her, he had not taken advantage of her, even though he had frightened her that night.

She shook her head. Over the years, Alaina's stories about her son had reached inside Victoria and touched a romantic chord in her, and she wondered if that might not be the real reason she wanted to find him.

Remembering all the times she'd caught herself thinking of Hawk, she knew it was a genuine possibility. One she might not have even been aware of herself until now. She smiled. Heavens. More times than she could recall, she'd tried to imagine what it would truly be like to share his home, to raise his children.

"Why do you smile?"

"Shadow!" Victoria gasped. "You nearly frightened the life out of me. Don't sneak up on me like that."

He stood close to her, his head bent. "You did not answer my question."

"I was smiling at a memory."

"From your childhood?"

"No. If you must know, I was thinking of my husband."

Shadow straightened abruptly. "You smile when you think of a man who *deserted* you—as you say? Why?"

"I don't know. I have seen him only three times in my life, yet during all the years I spent with his mother, listening to her talk of him, of his childhood escapades, I guess I found myself falling a little in love with him." She settled the blanket closer to her chin. "And even though he did try to . . . take advantage of me, he truly was kind. He bought me a trousseau, which doubled as my sixteenth birthday present, and the most magnificent bay. I named him Brandy."

A rush of sadness hit her. "I just wish he hadn't treated his mother so badly. I can understand his not wanting to correspond with me, feeling coerced into marriage as he was, but Alaina loves him, and he hasn't contacted her in years. Not that she complains; she doesn't. But I ache for her every time the post is delivered. Her eyes are always filled with such expectation . . . then pain."

A muscled tic jumped near his temple. "Perhaps there is much you do not know." He pulled up one of the spindly chairs and sat down. "Tell me of your life before your marriage."

She gritted her teeth at the way he made every question sound like a demand. Watching him warily, she haltingly told him about her life at Denwick, about her tomboyish ways when she was younger, and about her close companionship with Paddy. She told him of her love of horses and how her father had sold all but one for the carriage after her mother died, almost as if to punish Victoria.

Telling him about her mother's death was hard. But not as difficult as explaining how her father had turned against her afterward, since she didn't know the reason herself. He had seemed to despise her from then on. She told him about her visits to Paddy in his hovel near the docks and about that last visit, which had led to her being scandalously compromised by Hawk.

He studied her closely, almost as if weighing her words.

Then, ever so slowly, he leaned back in the chair and crossed his arms. "Tell me about Collier Parks."

"How do you know—"

"I know many things, *neewa*. Now answer the question."

How could he possibly know about her cousin? Had Hawk told him about Collier? "He's the son of my father's sister."

"Do you love him?"

Victoria shook her head. "Not as a woman loves a man. He's my cousin, and I do love him in that respect."

Something in Shadow's eyes resembled relief. "What of Dooley O'Ryan?"

"Who?"

"The red-haired seaman with one eye."

"I don't believe I've met him." She bristled inwardly. Shadow was acting just like her father with all these questions. Richard Townsend had enjoyed interrogating her over trivial incidents. Feeling an urgent need to end the queries, she posed a question of her own. "What do you do for entertainment around here?"

"That depends. If Jed is here, we play cards or argue. If I am alone, I read."

"And if you are with a woman?"

His gaze slowly moved down her body. "We make love."

Victoria swallowed at the erotic vision that conjured up. "Um, what if you aren't attracted to the woman?" *And surely he wasn't.* "Then how do you pass the time?"

Hawk's gaze slid to her mouth. "That situation does not arise."

She was certain her heart stopped. "Please, Shadow. Don't."

He lowered himself until he was at eye level with her. "Do not what, little one? Do not touch you like this?" He traced a finger down her cheek and neck, then along the curved shape of the blanket at her breasts, sending a quiver through her whole body. His eyes bored into hers, telling her without words that he would make love to her. "Do not kiss you like this?" He leaned forward and slid his tongue across her lips.

She inhaled sharply. Heat poured through her veins, and

her mouth softened. It was all the invitation he needed. He pressed closer, his tongue warm and wet as it penetrated her lips.

Victoria's head spun. No one except her husband had ever kissed her like that. Not even Collier had been so bold. She wanted to tell him to stop, but she didn't have the breath. She wanted to push him away, but her arms lacked strength. She wanted to pull back, but his lips held her as surely as if they were manacles. She sighed softly and melted into him.

Hawk groaned, drawing her tightly against the hardness of his chest. His mouth grew hot, demanding.

Something vaguely familiar flashed in her mind, but it faded when she felt him ease her down onto the cot, her lips aching from the half-tender, half-savage assault of his potent kiss.

"Oh, Shadow," she murmured low, "please . . ."

He bolted upright and swung his gaze to the door.

Shocked by the movement, Victoria sat up and yanked the front of her shirt together, fumbling as she tried to button it. How had he undone them? Before she could examine the extraordinary feat she'd seen performed by only one other, she heard the clop of an approaching horse.

Shadow stood, facing the door, his body tense, his eyes alert.

When the soft thud of boots sounded on the plank porch, Victoria, too, watched the door.

Silence reigned for a moment; then there was a loud knock.

Shadow didn't move.

Victoria didn't know what to do. Should she answer the door? Why didn't Shadow open it? Was there danger? Undecided, she kept still.

"Indian?" a man's voice called from the other side of the panel. "Open the blamed door!"

Shadow's shoulders seemed to visibly relax. Then he strode forward and wrenched it open.

A grizzled man with bristly graying red hair and beard stepped inside. Over his massive shoulder he carried a large burlap sack that looked extremely heavy.

"'Bout time," the man grumbled as he lowered his burden to the floor. "Damned hides weigh as much as ol' Molly out there." He gestured toward a swaybacked horse standing beyond the porch.

"I thought you said you would be gone for three days, old man."

The bearded man grinned. "I didn't 'spect the first set a traps ta be full, either." He slapped Shadow on the back. "Don't worry, breed. I jest come ta drop these off an' have a swig. Then I'll leave ya"—he glanced at Victoria—"ta yer privacy."

Victoria felt heat rush to her face. Then, realizing she wore only Shadow's shirt—which was half unbuttoned—she scrambled under the covers. Good heavens! How could she have forgotten her state of undress? That wretched Indian completely unnerved her!

Obviously ignoring her chagrin, the old man walked to the table and picked up the bottle and cup. "Join me?" he asked Shadow.

"Jed, you could have left the pelts anywhere. Why have you come?" Shadow asked, ignoring the man's invitation.

The old man set the cup and bottle down, then flicked a concerned glance at Victoria before answering. "Outside."

Completely baffled, Victoria watched the two men leave the cabin. What in the name of Providence was going on?

Several minutes later the door opened again, and Shadow entered alone. "Get up. We are leaving."

"What's happened?"

Shadow gave her a disgusted look, then crossed the room in three long strides and pulled her to her feet. He stood for a moment, staring down at her attire. Then he shot a searching glance around the room. His gaze stopped at a buckskin shirt hanging on a peg near the fireplace. He quickly snatched it up and tossed it to her. "Put this on." Turning, he began gathering things from the table and cupboards and shoving them inside an empty burlap sack he'd taken from a stack near the cot.

"I wish you'd tell me what's happening," Victoria mumbled. "Where are we going?"

Shadow placed another item in the bag, then tied it closed. He hesitated for just an instant, then said softly, "To your husband's village."

Victoria's pulse increased. Relief conflicted with a feeling of loss. He was going to set her free, return her to her husband. She stared at Shadow's scarred back as he bent to pick up a wrapped packet. She felt the unholy urge to kiss his streaked flesh, to take away the pain he must have suffered.

As she watched the play of muscles, she attempted to recall the night he said they'd made love, and she wondered if it could possibly be true. She tried to detect a soreness in her private region, but felt nothing. *It has been five days,* a little voice reminded her.

He glanced up and caught her staring. He didn't move for a moment, but just stood there watching her closely, as if trying to read her thoughts.

She blushed and looked away. Then, to take her mind off her traitorous thoughts, she hastily donned the shirt he'd given her. It hung on her small frame like a sack, the sleeves much too long for her arms, the V opening at the neck nearly reaching her navel. But at least, with the fringe, it was longer than the silk shirt—barely.

When she finished, she found Shadow standing before her, his hand outstretched, offering her a pair of calf-high moccasins like the ones he wore. "These will protect your feet."

Delighted, Victoria took them and slipped them on. They fit perfectly and felt so comfortable. "Where did you get these?"

He hefted the burlap sack over his shoulder. "I made them." He gripped her arm. "Come."

A thrill shot through her. He'd made them for her. Something warm encompassed her heart, but Shadow's hasty movements reminded her of the urgency of the moment, and she wondered what Jed had told him to warrant leaving with such speed.

Outside, Jed finished strapping two more bags he'd use to gather pelts onto the back of his mare. "Speedy as ever, I see." He nodded at Shadow, then smiled at Victoria. "Nice ta have met ya, missy."

"Thank you. And thank you, too, for the use of your cabin. I understand I was quite ill when Shadow brought me here."

"Ya sure was. Ragin' with fever and mumblin' the way ya was, I thought ya was a goner. But the breed here wouldn't let ya die, never once left your side till yer fever broke. He's real good at healin'. Even saved my own neck a time or two, he did. Ya couldn't a been in better hands."

"You talk too much, old man."

"Yep. And right now maybe it's a good thing I do," he returned sharply.

Victoria watched curiously as something seemed to pass between the two men. Then Shadow nodded, tightened his hold on Victoria's arm, and started forward.

"Ya might want ta stay ta the north, boy, since them varmints I was tellin' ya about is ta the south."

Shadow lifted a farewell hand toward the old man, then headed into the woods.

As the shady foliage engulfed them, Victoria sensed a feeling of peace. Strange, she thought. The forest didn't seem quite so frightening anymore, but she couldn't decide whether that was because of the bright, beautiful spring afternoon or because she felt so safe next to Shadow. Don't be ridiculous, she chided herself. Of course it's because of the daylight.

She scanned the distant horizon, visible through the trees, and wondered how long it would take to reach the Shawnee village—how long before she would come face to face with Hawk.

Chapter 16

For several hours they walked in silence, climbing hills, weaving their way through straggly thickets and tall underbrush. Shadow stopped frequently to allow her a brief rest before continuing.

Finally they emerged from the trees into a wide rocky ravine with a small stream running down the middle. Huge patches of white flowers dotted the half-rock, half-grass banks.

"Oh, how beautiful!" Victoria exclaimed, plucking a white daisylike blossom with a red stem. The yellow center looked like tiny upthrust fingers. "What is it called?" She raised her gaze to find Shadow studying her intently.

He seemed to shake himself. Then he turned his back to her and dropped the sack. "It is called bloodroot."

"Bloodroot! What a horrid name for such a pretty flower."

"It is named for the red stem." He crossed his ankles and sat down, then rested his elbows on his knees. "We will eat now." He untied the bag near his leg and withdrew a packet. After unwrapping it, he handed her a chunk of hard bread and a piece of dried meat.

As she nibbled, she listened to the sounds of the creek, the twittering of unseen birds in the trees, and the rustle of grass as some small animal scurried about.

She studied the wide riverbed. Everything looked fresh and green after the storm a few days ago, and the woods smelled of sweet blossoms. Then Jed's remarks came back to her. "Shadow? How did you learn about healing?"

He shrugged. "I watched the old shaman in our village perform his rituals. I would follow him when he searched for herbs."

"Why didn't you just go with him?"

"The shaman's rituals and herbs are sacred."

"Did you ever get caught?"

"Yes."

Victoria lifted a brow in surprise. Somehow she didn't think he would have. "What did he do?"

"He welcomed my curiosity, and over the years he taught me much about healing."

"Are you the shaman of your tribe now?"

He glanced away. "No."

"Is Hawk?"

"No." He gestured toward the water. "Drink and refresh yourself. We will not stop again before dark."

She knew he didn't like talking about Hawk, but this was becoming tiresome. "How long will it take us to reach the village?"

"Seven suns."

Victoria gave an inward groan. Another week in his company. "Will Hawk be there?"

He avoided her eyes. "Yes."

"I see." She watched him closely. Something about Hawk bothered him. "Is my husband the leader of the tribe now?"

The muscles across his shoulders bunched, and he mumbled something that sounded like "I pray not."

Uncertain whether she'd heard him correctly, Victoria frowned, then rose and crossed to the water a few feet away. Five days ago she would have sworn she never wanted to see another drop of water. But she was thirsty and so dirty. Heavens, what she'd give for a bath.

Shadow, too, came to his feet. He pointed to a bend in the stream. "The water pools behind that wall of flowers. It is better for washing."

Victoria blinked, surprised by his ability to seemingly read her mind. It was rather unnerving, especially after the thoughts she'd had about him this morning. Wretched thoughts that didn't belong in a married woman's mind. Anxious to retreat, she nodded and hurried off toward the sheltering curve.

As he had said, a small pool, about six feet wide, lay just beyond the bend. Victoria glanced down at the atrociously large shirt shrouding her frame, wondering if she'd have time to take it off and bathe before Shadow called to her. She glanced back the way she'd come, then pulled the buckskin off over her head. She'd make time.

Relieved of the heavy garment, she stared down at the silk shirt she still wore. At first she wasn't certain she should take it off. Then, frustrated, she tugged at the buttons. It didn't matter. Shadow had seen her without her clothing many times. Fleetingly she gave thought to her lost modesty and waning morals, but nonetheless dropped the garment to the ground and waded into the waist-deep pool.

As she bathed, she felt the cool water massage her skin. An unbelievable vision of Shadow caressing her body rose in her mind, and she again wondered if he had told the truth about making love to her. She couldn't imagine betraying her husband like that, but . . .

Curiously she touched the area between her legs. She felt nothing different, but an odd little tingle raced through her midsection. Surprised, she snatched her hand away and sank to her knees.

The water slithered between her thighs and lapped at her breasts. She looked down at the hardening nipples, trying to visualize Shadow's strong hands on them. Heat swirled between her thighs. The centers of her breasts tightened.

Shocked, she tore her thoughts from her abductor and bathed quickly.

But when she stepped onto the grassy bank and a breeze feathered her sensitized skin, Shadow's erotic declaration of their lovemaking echoed again in her mind, taunting her. She closed her eyes.

She tried to envision his mouth, gentle on hers, his long fingers moving over her skin. Her hands rose to her breasts, and she cupped them as she imagined he might have done.

A faded memory appeared of her abductor bending over her in the rain, his hot mouth sliding over her flesh, tasting, stimulating, teasing, arousing with exquisite expertise. Her belly constricted.

She heard a sharp intake of breath. Her eyes sprang open.

Shadow stood before her, a fierce light glowing in his silver eyes, his chest rising and falling heavily as he stared at her naked breasts. "Such perfection," he whispered hoarsely. He brought his hands up to cover hers, pressing them tight against her own flesh. "Such sweet perfection."

Dizziness blurred her vision, and she couldn't move. Couldn't think.

Slowly he eased back on her hands, rotating them, rolling the stiff peaks against her own palm, his eyes scorching her skin. "This is what I feel when I touch you," he rasped. "What sets flame to my blood."

Victoria thought she'd swoon. Those half-whispered words melted her insides. The movement of his hands on hers destroyed her logic.

Holding her captive with his eyes, he guided her hands slowly up and down her body, along the smoothness of her throat, around the swells of her breasts, over her sides, down the flat plain of her belly, then lower until they touched her thighs. "Feel what makes me burn, Victoria." He eased one of her hands between her legs. Fire leapt beneath her palm, startling her.

She jerked her hand back. "No!"

Hawk stared at her, his body pounding for release, his fingers still nestled near her soft curls. But the panic he saw in her eyes rapidly cooled his passion. Inhaling a much needed breath, he released her and stepped back. "Take care how you tempt me, *neewa*. I am only a man."

He inspected her closely. Golden sunlight bathed her dark hair, illuminating the reddish strands scattered in a maze of thick shiny curls. The delicate features of her face seemed almost angelic. The fine arch of her neck, the smooth slope of her shoulders, and the rich, wet fullness of her breasts looked as if they'd been molded in fine porcelain.

Unbelievably he felt his manhood stir again. Giving

himself a mental shake, he turned his back to her. Stiffly, his breeches clinging in several uncomfortable spots, he walked back around the bend.

A few minutes later Victoria joined him, her expression grim. "Shadow. About what happened . . ." Her cheeks flamed, and she looked down.

Hawk placed a finger under her chin, brought her gaze back to his. "Do not feel shame, little one. Giving or receiving pleasure should not be spoiled by embarrassment." He stroked the curve of her lips, repressing the urge to sample them. But he wanted to. This woman completely distorted his senses. He released her and lifted their bag of supplies. "It is time to go."

Victoria followed Shadow on unsteady legs. Every muscle in her body felt drained of strength, and she still couldn't believe that she'd allowed him to do those things at the pool. Her face grew hot at the mere memory. She was a wanton. A betrayer of vows—and quite obviously possessed. She glared at Shadow's back as they walked, wondering if he might have given her some wicked potion or herb. He knew about such things—and that would certainly explain her despicable behavior.

Suspiciously she eyed the burlap bag he carried. He could very easily have something in there, could have put it in the meat she ate. Or the bread. Yes, she decided. That must be it.

She narrowed her eyes. Well, she would fix him. She wouldn't eat another thing that *he* offered her. She would find her own food. Lifting her chin, she stared straight ahead as she walked behind her nemesis.

They followed the creek for most of the day, then walked back up into the trees. The mountainside was steep and the going rough for a while, and she was still extremely weak from her illness, but once they reached the top, Victoria couldn't believe the reality of the sight before her.

Miles of rolling, timber-covered hills fanned out in all directions. Some were dotted with pink, white, lavender, and yellow flowers; others alternated between granite formations, grass, and foliage. The blue, blue sky melded into a glow of pink and gold near the horizon. She stood next to a red cedar, its outstretched branches a silhouette of haunting black against the serene heavens. So beautiful.

She glanced down at the array of flowers and rich spring grass waving gently at the tree's thick base, wishing she could lie down and enjoy the view for a while.

Shadow startled her by tossing the burlap beneath the cedar. "We will rest here." Kneeling, he withdrew a canteen, two gray blankets, and another packet of food.

Pleased, and very tired, she dropped to her knees, then wearily sat down. Her stomach growled, and she glanced at the package he had just opened. Her mouth watered, but thoughts of what had happened the last time she'd accepted his offer of food intruded. "I'd prefer to find something else to eat," she said sweetly. "My stomach would cease to function if I forced down any more of that hard bread and leathery meat."

Shadow stared up at her curiously with those exquisite eyes, then shrugged and tore off a piece of meat with his strong teeth. He chewed thoughtfully before turning away to reach for the bread.

Realizing he'd dismissed her, she rose to her feet in a huff, determined to find something nearby that would fill the emptiness in her belly. She spied a blanket of green cabbage-like sprouts sloping down the other side of the hill.

"They are called cyme, and they are not edible," Shadow said without looking at her.

Victoria gnashed her teeth. Did the man have eyes in the back of his head? She swung her gaze to one side. It landed on a lone walnut tree. Her hopes soared.

"Too green," her captor offered smoothly.

Frustration swelled to bursting proportions. Curse him! Drawing on all her composure, she nodded. "It's just as well. I'm not very hungry anyway."

She could have sworn she saw amusement spark in his eyes before he lowered them and continued with his meal.

Knowing she would give in and eat, thus give in to his lust if she continued to watch him, she moved to the other side of the cedar and sat down with her back to it—and him.

195

"Why do you want to see Hawk?" he asked.

Victoria was so shocked she nearly choked on an indrawn breath. Until now he'd avoided the subject of her absent husband. She placed a hand to her throat and turned to look at him. "To ask for a divorce."

A shadow passed over his features. "Why? Do you not possess everything you wish?"

"It's not a matter of possessions. It's a matter of living." She'd never felt her loss more than she did at that moment. "I want a real home. I want children, and I need a husband I can depend on, not see only when I'm desperate enough to cross the ocean."

He took a moment before replying. "He does not want these things?"

She stood up. "Obviously not. He doesn't even bother about his responsibilities."

"What responsibilities?"

"Well, for instance, he doesn't do anything about the poverty in the villages under Silvercove's protection. His people go hungry, a young boy named Nigel is in desperate need of a physician because of an accident, clothing is as scarce as food. But Hawk does nothing." Her voice shook. "And there's still the fact that he deserted me."

Shadow threw down his food and rose. He faced her angrily. "Hawk did not know of these things in the village. And he did not *desert* you—" He clamped his lips together.

Victoria sprang to her feet and placed her hands on her hips. "Just how would you know? You weren't there. I was. I saw the poverty, the devastation. And *I* was the one who had to face the proprietor of the inn when he asked about my missing husband. *I* was the one who had to face the sneers and chuckles of the *ton* when I walked into a room. *I* was the one who had to endure the servants' pitying looks. Heavens! The *ton* even made up a song about Adam leaving me because I was frigid!"

All the hurt, pain, and embarrassment came back in full force. "Oh, God, I hate him for what he did to me!" Tears rolled down her cheeks, and she slammed a fist against the trunk of the cedar. Then, pressing her forehead against her balled hand, she cried for all the lonely years, the ugliness, the bitterness. "My mother left me, Paddy left me, my father hated me, then my husband—" She choked on a sob. "No one wants me. No one!"

Shadow turned her around and pulled her into his arms. "I want you, *neewa.*"

She sniffed. "It's not the same. You want to use me. I'm merely an object to satisfy your l-lust."

"What we shared went far beyond lust."

"No."

"Yes," he insisted. He placed a hand on either side of her face and raised it. His gaze slid into hers. "We made love."

"You mean we really did—"

"Yes," he said so quietly, so sincerely, that she had no choice but to believe him.

Her stomach fluttered, and for one wild second she wanted to remember. But quickly she placed her palms against his chest in a gesture meant to push him away. His muscles tightened beneath her hands, and her mouth went dry. She licked her bottom lip, then trembled at the way his hot gaze followed the movement.

She watched the slight flaring of his nostrils, smelled the warm, musky scent of his skin, felt the heavy thud of his heart beneath her hand. "Shadow, please, don't—"

"We joined our bodies during the fury of a storm," he stated softly, his eyes darkening as if he were recalling pleasurable memories. He leaned closer, his breath a warm caress against her lips. "The violence of nature could not compare with the intensity of our lovemaking. Passion so fierce it stole your consciousness." He lowered his mouth to hers. "And destroyed mine."

His erotic words were as explosive as his kiss. Her powers of resistance crumbled, and she closed her eyes, reveling in the sweet sensations stirred by his intimate possession. Heaven and earth blended into a magical abyss of gentle explosions in her secret place. A place she now knew only he had touched.

She felt him draw her closer, then mold her to his length. So much warmth. So much heat. Her knees wobbled, and she clung to him for support.

He stroked her spine, then pressed her hips closer.

The feel of his growing need propelled her over the edge of control. Her body arched into him.

As if to torment her, he let her go and stepped back. But only for an instant. He gathered the hem of the buckskin shirt and drew it up over her head.

Victoria couldn't stop shivering. Her heart jumped at the smoldering look in his eyes and the way his hands shook when he reached for the buttons of the silk shirt.

Instinctively she clung to the material. "Please." Her voice sounded like someone else's. "I'm not strong enough to stop you."

He pulled her hands down. "I will not take you against your will. But do not keep your splendor from me." His eyes grew hot. "I only want to look at you. Watch your body respond to my touch." He brushed his fingers lightly over the tips of her breasts. They tightened into hard pebbles beneath the silk shirt, and she felt the tremor in his hands as he watched her body betray itself.

His palms stroked her fullness, kneaded the sensitive flesh, then slid down to caress her rib cage and waist, then skimmed over the curve of her hips. Dear God, she couldn't take this. She wanted him so much she hurt.

His long fingers stroked her thighs, then glided slowly under her scant covering and back up her sides and ribs until they brushed over her bare nipples.

She swallowed, trying to ignore the burst of heat that seared her.

He circled the peaks of her breasts with his thumbs, then gently drew her down with him to the grass until they were facing each other on their knees. His mouth sought hers. Hot and hungry, he invaded her strength again and again, his tongue penetrating her defenses, conquering her innermost opposition, her soul.

When he finally pulled away, she fought for air, but her breath stopped when she felt his mouth slip lower, down the now gaping front of her shirt, over her naked skin. The vows she'd spoken to another nearly seven years ago rose to mock her. Her senses cleared, and she gripped his arms. "No. You said—"

He froze. For a long moment he didn't move. Didn't breathe. Then he released a long breath and dropped his forehead against her chest. "I know what I said," he admitted roughly. Slowly he climbed to his feet, his eyes dark as they met hers. "But next time I will make no promises."

If there was a next time, she wouldn't want him to. Her head fell back, and she breathed deeply, resisting the urge to call him back, to cast aside her vows as her husband obviously had. But she couldn't. *You already have,* a small voice reminded. Yet she still couldn't do it. This time she had her senses about her. Numbly, keeping her gaze downward, she rose from the grass and pulled on her clothes.

A moccasined foot stepped into view, and she glanced up. Shadow stood before her holding out a piece of dried meat. "You will eat now."

Unable to meet his gaze, and now certain that food had nothing to do with her wickedness, she nodded and took the offering, though she doubted her tight throat would allow her to swallow it. "Thank you." She placed the meal in her lap and stared down at it, then, still unable to meet his eyes, began eating.

Shadow knelt before her. "What troubles you, *neewa?*"

Another wretched burst of color fired her cheeks. "Nothing." She chewed doggedly, letting her gaze wander aimlessly.

He lifted her chin and stared into her eyes. "Then why do you blush?"

"You *know* why."

A rich, low chuckle rumbled from his chest. "You are ashamed of your explosive passion."

"It's not humorous. I feel like a—a harlot."

His features hardened instantly. "You are not a whore."

"Well, I certainly feel like one." She tightened her fists. "What *normal* woman would behave with you as I did?"

His mouth softened. "Victoria, there is nothing wrong with you." He stroked her cheek. "All women possess passion, but few will allow themselves to release it. They will not allow another to witness their true desire, their vulnerability." He laughed self-consciously. "Did I not lose control with you? Or do you believe I open my veins to any woman who shares my mat?"

She studied his handsome, yet strong features. No. He wouldn't lose control like that with just any woman. "What's so special about me?"

Shadow sat down beside her and leaned against the cedar, his gaze on the horizon. "I do not know. I only know that you touch my soul as no other ever has."

He turned to look at her, and she couldn't help noticing the way the firelight danced over the angles of his face.

"I will never let you go, Victoria."

Lost in the depths of those shimmering silver eyes, Victoria melted at his words.

Abruptly he sprang to his feet, then held out his hand and gestured toward the blankets spread near the fire. "Come, *neewa*. It is time to sleep."

As if in a daze, she set her remaining food aside and allowed him to pull her to her feet, then followed him to the pallet. She stood like an obedient slave as he turned back her blanket and lowered her to the bed.

He explored her face, then gently brushed a kiss over her lips and rose. "Good night, little one." On a sigh he left her and made his own bed on the opposite side of the fire.

But Victoria barely noticed the honorable gesture. Her thoughts hadn't gone beyond his vow never to let her go, or the fact that she desperately wanted it to become reality.

Chapter 17

She wanted to stay with Shadow. She had no doubt about that over the next few days as they continued through the mountains toward his village. Even though she was weary to the bone, dying for a bath, and aching from her head to the soles of her feet, she would not change a thing as long as she could be with him. Even the horrors of the forest didn't seem quite so frightening while he was there to protect her.

As she walked along behind him, she couldn't keep her eyes off the breadth of his shoulders and the tight flexing of his buttocks. But for the hundredth time she wondered where he had gotten the scars that marred that perfect back.

"*Neewa,* look." Shadow stopped and pointed.

Victoria followed his line of vision.

Not ten feet from them a tiny fawn and a beautiful doe grazed just beyond a wall of trees.

"They're superb," she whispered, but her voice must have carried.

The doe jerked her head up, then scrambled into the brush, quickly followed by her offspring.

Shadow glanced back at Victoria and smiled.

Her heart flopped over. The man looked positively delicious when he grinned at her like that. Just looking at him made her hungry—and not for food.

As if he'd read her thoughts, his eyes darkened then lowered to her lips. "If you continue to look at me like that, little one, we will not reach the surprise I have for you."

She attempted an innocent expression. "Look at you like what?"

He flicked the tip of her nose. "Witch."

"And what surprise?"

He started walking. "If I tell you, it will not be a surprise." He glanced back. "Come, woman, or we will not have enough time."

"Time for what?"

"You will see."

An hour later Victoria heard the roar of water before she stepped beyond a wall of dense undergrowth. She cried out in surprise. "Oh, Shadow. It's magnificent!"

She stood before a rock cliff covered with moss and spewing a shower of white water down across several boulders before it crashed into a crystal clear pool at the bottom. Late afternoon sunlight glinted over curling ripples as they glided toward shore.

"I've never seen anything so beautiful!" She stared in awe at a lone maple off to one side, its branches broken down to nubs, one long root protruding out of the water, its end cut short. Just beyond that, to the right of the falls, a cave receded into the base of the cliff, half concealed by a smooth, flat jutting slab of rock that resembled a table top.

Shadow lifted his arm in a gesture for her to proceed. "Your bath."

Victoria was so excited she wanted to race into the refreshing coolness, but she couldn't help teasing him a bit first. "Hmm. I don't think I'd better chance it. There might be horrible creatures lurking beneath the surface." Which was utterly ridiculous since she could see clear to the smooth, sandy bottom.

His eyes glinted mischievously. "Have no fear, *neewa*. I will bathe with you—for your protection, of course."

"How gallant of you," she returned lightly, but the image of the two of them together in that pool made her dizzy—and frightened.

As if he sensed her turmoil, he stepped closer and placed his finger under her chin. He tilted her face up. His gaze searched hers; then, ever so softly, he commanded, "Remove your clothes."

Those words went straight to her soul. "Shadow, I can't." She swallowed, trying to explain. "I know that Hawk and I haven't lived together as man and wife, but I can't betray him. Please understand that. What I feel for you is wrong. And no matter how much I want to"—she took a fortifying breath—"he's still my husband."

Something in Shadow's eyes softened. Almost like pride. Then he leaned forward and brushed his lips over hers. "There is much that you, also, do not understand, *neewa.*" He traced her lower lip with his thumb. "You belong to me."

Fighting back tears, she nodded. "In my heart, yes. But my vows to Hawk—"

He gripped her shoulders and shook her. "Enough. Hawk is not worthy of your devotion. Not after what he has done to you." Pain clouded his eyes, and his hold tightened. "I will say this once, *neewa,* and no more." He slid his hands down her arms. "What we share is not a betrayal."

Slowly, holding her gaze captive, he lifted the heavy buckskin shirt up to her chest. His eyes seemed to ask—no, to demand—her permission, and Victoria knew she couldn't resist. Everything about this man fired her emotions, her senses, her dreams. She didn't know how she would deal with her husband when the time came, but at the moment nothing mattered but Shadow.

Moments later, when they both stood naked—her trembling, him powerfully magnificent in his nudity—he picked her up, cradling her in his arms as he carried her into the crystal depths. Water lapped at her bottom, then rose, flowing over her belly and between her legs, causing her stomach to grow taut and her breasts to tingle.

His step faltered, and she looked up to see him mentally devouring the tight peaks. A rush of warmth surged through her belly, and her hand shook at the back of his neck.

He lifted his head, and a strained smile curved his lips. "If your body does not behave itself, the bath will have to wait until later." His attention drifted back to her breasts. "Much later."

Ignoring the way her pulse quickened, she smiled weakly. "I'll try to control it."

Looking unconvinced, he started walking again. As he waded deeper into the pool, spray from the falls feathered her cheek, and water tickled her upper arms.

But the farther he moved, the more her concern rose. Water sloshed against his shoulders, sending jolts of dread down her spine. It was getting too deep for her to stand.

She tightened her hold on his neck. "Please, go back."

He stopped abruptly. "Why?"

"I can't swim."

"Then I will teach you."

"No!" She clutched his neck. "I don't want to learn. Just take me back to shore." She tried desperately to keep the hysteria from her voice.

Shadow studied her for a moment, then walked toward the rock slab. When he reached it, he lifted her out of the water and sat her down, then braced a hand on either side of her hips, palms flat against the rock. "Why do you fear the water?"

She felt sick. He would never understand. The forest, the streams, and the lakes were his home. He'd probably learned to swim before he could crawl. She stared down into the shimmering depths, unable to answer.

"Because of your mother?" he asked softly.

She nodded.

"I am sorry, *neewa*. You suffered much." His eyes filled with compassion. "But if your *nikyah* had learned to swim, she might not have died." He gripped her shoulders. "I would not see this happen to you," he said fiercely. "I want nothing to take you from me." He pulled her into his arms and sank with her into the pool.

She clung to him, but whether from fear or from need she couldn't be certain.

He eased her back, keeping a hold on her arms. "It is not as difficult as it seems. But you must first learn to relax." He lowered her slowly.

When her feet touched the bottom, she let out a sigh of relief.

"Walk with me, little one. Until you can no longer touch." He smiled reassuringly. "I will not let go of you until you are ready."

She'd never be ready, she thought nervously, but didn't voice her opinion. Instead, she nodded. In that instant Victoria realized she was placing her life in this man's hands—and she trusted him with it. It was a shocking revelation, followed by an even more startling certainty. She loved him.

Afraid to meet his eyes, fearing that her own might give her away, she kept her attention focused on the water and stepped forward.

He eased back another pace.

She followed. Water lapped at her chin, and she lifted it then took another step. Liquid sloshed into her mouth and nose. She arched her head back and took a deep breath, knowing her next step would plunge her beneath the surface.

His hand braced her spine, while his other raised her lower body. "Loosen your muscles, *neewa*. Lie on your back."

To her amazement, when she did as he directed, she didn't sink. She was keeping herself afloat. Or was it his palm under her?

"I will remove my hand now."

"Shadow, please. I'm afraid."

"I will let nothing harm you, *neewa.*" His fingers glided up and down her back beneath the water. "Spread your arms and keep your legs still, as they are now."

Her throat worked, but she couldn't speak, and when his palm slid away, she felt a surge of panic.

"Do not tense your muscles," he ordered instantly, again supporting her. "Relax."

Willing herself to comply, she loosened her limbs, then opened her arms wide.

His hand disappeared.

But she didn't sink. She was doing it! Oh, God, she could float—and it felt wonderful. She'd never dreamed how sensuous water would feel against her naked skin. Her breasts bobbed gently; the movement of water against her legs caused swirling currents to tickle up between her thighs.

She turned her head just the tiniest bit and saw the raw desire in Shadow's expression as he stared down at her nakedness. Then he met her gaze, and she licked the sudden dryness from her lips.

Flames leapt into his eyes, and he reached for her, then pulled her against his nude body. "That is enough for now," he murmured huskily.

Victoria's blood ignited, and she pressed closer, enjoying the feel of skin against skin as their bodies rocked and slid against each other. She became aware of every inch of him. Of the way her breasts brushed the smooth, muscled expanse of his chest. Of the way their stomachs touched, the way his hardness glided smoothly against her thighs. She shivered and stared into his hot eyes.

"I need you, *neewa,*" he rasped hoarsely.

Victoria felt her belly turn to liquid, and thoughts of her marriage to Hawk disappeared. She closed her eyes and arched back over his arm, feeling the gentle slap of water against the back of her head.

His arms tightened around her waist, and she heard his quick intake of breath an instant before the warmth of his mouth closed over the cool tip of her breast. The heat was startling, igniting a flame between her thighs.

Ignoring the prick of conscience that demanded she stop this nonsense, she extended her arms, allowing them to float on the surface while Shadow hungrily worshiped first one tingling crest, then the other.

Vaguely she saw flashing images of another time, in the rain, and the feel of his body on hers. Her reason spun out of control.

She gave herself up to his delicious torment, reveling in the feel of his hard fullness brushing against her thighs.

He stepped forward into shallower water and stood her on her feet. Though he still held her firmly with one arm banded around her waist, his other hand slid down to caress her bottom. His lips took hers while the fingers on her backside moved lower, between her legs, stroking gently from behind. He penetrated her with his finger, then withdrew.

She gasped. Her muscles tightened. She'd never felt anything so erotic.

He lowered his head and grazed her nipple with his teeth, then soothed it with his tongue. He slid his hand around to her belly, then down. He pushed deeper into her core, then eased out, drawing his fingers slowly upward, brushing a pulsating spot that burned for his touch.

Her senses went wild. Her stomach fluttered, then jumped.

He filled her again. And again.

Pressure built between her thighs until she knew she would die from the sheer pleasure of it. "Oh, Shadow. Please. I can't take any more."

The desperation in her voice must have reached him, for, reluctantly, he withdrew his hand and pulled her limp body against his chest. He carried her to the flat rock and lifted her out. His eyes never left hers as he sprang up beside her and enfolded her in his arms. Voraciously, his mouth consumed hers. He leaned back and pulled her on top of him, never breaking contact with her lips.

Her body responded crazily to the rigid power throbbing between them. She felt dizzy with need.

"Ride me, *neewa,*" he said raggedly, his fingers digging into the flesh of her bottom. "Ride me hard and fast."

She raised her lashes and looked down at the man lying on the boulder beneath her. His eyes were closed, his face muscles taut, his lips parted to drag air into the straining hollow of his chest. God, how she loved him. How she wanted him.

Rising up, she placed her palms against his chest and straddled him.

He clasped her hands, then drew them up, holding them out to give her balance.

Her flesh seemed to dissolve, and she flowed down onto his pulsating maleness. He filled her completely. So fully. So deep.

His groan of pleasure echoed from the cave behind them,

and he thrust up into her. The impact took her breath. She laced her fingers through his and dug her nails into the backs of his hands. Easing herself up, she waited a heartbeat, then plunged down.

His breath whooshed out on a moan.

Again and again she tormented him by pausing, then plunging, until her own body could stand no more. Her motions became primitive, then frantic, as she took him deeper. Deeper. She twisted, thrust, ground herself into him.

He bucked. Arched his back. He gripped her hands so hard they shook.

But she wouldn't cease the feral onslaught. She rode him wildly, then slowed maddeningly, before increasing the pace to a savage frenzy.

He pressed his head back into the slick boulder, the cords in his neck bulging. His fingers tightened, nearly squeezing her hands flat.

Still she wouldn't stop the torture. She withdrew and paused, then slid back down, rotating her hips in sensuous circles.

A hoarse cry rumbled from his chest.

She pulled back and waited a breathless moment, trying to control her own spiraling senses.

But he wouldn't let her stop. He pulled her forward and drove himself up into her with such force that she screamed as reality shattered into a million fragments.

Through blinding ecstasy, she felt him spread his arms and bring her down to him. His tongue filled her as fully as his shaft. He thrust hard, then bowed and stiffened, his body shuddering violently as it found its own powerful release. Her body erupted into flames.

For a long time Hawk stroked her back soothingly, knowing she'd fainted again, as she had the night of the storm. His own heart thundered crazily, and lack of air hurt his lungs. But he was content. She had taken the worst of his anger, the fierce heat of his passion, and faced her greatest fears for him, and he knew she was not capable of the atrocities he had once blamed her for.

He slid his fingers through the damp length of her hair, wondering why he had not been able to bring himself to tell her the truth of his identity.

His hand paused. Because he loved her . . . and feared losing her, that was why. She trusted him now, but once she learned how he had deceived her . . .

Victoria moaned and stirred, then lifted her head to stare down at him. Her face flushed. "I swooned, didn't I?"

He smiled. "You deserved the rest."

Her color heightened to a deep shade of pink. "Will it always be like that?"

Hawk brushed a strand of hair out of her eyes and caressed her cheek. "I hope so." He drew his thumb across her passion-swollen lower lip, aching to touch it with his tongue. "When I am inside you, knowing that I can pleasure you until you lose consciousness does much for my vanity."

She pulled her mouth into a pout. "I don't do that to you. You never lose control."

Hawk bit back a surge of laughter. *"Neewa,* I have not been in control since the day I met you." He kissed her slowly, reverently. "And the things your body does to mine go far beyond pleasure." His tongue traced her lips. "Even beyond sinful. The way your touch sets flame to my sanity, I sometimes wonder if you truly are a witch." He swatted her bare bottom. "Now, up, woman. I still have not given you my surprise."

"But I thought the pool . . ."

"You thought wrong. Now get up."

Easing off of him, Victoria felt a moment's loss when he slid out of her. She moved to sit next to him, primly folding her legs to one side.

Shadow rose, his wet, magnificent body towering over her before he dived smoothly into the pool. Awed, she watched him glide through the water, then emerge near the bank and climb out.

She smiled to herself at the picture he presented. Naked against a backdrop of pine and granite, he looked like a majestic yet savage animal. Her smile slipped when he disappeared into the forest. He was so much a part of this land. Just like Hawk. Guilt churned inside her, but she forced it aside. Hawk didn't care about her; she'd be hanged before she'd writhe in remorse over something so beautiful and pure as what she and Shadow had shared.

Staring at the line of trees, she tried to imagine living in the woods with Shadow and knew that, as much as she loved him, she could never be happy within the dark confines of the forest. So where did that leave her? She couldn't ask him to give up the land he loved. Still, too, there was the problem of getting Hawk to release her.

Just as the thought formed, Shadow emerged from the trees carrying something. His eyes met hers across the pool. Regally her lover walked toward her, his bronze body gleaming wet in the dying sunlight. He stopped when he reached the center of the pool, water swirling against his shoulders. "Come to me, little one," he urged softly.

Refusing to worry about Hawk or the forest, Victoria took a fortifying breath and slid off the rock into the water. Knowing he wanted her to float to him as she had before, she turned her back to him and spread her arms. She pushed against the rock with her feet and glided over the sparkling surface of the pool. Once again she had moved out of her depth.

When Shadow's arms closed around her from behind, her heart soared. She'd done it! She'd conquered her fear of the water. Turning into his arms, she hugged him. "I love you."

For a moment he looked as if he were molded out of stone. Even his chest didn't move as he stared down at her. Then he hauled her up against him. Savagely he wrapped her in his strength, his face buried in the sensitive spot between her neck and shoulder.

He didn't move for a long while, and when he did, it was to ravish her mouth with hungry, fierce kisses. After several delicious moments, he pulled away and looked into her eyes. *"Nihaw kunahqa, ni kitehi."*

"What?"

Shadow seemed to shake himself mentally; then he eased back. "It was not important." He held up the hand clutching a bunch of tufted leaves and white flowers streaked with purple. At their base hung several bulbs. "Here. This is your surprise."

Not wanting to offend him, she took them and smiled weakly. "They're very pretty."

His lips twitched. "It is of the lilac plant. The bulbs are used as soap."

"Soap! Oh, Shadow, thank you. I thought the surprise was the flow— Oh, never mind. This is wonderful!"

After they'd returned to shore and he'd cut open the soap plant bulb then shown her how to use it, Shadow left her to her ablutions and sat on the grass. She watched him lift the buckskin shirt she'd been wearing. He did something to it, then tossed it aside and stretched out.

It was extremely hard for her to concentrate on bathing and washing her hair with her eyes on his magnificently naked form warming beneath the gold evening shadows. The man had no idea how beautiful he was. All powerful, primitive male.

Feeling herself go hot all over, she quickly turned her back to him.

When she'd at last, if shakily, finished her bath, she waded out of the water and went to stand over him.

He lazily opened his eyes and studied her from his supine position. His eyes smoldered as they held hers, then moved to explore her damp body.

Icy chills shook her, then melted into slow, simmering embers. Without a word she lowered herself into his arms.

Chapter 18

Hawk watched Victoria cast one last forlorn glance at their secluded haven by the pool. She sighed heavily, then turned to face him. "I guess, since we *have* to leave, I'm as ready as I can be."

He nodded, his own reluctance carefully hidden. And he *was* reluctant. After the night they had spent, the many times they had journeyed into pleasure's paradise, who would not have been? Realizing that if he dwelt on it, he would take her again this very minute, he turned his thoughts to their destination . . . and what he had to tell her before they reached it.

His gaze drifted back to his wife, and he wondered how she would accept the knowledge that he was her husband. He inspected her closely. She looked so adorable in his silk shirt and Jed's buckskin, now that Hawk had removed the sleeves to give her more freedom. He warmed, remembering how pleased she had been over that simple gesture—and how thoroughly she had shown her appreciation.

"How long before we reach the village?"

Hawk released a breath, then looked ahead of them, mentally following the path they would take. "A few hours. Flaming Wing's village is on the other side of that rise." He pointed to the crest of the mountain.

"Oh." Her tone sounded weak, strained, and Hawk wanted to shake her, to demand that she stop worrying over her fate with her husband, to assure her that she had nothing

212

to fear. Wanting to do just that, yet dreading her reaction, he turned his back to her. He would not destroy her pleasant memories of the pool. He would tell her when they reached the rise.

"Shadow? How did you get those scars?" she asked softly.

Hawk felt the muscles down his back stiffen, then forced himself to relax. "I was sold into slavery a few years ago. The scars are from a whip used by the taskmaster."

"Oh, God." Her voice trembled, as if she were fighting the urge to cry. Then he felt her small cool palm touch his back. "How you must have suffered." Her lips brushed the ridges on his back.

Hawk could not mistake the compassion, the devastation, in her shaky statement, and his love for her soared. Knowing if he turned around and saw her concern for him, he would take her again, he stepped forward. "It was a long time ago."

Making certain that he kept his pace slow to accommodate her smaller, less capable steps, he started the laborious climb.

As they rose higher, Hawk again and again formed in his mind the words that he would say to his wife. Words to explain why he had deceived her. Words of love and, he hoped, words that would extract her forgiveness.

He did not doubt that Victoria was innocent of the atrocities done to him. He had seen into her soul, seen her goodness. She had come to him whole and pure . . . and completely. For the first time in his life, he trusted a woman—this woman.

But he dreaded her anger, knew it would be volatile, and within her rights. He stirred, wondering if he could turn her anger into passion, let her use his body for the explosive outlet. His blood picked up speed, and his feet slowed. For a moment he considered abandoning the idea of going to the village. He could still take Victoria to his cabin. . . .

He shook off the cowardly plan, wondering what had caused this lapse in his strength. He had never feared another's wrath. His step faltered. But then, he had never been in love like this before, either. Not even with

Samantha. Angry, and not certain at whom, he quickened his pace, nearly overwhelmed by the need to put his apprehension behind him.

When he looked up again, he found that they had almost reached the top of the rise. Brushing aside a wave of anxiety, he concentrated on what lay just beyond the mountain—his father's village, if Jed's directions were correct. And they must have been. Hawk knew they were being watched. He had felt it for the last half hour.

A rush of anger struck him. The white man had forced his people from their homeland, taken their crops, their abundant game, and driven them over the mountains, most of them across the Mississippi. Hawk could not help wondering how his father had responded—and if he still lived. Jed had not mentioned Flaming Wing, and Hawk had not been able to ask about his *notha,* fearing the worst.

Knowing all of the answers lay on top of that rise and beyond, he hastened his step.

As they made their way up through the pines, Hawk's chest grew heavier. A feeling he had not experienced for a long time rose inside him. A foreboding of loss, much like the one he had felt the day his mother left him. He tried to shake the sensation aside.

He glanced back at his wife, struggling to keep up with him, and knew he would not allow her anger to separate them. He would make her understand—keep her his captive, if necessary—until she believed him.

When the terrain leveled off beneath his feet, Hawk stopped. Though they still stood among the shadowed pines, down the other side of the mountain he could see smoke rising and the protruding tops of the *wegiwa* in his father's village. Warmth enfolded him. He was home.

The need to see Flaming Wing was nearly as intense as the urge to make love to Victoria. He explored his wife's lovely face as she stared in wonder down at the hillside dotted with the tops of bark-covered dwellings and at the southern end of the Shenandoah Valley just beyond.

Hawk smiled at Victoria's worried expression, knowing she feared seeing Hawk, feared that he, Shadow, would be forced to give her to the other man. His happiness soared, then slipped when he realized the time for the truth had come.

Victoria touched his arm. "Is that your village?"

His muscle tensed beneath her hand. "Yes." He faced her—and nearly lost his resolve. She looked so adorable in Jed's baggy shirt, her dark red-brown hair tangled around her small face. But her pale blue eyes held a look of nervousness and worry beneath thick, silky lashes. And he knew that concern over her fate caused it.

Sliding an arm around her waist, he pulled her to him, filled with the need to hold her a moment longer, taste her giving lips one more time before he bared his soul.

Slowly he trailed kisses across her temple and down over the uptilted tip of her nose, then lower to mold his mouth to hers. He kissed her long and deep, reveling in the feel of her trembling in his arms. She wanted him as much as he wanted her.

Giving a mental sigh, he pulled back. *"Neewa,* there is something I must tell you before we reach the village." He cleared his throat. "It is about your husband."

Suddenly a vicious growl pierced the air.

"What was that?" Victoria swung around sharply.

"Shh." He silenced her with a wave of his hand, praying they were downwind of the bear. But just for caution's sake, he withdrew the knife from the top of his moccasin boots.

The bear roared again, this time closer, to their right.

Victoria gasped. "Oh, God!"

Hawk swore: They were *upwind.* The animal would catch their scent at any moment.

Quickly swinging his gaze to one side, Hawk spied a deep recess behind a mound of boulders. He had to get Victoria to safety. He gripped her arm. "Come."

Half dragging, half leading, he took her to the outcropping and pushed her into the narrow opening. Knowing his own large frame would never fit through the mouth of the crevice, he ordered brusquely, "Do not come out until I call you." He hesitated. "Do you understand? No matter what happens, no matter what you hear, do not come out."

She stared out at him with frightened eyes, her chin quivering. "Where are you going?" She clutched his hand, squeezing it tightly. "You can't stay out there."

He offered her a reassuring smile. *"Neewa,* I have lived in these woods most of my life. I will come to no harm. Do not be frightened for me."

She did not look convinced. "Please don't go."

His heart swelled at her concern for him. Unable to resist, he leaned forward and kissed her quick and hard. "Stay," he commanded one last time, then moved away from the barrier.

Just as he rounded the boulder she hid behind, he came face-to-face with the bear. Its ferocious roar sent chills up his spine. The beast stood only a few yards away, at least six feet tall on its hind legs, its massive body covered with shiny brown hair.

Hawk swore beneath his breath. Of all the bears in the forest, this one had to be a grizzly—the deadliest breed.

With his back to the descending side of the mountain, Hawk retreated slowly downward, desperate to lure it away from Victoria's hiding place.

Hawk did not try to fool himself. His chances of coming out of this encounter alive were not good. In truth, they ranked a little less than none.

The bear bawled again and lowered its head, ready to charge.

Hawk retreated another step, never taking his eyes off the animal. His back bumped against a boulder, and a nervous jolt hit him. He was cornered!

The bear lunged.

It slammed into Hawk with the force of a falling tree. Sharp claws sliced into his shoulder and knocked him to the ground.

He scrambled to his feet.

The bear turned on him and charged again.

Hawk jumped to one side and plunged his knife into its stomach.

An enraged screech bounced off the mountains.

Vaguely Hawk heard another sound. A scream. He leapt

to his feet and saw Victoria racing toward the bear swinging a thick branch. *No.* Damn her, she would get herself killed!

Before Hawk could move, she slammed her weapon into the back of the bear's head.

It roared wildly and turned on her.

Hawk had never known such fear as he did at that moment. He sprang forward, leapt on the beast's back, and frantically plunged his knife into its throat.

Gunfire exploded, and the bear's massive body convulsed.

Another blast sounded, and hot pain cut across Hawk's temple. He felt a falling sensation as the bear crumpled beneath him.

Hawk hit the ground, then rolled away from the animal. In the distance he heard the faint sound of sobbing. He shook his head, trying to gather his thoughts. *Victoria!* He twisted around. His gaze flew to his wife.

The massive animal lay before her, blood gushing from its throat and a hole in its chest. Who had shot it?

Victoria knelt beside the bear, her arms clutched to her stomach, rocking. She sobbed hysterically, her glazed eyes focused blankly on the ground.

His senses whirling with the impact of the sacrifice she had made for him by attacking the bear, he forced his leaden limbs to move. He dragged himself over to her, vaguely aware of blood oozing from his head.

When he pulled himself up beside her, he touched her arm. *"Neewa?"*

She did not respond. Did not look at him.

"Victoria?" He gripped one of her shoulders and shook it. *"Victoria,* damn it, answer me."

Her gaze did not rise. Her sobs came in gasping hiccups.

The naked agony in her cries pierced his heart. He forced his pain-riddled body up and pulled her into his arms, fighting the moisture threatening his own eyes. He held her close, cradled her, fearing her mind had wandered to a place he could not reach. He buried his forehead in the arch of her neck. Not since the day his mother deserted him had Hawk felt the consuming urge to cry. He nuzzled the soft flesh. "Do not leave me, little one. I need you."

"I didn't kill it, Shadow."

Her voice sounded weak but sane, thank Moneto.

"I tried to," she continued. "I thought it was going to kill you. I didn't care what happened to me then. I wanted to die, too." Her tears dropped onto his shoulder. "But I didn't kill it." She clutched his arm. "Oh, God. So much blood. . . ."

Hawk felt his eyes burn, and he tightened his embrace. "I know, *neewa*. I know." He rocked her, trying to hold on to his whirling senses. Light and shadow wavered in and out of his field of vision. Oh, Moneto, do not let me leave her now. Not now! But his thoughts reeled, and he felt himself slipping into unconsciousness. Why was she screaming? He shook his head, trying to clear it. Pain nearly blinded him, then faded. . . .

Victoria cried out again, tears blurring her vision as she watched Shadow slide limply to the ground, blood streaming from his temple. *Nooo. Oh, God, no.* He's been shot!

Who? How? Cradling his head, she glanced around frantically. She needed help. Her gaze darted toward the rise. If she could just get him down to the village. Surely the Shawnee would know how to help him. She pulled at his shoulder, trying to sit him up, but she didn't possess the strength. God in heaven, what could she do?

She flattened her palm against his temple and searched wildly for something to stem the bleeding. If she could slow the flow of blood, she could run down to the village and get help. Visions of her time with Adam at the inn came back in a rush. Pressure. She needed something, a cloth, to hold against the wound.

She reached for the hem of the shirt she wore.

"Ria! Oh, love, I thought he was going to kill you!"

Victoria jerked her head up to see her cousin scrambling toward her. "Collier? Bragen?" she said as the taller man appeared behind her cousin. "Oh, thank God. Help me. Quickly, he's been injured."

Collier blurted out a question: "You mean he's not dead?"

Victoria gasped.

"No thanks to you, Parks," Bragen spat as he knelt beside Shadow and pressed a handkerchief to the bleeding wound.

"I was only trying to kill the bear," Collier said defensively. "How was I to know the beast would turn just when I fired?"

"I'd already hit it," Bragen spat. "You fired while the bear was going down."

Stunned, and more furious than she'd ever been in her life, Victoria sprang to her feet. She walked straight up to Collier. *"You* shot him?" She slapped him hard. "Damn you!"

Collier stumbled backward and grabbed at his mouth. He stared at her in confusion. "God, Ria." He slurred the words between his fingers. "Why'd you hit me? I didn't mean to shoot the bastard. I was aiming at the bear!"

Realizing that her cousin had only tried to save them, she was instantly contrite. "Oh, Collier, I'm sorry." She touched his cheek. "It's just that . . ." She glanced down at Shadow and watched as Bragen tended him. "He means a great deal to me."

"What?"

"Damn ye, Parks, give me a hand," another man called to her cousin.

Collier spun around, scowling.

A burly man with a bushy beard and an eye patch was making his way up the side of the hill leading four horses, and Victoria numbly recognized one of them: Shadow's stallion.

"Make your own way, O'Ryan. I'm not hauling your fat arse up—" Collier froze, his eyes glued on something off to one side.

Bragen Alexander swore softly.

Victoria turned—and gasped. A dozen mahogany-skinned men stood before them, some dressed in just scraps of cloth while others wore buckskins similar to Shadow's. They all carried some type of weapon, ranging from muskets to bows and arrows. All looked extremely threatening.

At any other time she might have swooned at the savage

display, but worry over Shadow outweighed her fears. "Please help us." She knelt and stroked Shadow's bleeding brow. "He's hurt."

One of the Indians stepped forward, and Victoria felt a shock all the way to the soles of her feet. Wearing a headdress with white feathers like the one Alaina always carried, he was obviously the chief—and he looked exactly like an older version of Shadow.

No one breathed as the man's velvet black eyes, faintly lined at the corners, shifted from Bragen to O'Ryan to Collier. They narrowed slightly on her cousin, then moved to her.

The chief stared at her for a long time, then slid his glance to Shadow's prone figure. Something like pain flicked in his eyes before he turned them on Collier. The Indian's well-defined lips drew into a grim line. "If my son—" His throat bunched. "If Shadow Hawk dies, you will join him."

Collier gasped.

Victoria's gaze flew to the older man, then to the one lying on the ground. The chief's son? Shadow? Her blood started to pound. Shadow *Hawk*.

Chapter 19

Hawk. Victoria walked beside the litter, her gaze on the wounded man as they made their way toward the village. Deep concern warred with righteous anger. Shadow was Hawk. He was hurt. He was her *husband*. He might die.

She wrapped her arms around herself and tried to still the shaking in her limbs at the thought of losing him. She grasped onto her anger. He had lied to her. Obviously that was what he'd started to explain on the mountain. Either that or he wanted to tell her he'd give her the divorce she sought.

She stumbled. He had used her to salve his lust, knowing full well he was within his rights as her husband. It had all been a game to pass the time until they reached the Shawnee—and certainly much easier than dragging her behind a horse.

Her fury grew when she thought of the tortures he'd put her through, and she wanted to punch his arrogant nose. The cur. The miserable blackguard! But when she again thought of him lying there helpless, his eyes closed, the pale bandages around his head and shoulder looking ghostly against his dark skin, she couldn't hold on to her anger. She wanted him well—*so she could kill him.*

"Flaming Wing comes!" someone yelled in English.

Victoria snapped her attention to their surroundings and saw that they had entered the village. For a moment she forgot her mixed emotions over Shadow—*Hawk*—and focused on the sights and smells around her.

Dogs yelped, and children squealed. The heavy scent of woodsmoke and roasting meat filled the air. Rows of bark-covered huts with heavy buffalo hides over the doorways formed an uneven circle around a central clearing. In its core, meat hung over a fire in front of a single, much bigger structure. Along its log walls at eye level, thin vertical holes served as windows.

Victoria felt the first stirring of fear as she glanced at the dangerous savage-looking faces looming over her from all sides.

A woman gasped. "Shadow Hawk!"

Murmurs skittered through the people, then faded into an eerie silence.

The chief said something in Shawnee to a group of braves, then turned fierce eyes on Collier. He said something else that sounded ugly.

Victoria frowned and leaned toward Bragen, who stood next to her. "What does *cut-ta-ho-tha* mean?"

He bent to her, his voice low. "Condemned man."

"What do you mean?" Fear for Collier spiraled through her. "What are they going to do to him?"

As a brave approached, Bragen straightened but didn't answer.

Weary from the terror, confusion, and concern she'd been through in the last hour, Victoria watched them carry Hawk into a separate hut, then numbly followed the others into a large building.

"It's called a council house," Bragen offered as he passed through the log-framed door. "The leaders of the tribe meet here."

But she barely heard his comments. Her thoughts were too chaotic. Concern for Hawk battled with fear for Collier and the others. She didn't think the Shawnee would harm her. At least, she prayed they wouldn't.

It took several moments for her eyes to adjust to the dark interior of the council house. Then slowly the room came into focus. It was large and cool with tiny streams of light seeping in through the long narrow windows along both sides. At either end of the building a slender tree trunk supported the gabled roof, which rose in a crisscross pattern of interlocking poles. In the center a large hole yawned directly above a circle of rocks on the dirt floor below—obviously an opening for smoke to escape.

Bragen sauntered over to one of the support poles, sat down, and leaned back against it. "Might as well make yourself comfortable, Ria. We'll probably be here awhile."

O'Ryan edged toward one of the windows and peeked out, his single eye twitching nervously. "Damned heathens is prob'ly plannin' to eat us for supper."

"They're not cannibals," Bragen said.

Victoria wondered briefly where he'd acquired his knowledge of the Shawnee, but cast off the thought as unimportant. She rubbed her chilled arms and moved into a beam of sunshine.

"Damn me hide, will ye look at that!" O'Ryan exclaimed. "They're strippin' Parks."

Victoria rushed to a window. Horrified, she watched Collier twist wildly and scream obscenities as two braves held his arms outstretched while a third cut the clothing from his body.

"My God!"

Bragen moved up beside her, then swore softly.

"I was afraid o' this when the chief seen Collier shoot the redskin," O'Ryan croaked.

Victoria gasped. "What are they going to do?"

"Make him run the gauntlet," Bragen answered.

As he spoke, a group of women and children formed two lines between her cousin and the council house. Each held a stick, switch, club, or staff—some nearly six feet long. Panic exploded inside her. "They're going to kill him!"

"Not if he runs fast enough," Bragen offered solemnly.

In a daze, Victoria watched one of the braves lift his hand and point to the council house. *"Msi-kah-mi-qui,"* he snarled, then rapped out more unintelligible words.

"What's he saying?"

"The brave told Collier to run through the line to the

council house," Bragen answered. "But if he falls, he'll have to start again."

Collier's naked body shook. Then someone shoved him forward.

He screamed and stumbled toward the menacing row. Someone struck him in the back of the head. His face contorted, and he took great bounding strides as he tried to dodge the fierce attacks. He'd almost made it to the end when a huge woman stepped out in front of him, her club ready.

Victoria cried out when the woman slammed the heavy stick between Collier's eyes, knocking him to his knees. Blood spurted, and he grasped his head, whimpering like a child as the others closed in, raining blow after blow across his bare back and shoulders. Then they dragged him back to the beginning of the line.

"Stop them! Oh, God, somebody stop them!" Victoria cried hysterically.

Bragen pulled her away from the window and into his arms, turning her face into his shoulder. "Don't watch."

She clenched a fistful of his shirt and cried until her throat was raw. She hated these savages! And Hawk most of all!

It seemed to take a lifetime before the shouting and laughter finally stopped. Sick with fear and dread, she looked up to meet Bragen's compassion-filled eyes.

He offered her a reassuring smile. "It's over."

She whirled toward the window, and her knees nearly buckled in relief when she saw her cousin on his feet, supported between two Shawnee braves. Her stomach rolled at the sight of his bloody, beaten body. But he was alive.

As Collier struggled weakly, another brave approached him carrying a bowl of inky black fluid, with which he began painting her cousin's nude body.

"What are they doing?" She hoped that black stuff was medicine.

"They're marking him a condemned man," Bragen answered.

O'Ryan shifted, digging his fingers into the bark at the

base of the window where he stood, his eye glazed with fright. "What'll them savages do to me?"

"Nothing. Parks is the one who shot Remington. He's the only one they want."

The bearded man's breath whooshed out with his relief. Then he straightened suddenly. "What're they doin' now?"

Victoria's gaze shot back to the opening. Collier was now spread-eagled between two upright poles. Blood and black goo dripped on the dirt beneath him, and his head hung down in either exhaustion or unconsciousness. Tears pooled in her eyes. He looked so pitiful.

"They're finished torturing him, for now," Bragen replied. "They won't start again until tomorrow."

"And then what?" Victoria turned viciously on the tall man.

Sympathy filled his eyes. "I'm not sure. I guess a lot depends on Hawk, if he lives." Bragen shrugged. "If he doesn't, then Parks will run the gauntlet again. Then he'll endure whatever other forms of torture they choose. In the end they'll kill him. Until then, they'll torment him with descriptions of an agonizing death."

The room swirled threateningly, and Victoria grabbed Bragen's arm for support. This couldn't be happening.

At that moment another commotion reverberated from outside, and Victoria spun back to the window. Her gasp of surprise echoed through the room. "Alaina!"

Weak with relief, she watched her mother-in-law and Paddy and a strikingly attractive man on a black stallion ride straight into the Shawnee encampment. Fleetingly she realized they must have left the carriage somewhere, perhaps at Halcyon.

Her gaze slid back to the dark-haired stranger. Was this Jason Kincaid? Appreciatively she studied his powerful form in snug fawn-colored breeches, noticing the breadth of his wide shoulders beneath a white linen shirt.

She was so caught up in her inspection that it took a moment for her to realize that, for the second time that day, the village had gone silent. Everyone seemed to freeze, every eye on the beautiful Lady Remington.

Victoria watched in wonder as Alaina approached the hut where they had earlier taken Hawk.

Whispers skittered among the people, and the name Sand Blossom echoed several times.

One of the Shawnee women stepped forward and called out to someone, then scampered away.

Flaming Wing emerged from behind the hide door covering then stopped and stared unbelievingly at Alaina.

Victoria saw his expression go from shock to elation to fury, then tighten into an unreadable mask. He crossed his arms and stared straight ahead as if Alaina wasn't there.

A flicker of pain touched the older woman's eyes before they cleared into a somber stare. She leaned forward on the horse and said something to the chief.

He stiffened, his features momentarily slipping into a line of indecision before again becoming rigid.

For a breathless moment, no one moved; not even a bird dared to chirp. Then Flaming Wing nodded and walked back inside.

Alaina's composure didn't waver. Her head held high, she dismounted and followed him.

When they'd disappeared behind the hide door, the entire village erupted in activity, everyone seemingly anxious to look busy and avoid the chief's lodge.

Paddy and the other man remained on their horses.

It seemed like hours before Flaming Wing and Alaina finally emerged. Without speaking, the chief mounted Lady Remington's horse, then lifted her up and settled her in front of him before banding her slim waist with his arm. The Shawnee seemed to hold their breath as, without a word of explanation to anyone, the two rode off into the woods.

The attractive man mounted beside Victoria's old friend said something to Paddy, then spoke to one of the Indians before he eased his tall frame out of the saddle and strode toward Hawk's hut.

Paddy headed for the council house, his limp more pronounced. "Ah, Ria," he groaned as he entered and pulled her into his arms. "Ye will never know the worry I been through over ye." He stepped back to look at her. "Are ye all right, lass? They didna hurt ye?"

Tears stung Victoria's eyes, and she curled back into Paddy's comforting arms. "I'm all right, Paddy. Truly. I'm unharmed."

A quiver raced through the older man's body before he released her and moved back. "Thank the saints." He glanced toward the other men in the room. "Why's Parks trussed up?"

O'Ryan ignored him and stared at something out the window.

Bragen explained as quickly as possible.

Paddy frowned. "Ye mean he fired on the bear after ye'd already downed it? An' hit the chief's lad?"

"Yes, he fired afterward, but he never intended to hit anyone," Victoria added, defending her cousin. "And after what my beastly husband did to me, making me think I'd been kidnapped by some savage, the way he—well, I wish Collier's aim had been even worse."

Paddy narrowed his eyes but didn't comment.

Not liking that look, Victoria changed the subject. "How did you find me?"

"Alaina figured her boy'd take ye to the Shawnee camp. But when we got to Halcyon, Jason Kincaid—the lad we rode in with—said Flaming Wing'd been forced to move his village. The duchess got real sad. Then, 'afore ye ken, she was headin' to the Shawnees."

He shook his head. "Kincaid didna like that none. Shouted somethin' 'bout Flaming Wing havin' suffered enough." Paddy smiled. "You'da thought they was goin' to come to blows. But Lady Remington finally said somethin' quiet like, an' settled that lad, Jason, right down. He looked real surprised, then tole us he was takin' us to the village."

"I wonder what she said?"

The flap covering the door was lifted and a young woman entered, drawing everyone's attention.

O'Ryan whirled around, his expression at first fearful.

The girl spoke slowly, as if trying to pronounce each word carefully, but Victoria didn't understand any of it.

"She said she'd take us to our lodges," Bragen supplied.

The pretty Shawnee lifted the hide door and motioned them through.

As Victoria stepped out into the bright sunlight, her gaze automatically went to her cousin, still hanging limp between the poles. Sympathy churned at the awful sight he presented. But before she had a chance to dwell on his suffering, a lovely older woman approached them. She wore a clinging buckskin dress that was laced down the front. Only it wasn't tied. It gaped wide, revealing a daring expanse of full, mature breasts.

The woman stood silent for a moment and stared appreciatively at Bragen and Paddy. Then, heaving a sigh, she turned to O'Ryan. "You come with Winter Flower," she said in broken English.

O'Ryan's chest puffed out, and he cast the two men a smirk. "The squaw be knowin' a *real* man when she sees one."

Victoria noticed the flash of distaste in the woman's eyes before she quickly concealed it and looped her arm through O'Ryan's. She smiled warmly, if falsely, then led him toward a bark hut.

"Where are they going?" Victoria asked before she thought.

Bragen seemed to search for words. "To share a mat."

Victoria felt her face go up in flames, especially when Paddy chuckled. The cur.

After O'Ryan and the woman disappeared inside the lodge, the girl who'd led them out of the council house raised a hand and pointed to a shelter near Flaming Wing's. Then she pointed to Paddy and Bragen.

Bragen watched Paddy walk toward the hut, but didn't move. "I want to speak to Kincaid first," he told Victoria before repeating the request in Shawnee to their guide.

The girl lifted a narrow shoulder, then started forward, motioning for Victoria to follow her. She led the way to yet another dwelling.

A fine-boned young woman with silky, straight black hair stepped out. She waved the other Shawnee girl away, then nodded to Victoria. "You share *wegiwa* with Summer Wind." She touched her chest. "And *nikyah*—mother—Cooing Dove." She lifted the flap and pointed to a frail old woman who sat bent over a half-woven basket in her lap. *"Nikyah* no hear."

The aging woman, as if sensing their presence, looked up, startled, then made rapid movements with her hands.

Summer Wind shook her head and said something in sign language. "Cooing Dove fears you *tha-tha,* enemy. I tell no *tha-tha.*"

Obviously relieved, the old woman made another sign, then lowered her head and resumed weaving.

Summer Wind moved deeper into the dwelling, then gracefully eased down onto a mat. "What name?"

"Victoria."

She repeated the name slowly. "Vic-tor-i-a. Pretty." She waved a hand toward a crudely carved wooden bowl filled with what looked like flat scones. "Want food?"

Victoria's stomach rebelled at the mere thought. "No, thank you." After a silent moment passed, Victoria began to feel awkward. She glanced around the hut. "How did your people learn English?"

"Sand Blossom teach Shawnee for many suns."

"Sand Blossom?"

"Al-ai-na." The girl pronounced the name roughly. *"Nikyah* to Shadow Hawk."

"How did she come by the name Sand Blossom?"

"Hair color of sand." Summer Wind lifted a slim shoulder. "Little Shadow Hawk bring many flowers to *nikyah.* Sand Blossom put here." She pointed to her hair.

Something touched Victoria's heart at the vision of her husband, as a small boy, bringing flowers to his mother. How he must have adored her then. Sadly, she couldn't help wondering what happened to cause his bitterness toward Alaina.

"Chief say you *neewa*—wife—to Hawk."

Victoria sucked in a sharp breath. *Neewa* meant *wife!*

229

That wretched, no-good, vile, blasphemous blackguard! All this time he'd been calling her his wife! She clenched her jaw. Oh, he would pay for this. "Yes. I'm his *neewa.*"

Summer Wind's pretty mouth curled into a smile. "Women of village no happy. Many moons Shadow Hawk seek pleasure in many *wegiwa.*" Her smile grew wider. "Winter Flower teach good. Hawk much brave."

Victoria couldn't deny that, or the fact that she was burning with jealousy. Just the thought of Hawk in the arms of the sultry Winter Flower, not to mention the others, made her want to kill. Feeling suddenly claustrophobic, she looked toward the opening. "Am I allowed to go outside?"

"You no prisoner."

"Then, if you don't mind, I'd like to walk around for a while."

Summer Wind nodded, her expression concerned, as if she realized she'd said something she shouldn't have.

Victoria turned for the door just as someone approached from the other side.

Summer Wind moved past her and brushed aside the flap.

"Beggin' yer pardon, missy. But is me girl, Ria, in there?"

Victoria hurried to the door, anxious to talk to Paddy, to know how Hawk was. But she never expected to see her old friend looking so strained and tired. His throat worked; then he spoke quietly. "I need to talk to ye, lass."

Fear tightened her muscles. "It's Hawk, isn't it? Something's happened to him."

"What? No. No, lass. The boy's fine."

Relief nearly folded her knees, and she motioned for him to come in.

But he hesitated. "Can we be goin' for a walk? What I need to say isna for others' ears."

"Of course." Confused, Victoria left the hut and walked with Paddy to the edge of the woods. "What is it?"

He shifted uncomfortably, his hands shoved deep in his pockets as he stared down at a pile of pine needles. He looked so nervous, she fought the urge to smile.

"Ria, I dunna ken how to tell ye this, so I'll come right out with it." He took a deep breath. "Richard Townsend wasna yer pa."

If he'd slapped her, he couldn't have stunned her any more than he did at that moment. "What?"

"Ye heard me, lass."

"But if *he* wasn't my father, then who *is?*" Her mind searched frantically for any man she'd seen her mother with. None came to mind—except Paddy, of course. Her heart picked up speed. *Paddy?* Her gaze flew to his, and she knew. She could see it. "You?"

"Dunna look at me like that, lass. I wanted to tell ye for many a year. But yer mama didna want ye upset." He closed his eyes. "But when ye were kidnapped, I couldna help but think ye might be killed." His eyes met hers. "I couldna live with meself if anythin' happened to ye, an' ye not be knowin' the truth."

Still shocked, she stared at him, for the first time noticing things she'd never given thought to before. His dark chestnut hair, though gray at the temples, closely resembled her own coloring, as did his light blue eyes. Conflicting emotions battled inside her. Everyone she cared about had deceived her. She loved Paddy. She hated him. But after her ordeal with Hawk, she wouldn't judge him until she knew all the facts. "Why are *you* my father instead of Richard Townsend?" she asked as calmly as she could.

He cleared his throat. "It isna a short story, Ria."

"I've got plenty of time."

Paddy turned his back to her and stared out across the vast wilderness, and when he began to speak, his voice shook. "I fell in love with yer mama when we were wee tykes," he said in a low, gravelly tone. "I was a lackey then, workin' for her pa in the stables. I grew up lovin' her from afar, knowin' it was hopeless. She couldna marry one o' my station."

He rubbed the back of his neck. "When she married the earl, it near broke me heart. But she took me with her to Denwick as her personal groom. That didna please the likes o' Richard, but he didna have reason to deny her. I was happy just bein' near me love."

He turned around to face her, his eyes hard. "But she wasna happy with him. I saw how he treated her—his cruel words, his heavy fist. . . ." He closed his eyes and took a breath. "I seen the way she was sufferin' year after year. I hated him, and I ken she did, too. Yet she didna turn away from his meanness. She be wantin' a babe too much. But after near a decade she finally realized the earl couldna give her one, and she decided to leave him."

He swallowed and blinked back a hint of moisture in his eyes. "She planned that journey to the colonies, supposedly to visit her sister, but she wasna comin' back. All of us, along with old Louise, her maid, was to leave on the same ship. Only the king sent for the earl, an' we couldna wait for him. We went on ahead."

Pulling the other hand from his pocket, he wiped it across his brow. "The maid, Louise, didna fare well on the ship. She took to her bed with sickness, leavin' me an' yer mama alone most o' the time." Pain etched his features. "Too much o' the time. Before we reached the colonies, yer mama already knew she carried me babe."

He met her gaze, his filled with a combination of warmth and sadness. "She couldna tell the earl the truth when he joined us later. It woulda meant me death. So she lied. She convinced him ye was of the earl's loins."

"Did she love you?" Victoria asked through a tight throat.

He nodded his dark head, sadness visible in every line of his handsome face. "She told me on the ship. Said she'd loved me most o' her life."

Victoria felt Paddy's agony as if it were her own. She knew what it felt like to love someone . . . hopelessly. On unsteady legs she moved closer to her father. Father. The word echoed through her heart. She touched his cheek tenderly, remembering all the times he'd taken care of her. "You were always more of a father to me than Richard Townsend was." She kissed him. "Nothing's changed."

Paddy took her hand and clutched it fiercely. Tears brimmed his eyes, and his shoulders shook. "God, how I love ye, lass."

A sob broke from her throat, and she buried her face in his strong shoulder.

When Victoria and Paddy finally returned to camp sometime later, Paddy, after a last fierce hug, headed toward his *wegiwa*. Watching the proud set of his shoulders and the slight limp, she felt warmed. They had talked as they never had before. She told him of Hawk and her love for him—*before* she realized how he'd lied to her. She explained how she'd always felt so much closer to Paddy than to Richard, but had not even an inkling that he was her true father. She knew now that Paddy loved her, too, as much as she did him, and he'd never deceived her intentionally—nor had he left her. He'd stayed to watch his child grow, even though it meant seeing the woman he loved with another man day after day.

Victoria glanced toward Summer Wind's hut, remembering the pain of jealousy she'd felt over the girl's innocent tales of Hawk's other women. How Paddy must have hurt all those years. Yet he'd remained at Denwick for Victoria.

Not wanting to dwell on thoughts of her father's misery and her husband's sexual prowess, she searched the village for any familiar person. She didn't want to talk to Summer Wind again. Not right now. And she certainly didn't want to see Hawk. Not until he was well enough to withstand the force of her anger.

Bragen wasn't anywhere to be seen. Obviously he was still in the lodge with Hawk and Jason Kincaid. Victoria fought the urge to go there, to make certain her husband was all right. Instead, she walked toward Collier. She didn't care about Hawk. He was a liar and a bounder—and an unprincipled womanizer.

As she neared her cousin, she noticed that he had regained consciousness and was talking to O'Ryan. No, *arguing* with him in a low voice. The one-eyed man snarled something and stomped off. He headed back toward Winter Flower's hut where the exquisite woman stood in the opening, an inviting smile playing across her lips.

Victoria nearly drowned in a sudden swell of jealousy when she thought of Hawk with the woman.

O'Ryan quickened his pace; then the two of them disappeared inside the lodge and lowered the flap.

"Ria!" Collier called hoarsely. "Come here."

Victoria hurried to her cousin, relieved that he was able to converse, and grateful to take her mind off other matters.

"God, Ria. You've got to help me. The chief thinks I shot his son on purpose." Collier's eyes shifted fearfully. "I told him I shot at the bear, but he doesn't believe me."

Sweat beaded on her cousin's brow and mingled with the blood. "They're going to kill me." His body trembled. "One of the braves who spoke English told me. He even told me when . . . and how I would die." He shuddered, and his voice rose to a raspy squeak. "Tomorrow at sunrise, I'm to run the gauntlet again. When they tire of that, they're going to skin the flesh from my body." His eyes looked wild. "If I live through that, they'll burn me alive."

Victoria's stomach rolled, and she pressed a hand over her mouth.

"Please, Ria," Collier begged. "O'Ryan's turned against me. For the love of God, you've got to help me."

Taking a great gulp of air to compose herself, Victoria swallowed. "How?"

"Cut me free."

Victoria glanced around at the throng of Shawnee milling about. "Now?"

"Tonight. When everyone's sleeping. All you have to do is steal a knife."

Victoria clutched her throat. Her pulse beat crazily. What would Hawk do if she freed Collier? What would Flaming Wing say? Could she even do it? God. She *had* to. "I'll try."

Relief flooded Collier's features.

Turning quickly, fearing she might be sick from her cousin's description of the planned tortures, she hurried back inside Summer Wind's lodge.

Hawk stared groggily at Jason, sitting cross-legged on the floor beside Hawk's mat, wishing he could rise and embrace his friend. But he could not. And for the first time he cursed the shaman's healing herbs that made him feel so listless. He knew the wound on his head and the gash on his shoulder were not bad. But the old medicine man wanted him to stay lying down for the rest of the day. And he had made certain that Hawk would obey. Damn him.

"Are you hurting, Hawk? Do you want us to leave you alone for a while so you can rest?" Jason asked quietly, sending a glance at Bragen Alexander, who was leaning against the center pole.

Hawk tried to shake his head but winced. "No, my brother. I want to get up. And I want to see my wife. I must explain."

Jason smiled. "Obviously Healing One remembers how hard you were to tend when you were a child. He gave you enough crushed poppy leaves to keep you down for a week."

Hawk snorted and looked around. "Where is my *neewa?*"

"Your wife is in another lodge," Bragen answered.

"Is she very angry?"

Jason's smile grew. "After what Alaina told me about you kidnapping the girl, I don't doubt it. If it was Samantha, I'd be watching my back."

Hawk chuckled, recalling the beautiful, fiery-tempered Samantha Fleming Kincaid. "That would be wise on your part, my brother. But fortunately my *neewa* is not quite as hostile as your Samantha." He shifted beneath the covers. "At least I *hope* she is not."

"Why'd you do it, Hawk?" Bragen asked suddenly, coldly.

After releasing a tired breath, Hawk told them of his forced wedding, of his abduction and years in the salt mines, how he'd believed Victoria responsible. But before he could finish, Paddington McDaniels entered the lodge.

"Where is my *neewa?*" Hawk demanded.

"In one o' the huts."

Hawk fixed his blurry gaze on the older man. "Send her to me."

McDaniels's eyes softened. "I know ye want to right yer troubles, lad. But I'd be givin' the lass a little more time yet." He offered a sympathetic smile. "She's still in a fit o' temper over ye lyin' to her like ye did."

"Lying how?" Bragen Alexander asked from where he stood near the back.

Paddy shrugged. "Well, not exactly lyin'," he corrected. "When his lordship here kidnapped Victoria, he just forgot to tell her he was her husband. She thought some wild heathen had snatched her up." His eyes met Hawk's. "It were real hard on the little lass, fallin' in love with one man while thinkin' she was wed to another. A real blow to them rigid morals o' hers."

Bragen threw Hawk a nasty glance, but he said nothing.

Jason bristled. "God's teeth, McDaniels. Don't you know what Hawk's been through? Hell, if I thought a woman had me kidnapped and sent to suffer in the Algerian salt mines, I'd have killed her the instant I saw her."

Hawk hid a smile, knowing full well Jason had nearly died—twice—at the hands of a woman and had ended up marrying her. Hawk reflected on memories of the exquisite Samantha, and for the first time he felt no pain. Samantha would always possess a place in his heart, but she was Jason's wife . . . and she was not Victoria.

"What are ye sayin'?" McDaniels piped in. "Ria wouldna do that."

Hawk looked at the older man, noticing something different about him. A new calmness. A confidence. "I realized that some time ago."

"Then who—"

"I do not know," Hawk interrupted. "But I will find out."

"Am I free to leave the village?" Bragen asked, rising.

"Yes."

Jason frowned. "Are you in a rush?"

Alexander raised his chin. "No, but I still have some business to conclude. So if it's all the same to you, I'd like to leave before it gets dark."

"I'll be goin', too," McDaniels added. "To find me some food, that is."

Hawk nodded, then extended his hand to Bragen. "Go safely. And thank you for my life. You are a friend to the Shawnee and always welcome."

Bragen met his gaze steadily. "Don't give me too much credit, Hawk. I did it for Victoria."

"I know," Hawk replied solemnly. He watched the men depart, wondering at Alexander's strangeness. He had a very thorough knowledge of the Shawnee people and their language. Hawk turned to Jason. "Do you know him well?"

"I've seen him a few times in Richmond and Yorktown. But we're not really acquainted." Kincaid leaned back on his hands. "I have heard stories, though, that he married a Shawnee woman some time back. Last I heard, she had died."

Jason rose and stretched his long frame. "Speaking of dying, did you know that for a while I thought you were dead? Only after I found a passel of letters from your mother at Crystal Terrace did I think otherwise. I figured if she was still writing to you, then you must be alive, somewhere. And I kept them all to give to you when I saw you again."

"I do not want them."

"There's more to it than you know," Jason defended. "She told me—"

"Do not speak of my *nikyah.*"

"God's teeth, but you're pigheaded!" Jason clamped his mouth shut, then took a deep breath, a muscle throbbing in his temple. "Whatever you say, Hawk." He turned for the door. "Is there anything I can do for you?"

Hawk stared at his friend. He knew Jason was angry, but it did not matter. Hawk would not speak of his mother's desertion. Not even to his blood brother.

He took a moment to subdue his emotions, then considered Jason's offer. An idea struck him, and he nearly smiled. "Yes, my friend, there are several things you can do." He did smile this time. "First. You have something I wish to purchase. . . ."

Chapter 20

Alaina and Flaming Wing still hadn't returned by the time the village quieted for the night, and Victoria was beginning to wonder if they ever would.

Oddly uncomfortable on the mat-covered ground, she drew the blanket closer and turned on her side facing the two women sleeping across from her. She tried not to think about how cozy she'd been in Hawk's arms. How safe she'd felt. But it had been a false sense of security. Just like everything else about Hawk. False.

Hearing the deep, steady rhythm of her companions' breathing, Victoria turned her thoughts to Collier and fought to suppress a shiver.

It was time.

Quietly she brushed the cover aside and sat up, instantly wishing she'd taken Cooing Dove up on her offer of a deerskin dress. Why she hadn't wanted to part with the wretched silk shirt she wore was a mystery even to her.

Refusing to consider it further, she crawled quietly to the corner of the lodge where she'd seen Cooing Dove place the baskets and corn husks. A pile of tall grass and a couple of sturdy knives lay beside them.

She picked up one of the knives and rose to her feet, then carefully crossed to the door. Her heart slammed against her ribs, and moisture dotted her upper lip. If she was caught, Flaming Wing might decide to let her join Collier. And Hawk would probably encourage him!

Raising a shaky hand, she edged the door flap aside and peeked out. Since—according to Summer Wind—the Shawnee had no threatening enemies in the area, they merely posted a few guards near the top of the rise. She let out her breath when she saw only the low glow of a dying fire in the center of the encampment.

After slipping out of the lodge, Victoria again searched the area before creeping toward Collier.

When she stopped in front of him, she felt a wave of sympathy. He looked so pathetic there, his arms outstretched and tied to the two trees, his chest crusted with blood, his head bowed, his naked, paint-covered body swollen and lumpy.

She kept her gaze away from his torso as she moved forward. Stopping close to him, she placed a hand over his mouth. "Collier, wake up."

She felt the rush of air between her fingers when he sucked in his breath. He jerked his head up, his eyes at first wild, then relieved when he saw who it was.

"Thank God," he croaked as she removed her hand.

Victoria pressed a finger to her lips, motioning him silent. Then she lifted the knife to the strip binding his right hand. It seemed to take forever to cut through the tough leather.

When the thong broke, Collier took a moment to shake some circulation into his hand, then immediately grabbed the knife from her and started slicing frantically at the ties on his other wrist. At last the leather snapped, and he quickly freed his feet. He sagged for a minute, his hands on his knees, his head lowered.

Then, taking a deep breath, he straightened and clutched her arm. "Come on. Let's get out of here."

Victoria froze. She hadn't planned to leave with him. Her gaze slid to her husband's lodge. Leave Hawk? The mere thought of never seeing him again drained her insides until she felt hollow. She was very, very angry at him, but she *couldn't* leave. "No. You go on without me."

Her cousin's grip tightened. "What are you saying, Ria? You couldn't possibly want to stay with that savage."

"He's not a savage." Why was Collier acting like this? She

tried to wrench her arm free. "I may be furious with him for deceiving me, but I won't leave him."

Something maniacal flashed in Collier's eyes, and before Victoria could react to it, he clamped a hand over her mouth and hauled her up against him, the knife pressed against her chest. "The hell you won't," he spat in a shrill whisper. "You're mine. You've always been mine. And no skin-flaying heathen is going to take you away from me."

Gut-twisting fear enveloped her. Collier spoke like a demented man.

He pressed the knife deeper, piercing her flesh.

She flinched against the pain and felt the warm trickle of blood slip down between her breasts. Confusion and terror spun her into a rush of hysterical struggles.

"Don't fight me, Ria, or I'll have to hurt you," he grated fiercely.

Ignoring his threat, she pushed at the hand holding the knife, twisting her body recklessly.

He swore vilely. The hand over her mouth moved. He pinched her nostrils shut with his thumb and forefinger, cutting off her air.

She clawed savagely at his arms, fought to push his hand away. Pain seared her lungs. *She couldn't breathe!* A horrible ringing wailed in her ears. Everything swayed. Her body thrashed, then bowed. The suffocating hand pressed harder. She kicked out. Sucked frantically. But the world darkened, then stilled. . . .

Dawn was peeking through the smoke hole in the top of the lodge when Hawk opened his eyes. Then he realized it was not the light but the sound of his father's voice issuing urgent orders that had awakened him.

Hawk sat up and blinked, trying to clear his head. It pounded in response. He glanced around the lodge but found it empty.

After pushing himself up, he rose, then wavered unsteadily. Damn those poppy leaves. He gripped the center pole. On shaky legs, he made his way to the opening and looked out.

The village was frantic with activity. Braves rushed to gather weapons. The women huddled together with their children.

Hawk frowned. They sounded frightened. He looked around the encampment until he saw his father. Instantly Hawk understood their fears. Flaming Wing's expression resembled a demon's. Even Hawk felt a trickle of nervousness.

After stepping outside, he weaved his way toward the angry man. *"Notha?* What is it?"

Flaming Wing swung around, then froze. He at first looked concerned; then his features hardened and he lifted his chin. "Light-hair escaped." The chief's neck muscles tightened. "Your *neewa* has gone with him."

For just an instant Hawk's world spun crazily. No! She would not *do* that to him. She would not leave.

But she had.

It took every ounce of will he possessed to force down the killing pain that threatened to unman him. He dragged in a breath and straightened his spine, ignoring the cold, heavy feeling in his chest. Not yet trusting his voice, he nodded, then turned his back on the chief and walked away.

But as he strode across the grounds toward his hut, a thousand visions rose to taunt him. Victoria naked and stumbling beside his horse. Victoria in the tree, terrified of the cub, then clinging to him in the creek. The pain and terror in her eyes when she told him of her childhood trauma. The way she gave herself to him, so completely that she lost consciousness.

He could again see her fear of the water and her trust when he taught her how to float. He recalled her soft words of love and saw her swinging the branch, endangering her own life to save him from the bear.

Hawk stopped in mid-stride. She would not leave him. She would be angry. She would shout at him, curse him, strike out at him, *but she would not leave*.

He felt a jolt of fear. And if she did not, then she was taken against her will. He whirled back around to see his father speaking to Victoria's friend Paddy—and to Hawk's mother.

Too concerned over Victoria to ponder his *nikyah*'s presence in the village, he rushed forward. "Was the one-eyed seaman with the others when you captured them?"

Flaming Wing nodded. "He shares a mat with Winter Flower." Then as if in answer to Hawk's next question, his father added, "He did not escape."

Hawk started to turn. "Son?" McDaniels placed a hand on Hawk's arm. "Let her go. She wouldna be happy here in the woods. Come to England an' court her there."

"No," Hawk hissed, unable to explain the dread he felt in his midsection. "She did not go willingly."

The older man's eyes softened. "It isna true, lad. Ria stole one o' Summer Wind's knives and helped Parks escape. She went because she be wantin' to. Dunna force her to come back. Ye'll both regret it."

Hawk stared at the man for a long time, hurting from the blow of his words. But he could not shake the feeling that McDaniels was wrong. Victoria might have helped her cousin escape, but she would not have left Hawk. He knew that as surely as he breathed. "You are wrong, white man."

He spun on his heel toward Winter Flower's lodge. When he entered, he found O'Ryan huddled in one corner, completely alone.

Hawk approached the man. "Where are they?"

O'Ryan glanced around nervously. "How would I be knowin'? I swear to ye, breed. I ain't seen 'em. The blighter tried to get me to help him last night, but I wouldn't." He licked his lips and stared anxiously at something behind Hawk. "I told Parks he deserved what Flaming Wing give him. The bastard paid me two hundred pounds to have ye killed. But I didn't. I ain't no murderer. Yer only alive today 'cause o' me." He scooted deeper into the corner. "After I took ye 'board that ship and found out who ye was, I tried to tell the cap'n, but he wouldn't listen." He swallowed with difficulty. "Sellin' ye to the slavers was, um, his idea."

The man spoke only half-truths. Hawk could see it in every flick of his eyelashes. "Victoria?"

"What 'bout her? She didn't know nothin'. Collier be settin' it up so she wouldn't find out."

Hawk released the breath he did not know he'd held, then turned to see his father, Jason, and McDaniels standing in the door. Flaming Wing's face was a terrible thing to behold, and Hawk knew beyond a doubt that his father had heard the seaman's confession. Dooley O'Ryan would suffer very painfully. As Hawk had.

"I'll go with ye," Paddy offered when Hawk brushed past him.

"No." He turned to his father, and their gazes locked. *"I* will bring my wife back."

Flaming Wing's features did not reveal his thoughts, but Hawk saw a flash of uncertainty in those dark depths.

Jason moved forward and placed a hand on Hawk's arm, his expression determined. "I'm going."

"No."

Kincaid's crystalline eyes flashed, and he lowered his voice. "Don't deny me this, my brother. You were there for me when I needed you."

This was the Jason Kincaid Hawk remembered well. The cold, deadly calm Jason. But Hawk would not put his friend's life in danger. Straightening his shoulders, Hawk spoke softly, but left no room for further discussion. "I go alone."

Victoria smelled damp earth and musky granite before she opened her eyes. Sunlight, streaming in from the opening of a cave, momentarily blinded her. *Cave.* She sat upright and looked around. She *was* in a cave. With Collier.

Her cousin glanced up and smiled. "Well, Ria. You're finally awake. 'Bout time. It's damned boring in here without someone to talk to." He tossed aside the wood he'd been carving on and rose, obviously unconcerned that he was still naked and covered with black paint. "I've made you breakfast."

He crossed to a flat boulder near the back of the cave and returned with a piece of raw meat. "It's snake. I killed it this morning when I found it curled up in a corner."

Victoria's stomach heaved. Good God! She pulled at the cloth binding her hands and realized it was a strip off the silk shirt she wore. When had he done that? Vaguely she recalled waking up last night while he was dragging her into the trees, and she remembered fighting him again and again as he pulled her through the woods until they reached the foot of a cliff. Realizing he intended to take her up into a cave barely visible overhead she went wild. An ache throbbed in her jaw. That was when he hit her. "Collier, why are you doing this? Please, let me go."

"Don't be obtuse, Ria. I can't do that. You belong to me. You need me to take care of you." His crude gaze explored her scantily clad body. "You need me to keep you happy."

Never in all her years had she feared her cousin. But now she did. Something in his eyes, something frightening and horrifying, told her he'd gone over the edge of sanity.

She'd seen it last night. Seen the way he looked at her vacantly, heard the way his voice rose to a maniacal shrill pitch. But seeing his blackened face in the light, the way it twitched and pulled, the way his eyes remained open wide, bulging, squeezed her chest with terror.

He tossed a slimy chunk of snake meat into her lap. "Eat your breakfast, love. There's a good girl."

Aghast, Victoria slapped it away.

Collier watched it thud into the dirt, then pinned her with a disapproving look. "You didn't have to do that. You could have just told me you weren't hungry yet."

Fearing his unstable mentality and afraid she might anger him, she sought to change the subject. God, where was Hawk when she needed him? "Um, where are we?"

"You don't know?" He waved his hand airily. "Of course you don't. You slept all the way." He pursed his lips into a pout. "I had to drag you the whole way up that mountain trail. Bloody task, too. You really should do something about your weight, love."

He walked to the opening of the cave and peeked over its jutting ledge. "I brought you here because it was the only safe place I knew. Alexander and McDaniels and I stayed in it night before last when we were following you and that

Indian bastard. Not that we got much rest. That fool
Alexander was obsessed with pushing on. He was so worried." Collier scowled. "Of course he had no idea you were
enjoying yourself with that savage scum." His eyes blazed
brightly. "Tell me, Ria. Did you spread your legs for him?"
He stepped threateningly toward her. "Did he take what
belongs to me?"

"Collier, stop this at once. I *do not* belong to you. I'm
married to Hawk."

"No!" he screeched hysterically. His eyes burned with
insanity. "You're mine. You're over eighteen now. We can
be married just as I planned. That filthy savage'll never have
you." He lunged at her, grabbing her by the shoulders. He
shook her wildly. "Never! I'll kill you before I let him take
you away from me." He jerked her up against his naked
chest and ground his mouth down on hers, then nearly
gagged her when he plunged his tongue to the back of her
throat.

She grabbed his hair and yanked, trying to force him
away.

He kissed her harder, violating her mouth with his saliva
and teeth.

She tried to turn her face, but he held her by the hair,
twisting the strands until she groaned in pain. *Oh, God. Help
me.*

She didn't realize she'd stopped fighting him until he let
her go.

"That's a good girl. Now we understand each other." He
pulled her back to him. "You're mine now." His breath blew
hot against her cheek. "You'll be glad of that once we get out
of this hellish country." He squeezed one of her breasts.
"You'll be surprised at the marvelous tricks I've learned
about fornicating." He laughed shrilly. "I'm considered
quite good at it . . . by both sexes."

Revulsion curled through her, and she prayed for her
husband to find her as she'd never prayed for anything in her
life. "Hawk will come after me."

"No!" Collier screamed. "Your bastard half-breed won't
come. He knows you're mine. He knows I'll kill him. I did it

once; I can do it again." His eyes rolled, and he blinked in confusion. "Yes, I had him killed, but he didn't die. All because of that one-eyed jackal, O'Ryan. He wanted Remington to suffer, so he sold him to the slavers. By all that's right, your savage husband should have died in the salt mines like the others."

Collier snorted. "But, oh, no. Not his lordship, the haughty duke of Silvercove. He's too high and mighty for such a lowly death. He cheated death. Cheated me." Her cousin shook his matted blond head. "He should have died. I kept waiting for his body to show up, knowing when it did that you'd turn to me. Marry me. I would have had you *and* the duke's fortune." He glared down at her. "But he cheated me, and I ran out of time. My creditors were going to make an example of me by slitting my throat.

"Gad, I was so desperate then." He grinned like a small boy. "But I had an alternative plan. Since your father had named me the sole heir to his estate, I only had to arrange a small accident for Uncle Richard."

Victoria gasped. "You had him *killed?*"

"Now, don't look at me like that." He pulled his mouth into a childish pout. "He wasn't really your father, you know. He told me that the night of your wedding, the night he disinherited you."

Her world tilted crazily. Collier, a murderer?

"I hated him for that," he went on. "But mostly I hated myself, because it was all my fault that Uncle Richard found out." He clasped her hands and pressed them to his beaten chest. "I didn't know he'd turn on you. If I had, I'd never have told him about seeing your mama and that man in the stables together."

Victoria felt as if she were walking in a dream. "What are you talking about?"

Collier pushed her head down onto his shoulder and patted it consolingly. "The day your mother died, of course. I came over to ask Uncle Richard for a loan. He wasn't about when I arrived, so I went out to the stables, thinking he might be there. That's when I found your mother in the arms of the other man."

Victoria gasped. "What are you saying?"

Collier kissed the top of her head. "There, there, love. Anyway, I slipped out unnoticed. And I probably wouldn't have said anything to Uncle Richard when I found him snoozing in the garden. But he refused to lend me any money. Gad, Ria. I had to have it." He giggled. "So I bribed him. I told him that for fifty pounds I would give him some information that would change his life."

Her cousin grunted disgustedly. "When I told him, he went wild. It was quite a grand sight, and it took me the better part of an hour to settle him down. But I finally did, and he gave me the money. It was only much later, the night of your wedding, that I found out what had happened that day after I left."

Something ugly and frightening slithered through Victoria, but she had to know. "What?"

Collier loosened his hold a bit. "Uncle Richard went out to the stables—he said he made a lot of noise so he wouldn't catch them in the act—and cheerfully asked your mother to go for a ride in the chaise. He waited until they got to the cliff overlooking the lake before he confronted her about her lover. When she told him that she'd been in love with Paddington McDaniels for years, that you were *his* child, and that she wanted a divorce, your father went berserk. He hit her. Beat her to death. . . ."

Victoria's throat closed. Her surroundings spun.

"When Richard came to his senses and realized what he'd done, he threw your mama's body over the cliff into the lake. After that he climbed down, dived into the water, and dragged her corpse up on shore, wanting everyone to believe it was an accident, that he'd tried to save her. Pretending hysteria, he raced for Denwick, but when he saw McDaniels coming out of the paddock, something snapped. He ran him down, tried to kill McDaniels as he had your mother." Collier's hold tightened again. "Then the bastard turned on you. I hated him for that. I'm glad he's dead."

Victoria couldn't even gather the strength to raise her head. Everything drained out of her. Her mother was killed by her husband, Richard Townsend. And she still reeled from the knowledge that Paddy was her true father.

Too many emotions, too many thoughts, crowded in on her at once. All the people she'd loved and trusted had deceived her. Even Hawk. A heavy, blank fog swirled around her, and she welcomed it, embraced it.

Collier lowered her to the ground and stared at her sweet face. Gad, how he loved her. Had always loved her. He smiled. No one could take her away from him now. They would live . . . and die . . . together.

He stroked her springy breast through the white silk, then planted a kiss on its peak. Everything would be all right soon, once he possessed that glorious body. She'd never want another man then. Never. A smile touched his lips. He would show her things her Indian lover had never dreamed of.

Victoria soared up through mounds of thick black. She opened her eyes and tried to focus on her surroundings. The cave! Oh, God. It hadn't been a dream. She lurched up.

"Easy, love. There's a good girl." Her cousin patted her shoulder.

She cringed and edged away.

"Tsk-tsk, Ria. You've no reason to be frightened of me. I'm not going to hurt you."

Fear shot through her. Collier's eyes were wild and glazed. "Please. Let me go." She tried to keep the desperate whimper from her voice. "If you truly love me, let me go."

"Gad, it excites me when you beg." He brushed his hand down over his nude chest. "Do you know what your whimpers do to me?"

Victoria shuddered.

Collier grabbed her hand and pressed it over his heart. "Feel."

Realizing that he'd untied her hands, she tried to pull away, but he held her fast. "Collier, stop this." She tried to sound authoritative.

He laughed dementedly, then raised her hand to his lips. He kissed it, then bit her viciously.

She cried out and jerked her hand back. "Get away from me!"

"No," he whined. "You don't mean that. You love me. I know you do." He knelt in front of her. "We're going to be married. Gad, Ria. I've been planning it since you were a child."

Victoria tried to reason with him. "Collier, you must listen to me. I cannot marry you. I already have a husband, and I love him very much."

"No! He can't have you! You're mine! *Mine.* Do you hear me?" He lunged at her, slamming her onto the ground. He pinned her hands above her head. "You're *my* wife." He kissed her brutally. Moaning harshly, he thrust his lower body hard against hers.

His mouth left her cheek and moved to her neck. He bit her, then licked at the injured area. "We'll be good together, love. We will. You'll see." He sank his teeth into the swell of her breast.

Pain nearly blinded her. She screamed and twisted.

He ground his hips down on hers so hard, she cried out again.

He threw his head back and laughed, then straddled her and frantically tore the shirt from her body.

With her hands free she swung wildly, striking him in the face and chest.

He giggled insanely. "I never dreamed it would be this good with you. You've got more spunk than I ever hoped." He squeezed her breast. "You feel so good."

"No!" She grabbed at his hand, trying to loosen it.

Something jerked Collier backward.

Victoria gasped and looked up to see Hawk's deadly fist slam into her cousin's face.

Collier screamed, then crumpled.

Hawk's fury-brightened eyes bored into her cousin's supine figure, and relief swept through her with the force of a spring flood.

"Get up, Parks," Hawk ordered in a lethal voice. "We will see how much you like the *feel* of death."

The crazed man's eyes widened, then gleamed, and Victoria knew in that instant that he'd lost all hold on reality. He staggered to his feet. "You'll never have her. I'll kill her first."

Hawk's face paled.

Collier smiled as he raised his hand clutching dirt and the knife Victoria had stolen.

Hawk didn't even flinch. With a speed she'd never witnessed in anyone, he grabbed Collier's hand and wrenched it to one side, forcing him to drop the weapon.

Collier cried out, then cackled insanely. "Are you afraid of me, Indian? Afraid that I can make her want *me?*" He glanced at Victoria and giggled. "I can, you know. I can please you like he never could." He reached for her. "I'll show you."

Nausea threatened, and she shrank back.

An enraged growl erupted from Hawk an instant before he rammed his fist into Collier's stomach, knocking him away from her.

Collier whimpered, then stumbled back to his feet, clutching his middle. "Still afraid I can please her?" he giggled on a half-winded breath.

"You are insane."

Collier chuckled wildly. "Insane? Just because I want to show her the joys of sex beyond worldly pleasures? That's not insanity." He raised his hands to the heavens. "It's a gift. A magnificent gift." He lowered his gaze to Hawk. "From me to Victoria."

Her husband looked ready to kill. He grasped her by the arm and hauled her to her feet. "Come on." He glared at Collier. "Leave him to the bears." Hawk moved to the cave opening, taking her with him.

"Nooo!" Collier shrieked like a madman. "She's mine!"

With wild, flaring eyes, he dived at Hawk's midsection.

Hawk flung Victoria to one side just as Collier slammed into him.

"Hawk!" Victoria screamed, as both men catapulted over the ledge.

Chapter 21

When Victoria next became aware of her surroundings, she was standing in Summer Wind's lodge, facing her worried mother-in-law. Blinking the haze from her eyes, Victoria attempted to focus on the older woman.

"Are you all right, dear?"

She tried to think, but she didn't possess the strength. She sat down on a deerskin mat. "How did I get here?"

Alaina covered her shoulders with a blanket. "Jason found you wandering aimlessly at the base of a mountain." She brushed the hair out of Victoria's eyes. "When he brought you to the village, he said you were dazed and kept mumbling something about Hawk."

Closing her eyes, Victoria tried to think, tried to recall why she was in the mountains. Memory erupted like an angry volcano. She lurched up and cried out. "Where's Hawk?"

Alaina's drawn features paled. "I don't know, Victoria. They haven't found him yet."

Pain exploded on a burst of uncontrollable tears. "Oh, Alaina, he's dead! Hawk and Collier went over the edge of the cliff. They're both dead. I know it!"

"No. We don't know that—" Her voice broke. "At least not about my son."

Victoria's hopes took flight, and she clutched the older woman's hand like a lifeline. "What are you saying?"

"Only that they found your cousin's body but not Adam's. Collier's remains were amid some rocks below a cave, not far from where Jason found you." Her chest rose shakily. "Flaming Wing and the others are searching for Adam now."

Victoria closed her eyes, the ache in her chest nearly unbearable. Hawk was dead. It was only a matter of time before they found his crumpled body. Her heart burned with agony so intense she prayed for her own death to ease the hurt. She dropped to the mat and curled up into a ball on her side.

Jason glanced up at the hot sun, then took a drink from his canteen and handed it to Paddy. He rubbed the sleeve of his shirt over his brow and looked at Flaming Wing. "No sign of him yet?"

The chief stared toward a line of braves combing the craggy mountainside and shook his head.

"By the saints!" Paddy exclaimed. "A body doesna get up an' stroll away after he falls off a cliff. The lad's got to be here."

Jason rigidly clamped down on the leap of panic he experienced at McDaniels's summation. Damn it. Hawk wasn't dead. "We'll find him." He looked at Flaming Wing's tight features. "And we'll find him alive."

"Find who?" a tired, raspy voice asked from directly behind them.

McDaniels's eyes bulged, and he sputtered something unintelligible.

Jason whirled around and nearly buckled over in shock. *"Hawk!"*

The Shawnee stood before him looking as pale as death, silk bandages on his head and shoulder, his eyes glazed.

"God's teeth!" Jason grabbed his friend and hugged him fiercely, then angrily shoved him back. "Where the hell have you been? We've been nearly out of our senses with worry." He clenched his fist. "God damn you! Don't you ever put me through that again! Do you hear me? Not ever!" Tears welled up in Jason's eyes, and he pulled Hawk back into his embrace.

Flaming Wing cleared his throat and placed a hand on Hawk's shoulder. "You are not injured, *neequithah?*"

Hawk stepped away from Jason and clutched his father's arm. "I will live."

The chief's hand shook; his eyes grew bright. Lines of worry seemed to melt from his face, and his mouth spread into a slow smile. Then, before the astonished onlookers, Flaming Wing pulled his son to him.

Alone in the hut, Victoria hadn't moved from her curled-up position on the sleeping mat—and she didn't care if she never did again. Hawk was dead. She didn't doubt it now. She couldn't. She had seen him die . . . in her arms.

She caught her breath as a spark of memory flashed. She *had* seen him die. She pushed herself up into a sitting position and forced herself to concentrate. With blinding clarity, the memories came back in a rush. After the men went over the cliff, she had frantically scrambled down the mountain . . . and found Hawk lying beside Collier's mangled body.

Her stomach rolled, and she raised a shaky hand to her head. Hawk had been unconscious, bleeding from his shoulder and from the gunshot wound near his temple. Terrified, she had rushed back up to the cave and retrieved the silk shirt to use for bandages. In a hazy fog, she remembered tearing two strips from it before putting on the tattered remains.

After she bound Hawk's head and shoulder, he had opened his eyes and smiled so beautifully. Her chest heaved. God, how relieved she'd been that he was alive. Together they'd staggered nearly half a mile down the mountain to a creek.

Her pulse began to pound as she remembered what had happened, and moisture dampened her brow. The laborious trek to the stream had been too much for him. His face had gone pale, then deathly gray. Victoria clamped a hand over her mouth at the memory. He had asked her forgiveness, then closed his eyes in death.

Another wave of pain slammed into her, and she crumpled onto the mat. "Oh, God. *No.*" Gut-wrenching sobs tore from her throat, the agony like none she'd ever known. She cried for Hawk, for the vibrant life so viciously destroyed. She cried for herself, for the lonely years that lay ahead, for the beautiful children she and Hawk would never have. Grief, so intense it bordered on death, consumed her.

"Your tears are killing me, *neewa.*"

At first Victoria thought she had imagined the sound of his voice.

"Neewa?"

She leapt to her feet and whipped her head around. *"Hawk!"* She barreled into his arms. "Oh, God. I thought you were dead." She hugged him, kissed him wildly.

His arms closed around her, and he returned her passion with a fierceness of his own. He caught her mouth and ravaged it, plundered it, devoured it, while his hands raced urgently over her body as if he wanted to touch her everywhere at once.

Her senses exploded in a torrent of frenzied need. The need to hold on to him, to reassure herself he was real. She wrapped her arms around his lean waist and kissed his neck and chest, not willing to let an inch separate their bodies.

Hawk sucked in a sharp breath, shaking as he slid his hands down to cup her bottom. "Ah, *neewa.* Now you are going to kill me with your passion."

Victoria instantly pulled back. "I'm hurting you!"

He chuckled low. "Only because I do not possess the strength to make love to you."

She felt a surge of shame as she looked into his tired gray eyes. He looked ready to collapse. She backed up, clutching his hands. "Come over here. You need to lie down."

His body weaved slightly, but he smiled. "Only if you lie beside me."

Thrilled by his words, she nodded and led him to the mat, then gently helped him lie down before joining him. She turned on her back and brought his head to her breast, content to just hold him, smooth his bandaged brow. A satisfying peace settled over her, and she pushed away thoughts of her anger . . . of how close she'd come to losing him. He was safe, and he was hers.

Early the following day, Victoria lay snuggled next to her husband, in Summer Wind's lodge, thankful the woman and her mother had slept elsewhere. Yawning, Victoria opened her eyes just in time to see the buffalo skin covering the door move.

She gasped.

Hawk's eyes sprang open. "What?"

Flaming Wing entered the lodge unannounced. He met first Victoria's stunned gaze, then Hawk's questioning one. He held his son's eyes steadily. "Your *nikyah* would speak to you."

Victoria saw the muscles across Hawk's shoulders bunch as he sat up on the mat, looking deliciously attractive in his half-asleep state. But the harshness in his voice belied his tousled appearance. "You have forgiven her, *Notha*. I cannot."

Flaming Wing straightened, looking every inch the powerful Shawnee chief. His glare bored into his son's. "You will listen to your *nikyah*."

A flash of defiance entered Hawk's eyes. But she could see that it warred with the deep respect for his father that would not allow him to disobey.

Hawk rose, but he didn't move to go with his father.

Flaming Wing's eyes hardened. Then a flash of understanding lit their ebony depths, and he turned toward the entrance. "Sand Blossom, come."

Victoria held her breath and waited expectantly for the hide flap to lift. When Lady Remington slipped in, Victoria could tell how nervous she was by the way she held her chin at that proud angle.

She walked toward Hawk, but stopped a few feet from him.

Flaming Wing gave an irritated snort. "Speak, woman. You have convinced me. Now ease our son's mind."

Alaina met Hawk's cold gaze, then lowered her own. "I

would like to tell you why I left you." She folded her arms across her stomach.

Hawk's jaw tightened. "It does not matter."

"It does," Alaina whispered.

"No—"

"Shadow Hawk!" The chief glared angrily.

Taking a deep breath, Hawk nodded to his mother.

Looking somewhat relieved, she cast a quick look at her husband, almost as if to thank him for his support, then spoke quietly. "My father worshiped my brother, Stephen, and barely tolerated me. I won't go into all the unhappy details of my life, but when I had the chance to escape England and come to the colonies to stay with my friend Lucinda, Jason's mother, I took it. It was through her that I met your father, fell in love with him, and married him according to Shawnee law."

She shot a tender glance at her husband, then continued. "For eleven years I couldn't have been happier. I loved the village, the people, Flaming Wing . . . you. Then one day I got a message from my father through the trapper, Jed. You were taking your lessons at Jason's, and Flaming Wing was out on a hunt. My father's note sounded so distraught that I went to meet him by myself. In a little glen not far from where you built your cabin."

She swallowed with difficulty, as if the words hurt. "My father informed me of my brother's death and of the absence of direct-line heirs unless I returned to England and married. Of course, I refused. But in doing so, I made the mistake of telling him about my husband and son." Her lower lip quivered. "He became enraged and told me I was returning with him. When I flatly refused, he ordered one of the soldiers he'd traveled with to ready his men and attack the Shawnee village—to kill the chief and his son."

Alaina's composure collapsed. "I couldn't let them hurt you or your father. I loved you both too much. I agreed to go with them, but only on one condition—that I could send a message to Flaming Wing through Jed, telling him I was unhappy in the village and had willingly returned to England." She smiled at her husband through tears. "I knew your father well enough to know that if I had just disappeared, he would have come after me, all the way to Europe if necessary. I had to hurt you both to keep you safe." A tear glided down her cheek. "But my father never got what he wanted from me. I refused to be courted, and I never gave myself to another man. In the end, when my father lay dying, he sent for his solicitor and acknowledged you, Adam Remington of the colonies, as his heir."

"Why did you not tell me of this before?" Hawk asked in an uneven voice.

"I sent you dozens of missives over the years, hoping you might read one of them. I couldn't tell your father, but I wanted you to know. But you didn't read them. The only letter that managed to reach you was the one in which I asked you to come to England after my father died." She and Flaming Wing exchanged a look. "I was surprised when you did, but I know now why you chose to make the trip. Nonetheless, I'm thankful for it. I got to see you again, touch you, be near you"—her voice broke—"even if you couldn't bear to be in the same room with me."

Hawk stood silent for a long breathless time, staring straight ahead. Then he met Victoria's gaze, and she saw all the uncertainty, all the hurt the little boy in him had endured.

Through tear-filled eyes, she mentally gave him her support, then watched as inch by inch, his body seemed to visibly relax as if some heavy burden had been lifted from his shoulders. When his gaze focused again on Alaina, it was filled with compassion. Slowly, almost hesitantly, he held out his hands to her.

Alaina burrowed past his outstretched arms and crumpled against him, her body convulsing with sobs.

Flaming Wing turned away so that Victoria couldn't see his expression.

After a strained moment she saw Hawk slowly, almost warily, fold his mother into his embrace, his arms trembling against her back. He closed his eyes as if in pain, then buried his face in her hair. His hold tightened, and he crushed her to him.

Tears streamed down Victoria's face as she watched her husband's big shoulders shake. Then in a low, constricted voice, she heard him whisper, "I have missed you, *Nikyah.*"

Hawk was up before her the next morning, and she could tell that he'd already bathed. His hair was still damp and gleaming, tied back behind his neck. Damp spots marked strategic areas on his clinging buckskins. Victoria groaned. There should be a law against breeches like that.

Her husband's eyes flashed as he stared down at her, and she had the ungodly feeling that he could tell what she was thinking.

She averted her gaze. "Good morning."

"It is a beautiful morning," Hawk returned softly, "within the walls of this *wegiwa.*"

Self-consciously she shoved the hair out of her eyes and tried to change the topic. "It must be early. The village is so quiet."

Hawk's expression changed to one of discomfort, and he glanced toward the door flap.

"What is it? What's wrong?"

"Nothing is wrong, *neewa,*" he assured her. "Just unpleasant."

"What?"

He knelt before her and smoothed a lock of hair over her bare shoulder. "O'Ryan. The silence means . . . his punishment has finally ended."

All the screams and boisterous laughter she'd heard outside came back to haunt her. She had thought the Shawnee were celebrating Hawk's and Alaina's return. She hadn't given thought to the seaman. She shuddered. All that time they must have been enjoying O'Ryan's torture. "What did they do to him?"

"You do not want to know."

He was right. She didn't. His expression told her enough. Shakily she rose to her feet. She knew the seaman deserved anything the Indians did to him after all he'd put Hawk through, but she still couldn't shake the sick feeling in her stomach. As she pulled on the buckskin dress Summer Wind had loaned her, she felt the bark walls closing in. "I'm going for a walk."

She fled toward the opening.

"Victoria, wait!" Hawk called urgently.

But it was too late. She'd already raised the flap, already seen what he didn't want her to witness.

In the middle of the village O'Ryan was spread-eagled between two poles, his head slumped forward in death. He had been stripped to the waist. Deep, bloody gouges scored his back where he'd been repeatedly struck with a whip. At his feet lay the black coil of leather she'd seen strapped to his own belt.

Victoria clamped a hand over her mouth and swung back around. She felt Hawk pull her into his arms and stroke her spine.

"I did not want you to look upon this sight, *neewa*. I do not wish you to think the Shawnee people cruel. They sought only to torture him as I was tortured, not to kill him. Do not blame them for O'Ryan's weakness."

She wrapped her arms around him, trying to banish the savageness she'd just witnessed, and her fingers touched his scarred back—flesh that had been mercilessly slashed open again and again before it had later healed. Visions of him writhing in agony day after day beneath the lash struck her with the force of a blow. O'Ryan had done this. But his suffering had been quick and mild compared to Hawk's.

Inhaling a shaky breath, she leaned back. "Your people aren't cruel. They're just." She smiled bravely. "I don't blame them."

Hawk didn't look convinced. He touched her cheek. "If he had lived through the torture, as I did, *neewa*, he would have gone free. Though my suffering was great, I still live."

"For that I'm eternally grateful." Her smile was genuine this time. "And I still want to go for that walk."

A contented smile graced his mouth, and his eyes held all the love she'd ever hoped to see. She was still awed by how Alaina's confession had strengthened something inside him. Something tender and wonderful.

He pressed a hand against her spine and guided her up the

mountain beyond the place where they'd first seen the village—and the bear. Recalling what had happened there, she felt a moment's reluctance, but Hawk's reassuring squeeze on her waist gave her courage. Besides, she knew the bear wasn't there any longer. According to Alaina, the Shawnee had preserved the meat and processed the hide. Relieved, Victoria relaxed her step.

When they reached the top, Hawk knelt in the grass and pulled her down beside him. He studied her upturned face with a look that resembled reverence, and when he at last spoke, his voice sounded strained. "I, too, am in need of punishment, *neewa*. I have wronged you."

Staring into those sensuous gray eyes, knowing all he'd been through, she felt her misgivings dissolve. But she needed to know his reasons. "Why did you kidnap me? Want to hurt me?"

Hawk took a deep breath and twisted one of her long curls around his finger. "I went to England because of a woman named Samantha. I felt . . . things for her that one should not feel for the wife of a close friend."

"Jason's wife? The Sam you called out to in your delirium?"

He nodded.

Victoria felt the tiniest bite of jealousy, but tried not to let it show.

"When I left the colonies," Hawk continued, "Jason had just learned of his half sister's existence. Shortly after my arrival in London, he discovered that the child had been taken to England. He sought my help in finding her."

"What has this to do with me?"

Hawk smiled. "Because of what I believed my mother did to me, I did not trust white women. I agreed to wed you only because I believed you to be Jason's sister. Otherwise, I would not have married you. It was an unfortunate, but very welcome error."

He slid his hand up her back. "But that was not the only mistake I made." His voice grew harsh with self-recrimination. "On the night I was abducted—our wedding night—O'Ryan claimed you were responsible for my capture, and I believed him." He curled his fingers into her side. "For seven years my hatred for you kept me alive, and when I escaped the slavers, I wanted revenge."

He smiled down at her. "But soon after I captured you, I found that I could not bring myself to harm you. Not that I did not try. I did. Then I hated myself for my weakness. I blamed that, too, on you. Yet somewhere, between all the hatred and anger"—he nuzzled her ear—"I fell in love with you."

Victoria thought she'd burst with love for this man.

He pulled her into his arms. "I learned from O'Ryan that Collier Parks was the one who ordered my death. I live only because the one-eyed seaman sold me into slavery instead of killing me."

Oh, God, how he must have suffered. Tears welled up in her eyes at the thought of all he'd been through and how he must have despised her, thinking she had done those awful things to him. And she thought of her cousin. Money and greed had driven him to desperate measures, driven him insane. Her heart ached for the man he had been before. "Collier wasn't always like that, Hawk. Honestly he wasn't."

Hawk pulled back, and his eyes softened. "I know. You would not have cared for him if he had been."

"What changed him?"

"The war."

When she frowned, he explained. "I spoke with Winter Flower. Under my father's orders she took O'Ryan to her mat to learn from him, and he told her much. The seaman and Parks spoke often on the voyage over here. It seems that, until the war, Collier never had the stomach for killing. He could pay to have it done, as long as he did not have to see it—be a part of it. But in the war he was forced to kill many men. It affected his logic, and he continued to kill, not only the enemy but others as well, most often for profit. It destroyed him. He did not possess the strength to take a human life, so in his mind he turned the deed into something else. I do not know why or how, but he somehow convinced himself that every murder was necessary. The one thing that kept him rational was his love for you. When he realized in the cave that you did not love him, would never love him, he lost all touch with sanity."

Victoria shuddered, remembering the look in her cousin's eyes, something she prayed she'd never see again in her lifetime. Then overwhelming guilt consumed her, and she buried her cheek in Hawk's shoulder. "It's my fault. All of it. I made him join the king's forces."

"No, *neewa.*" Her husband corrected her gently. "Your cousin was unstable long before that. If he had not joined the king's service, the madness would have surfaced somewhere else—in a tavern brawl, during an argument, or on the dueling field. He would have taken a life, and the results would have been the same."

A tear slid down her cheek. "I'm sorry for what he did to you."

"Not all he did was bad. In the end he actually did save my life by breaking my fall from the cliff."

She laid her hand on his chest, so thankful for the strong, steady beat. She closed her eyes. "How you must have hated me."

"I wanted to," he confessed, then kissed her lovingly. "But my heart knew you were my life mate even when you were a child of fifteen." He brushed his nose against hers. "I had first planned to leave you after the wedding, but knew I could not. The night I was abducted, I was on my way to carry your luggage aboard the ship that would take us to the colonies." He met her gaze warmly. "If it had not been for O'Ryan, I would have returned to you."

Victoria felt her love swell. "I wish you could have. By now I'd not only have you to love but possibly a son as well."

Hawk smiled that beautiful, breathtaking smile. He placed his palm on her stomach. "Perhaps you carry my son now." He caressed her belly. "Or my daughter."

Excitement swelled through Victoria. A child. Hawk's child. Through misty eyes, she smiled. "I pray it's so." She touched his cheek. God, how she loved him. "But where will we live? Here?"

Hawk turned his face and kissed her palm. "No, *neewa.* You would not be happy in the forest."

She ran her thumb over his firm lower lip. "I'd be happy anywhere you were." *Even if it killed her.* She suddenly remembered something. "What did you say to me in Shawnee that day at the pool?"

Hawk slid his tongue along her lower lip. *"Nihaw kunahqa, ni kitehi."*

Victoria sighed. "What does it mean?"

He brushed his lips over hers. "'You are my wife, my heart.' Now, do not change the subject."

She made circles on his chest with her finger. "What was it?"

"About where we will live." He nibbled her jaw. "I have purchased Crystal Terrace plantation from Jason, or at least the duke of Silvercove has." He hesitated. "It is not as grand as Silvercove, but it is on the river, near Lynch's Ferry . . . and not *too* close to the forest."

Victoria hugged him. "Oh, Hawk, you don't have to do that. I'll learn to love the forest, honest I will."

"Then I will take you to my cabin deep in the pines." He smiled. "But we will live in the plantation house."

"It sounds perfect."

"It will be . . . when your horse arrives from England."

She sucked in a surprised breath. "Brandy? How?"

"I have asked Jason to take care of the animal's transport. He will make arrangements to have the stallion brought to the colonies." He kissed her quickly. "I have also arranged financing for the villagers. And since I am still head of the manse, I have ordered that the boy, Nigel, be taken to a physician and cared for properly. He will not be returned to his drunken father, but educated before he returns to oversee the care of Silvercove."

A sob tore from her throat. "You did all that for me, didn't you?"

"Yes. But in truth, I did not know of the villagers, or I would have seen to them." He ran his hand up and down her back. "I would also see your friend Paddy care for the stables at Crystal Terrace."

She didn't think it was possible to love another human any more than she did Hawk. "Thank you. I'm sure he'll like